THE
UNLOVE

SPELL

ISBN : 978-1-62251-031-3

Cover artwork by Dante Saunders
Interior Layout by Jennifer Carson

Summary: Marling can't really make Viktor fall in love with her, but she
can make damn sure he doesn't fall in love with anyone else.

First Edition: October 2016

Unlove Spell: a novel by Kendra L. Saunders

Published by Bellatrix Press, an imprint of Prince & Pauper Press

THE
UNLOVE
SPELL

Kendra L. Saunders

chapter one

Every girl living in a magical place like Manhattan is supposed to be the princess of her own modern fairy tale, complete with great designer clothes and lovely roommates waiting at home after a bad day to offer words of wisdom and appropriate feel-good movie rentals.

In Marling's experience, though, such roommates did not exist. Her roommates were a married couple who weren't familiar with opportune moments, rarely watched movies, and had never offered even one piece of helpful advice to her. Well, other than the time that the husband, Tim, had quietly suggested that Marling keep her hair dryer a bit further from the bathtub to avoid electrocution.

Today was not a good day, though, and Marling felt more than a little relieved to find the apartment empty when she finally dragged herself home.

Downsize. Productivity. They were little words Marling had encountered a thousand times, but they were suddenly more serious when strung together in front of her face along with a printed chart about input and output. Her boss hadn't specifically threatened Marling's job, but she had mentioned that there would be some layoffs soon, very soon. She had also done that thing with her eyes where she looked like she was trying to develop laser-eye-powers. That always made Marling uncomfortable.

But, oh God. If she lost her job and she couldn't make rent, the roomies would kick her out. And then what? Would she end up singing for pennies in Grand Central Station? Would she put glow-in-the-dark rods in her hair and sit with a cardboard sign on a street corner in Chinatown and ask people to throw change at her? Would she take up residence on a bench in Central Park for so long that she became a cautionary tale that international tourists would visit to photograph?

Just as Marling had concocted a detailed fantasy about how she might achieve notoriety as a national landmark, she heard an insistent knock at the apartment door. No one ever knocked at the door except for the occasional pizza delivery person and an old guy from upstairs who liked to hand out pamphlets about aliens.

"Errr, hold on!" Marling called, stopping in the kitchen to pick up a butter knife and carry it with her to the door. On a day like this, you could never be too safe. "Who is it?" Before she could finish swinging open the door, the high pitched voice of her former witch-school classmate, Emma, cut through.

"You're not going to believe this, Marling, but another witch is missing. Another one. What did I tell you?! It's just the beginning, I know it is. Juniper agrees with me. She says you need to be careful. Oh, I agree, Marling, you should be very careful. Have you put any protection spells on yourself?"

Emma Chatham was actually a twenty-eight year old blonde from a small town in Pennsylvania, but she insisted that everyone call her Primrose Redhaven and talked with a fake English accent. As much as Marling tried to refer to her as Primrose, it felt uncomfortable and borderline silly when the time came to say it out loud, so she made special effort to never say Emma's name. At all.

Having a friend, even one as strange as Emma, was better than not having a friend at all. And Marling always felt dangerously close to being friendless and alone, so she clung to Emma, even through the bad accent and alarmist visits.

"I haven't," Marling said, when it felt safe to speak again. She hated interrupting Emma when she went into one of her tirades or passionate speeches.

"You're just tempting fate, darling. Five people missing in a month. It's not some accident, that's clear by now. You don't still think it's an accident do you? Or coincidence? I think it's Morgana. According to Juniper, Morgana is quite the villain. She's a dark witch."

Emma always worried about dark witches.

"Five! In a *month*. Marling. In a month. It makes me wish that Kyran Gray would come back. He's quite skilled, even if Lady Grieve won't forgive him."

Kyran Gray had once been their tutor, second in command only to Lady Grieve. Between his impeccable fashion sense, hipster-boy beard and extensive magic knowledge, he was the perfect bait for someone like Emma.

"I do miss Kyran," Emma said. "He was so dedicated."

"Mmmhmmm."

"I've never seen anyone invoke truth out of someone as fast as he did. He just snapped his fingers and that kid started talking. Remember that? He was wearing the black sweater with the little shirt and tie underneath?" Emma shed her jacket and scarf and then moved to the refrigerator, opening it and helping herself to the mostly-empty bottle of red wine on the top shelf. "He's quite a handsome witch."

Marling sighed. "I think he's gay."

"That doesn't change how handsome he is. And, anyway, I wish we could talk to him about this. I might call him, you know, see what he thinks about the missing witches. Now, where are your wine glasses again? I simply must have a glass of wine after this stressful, stressful day. Witches! Disappearing!"

It wasn't that Marling wasn't worried about witches disappearing. Rather, she knew from experience that many of the young women who called themselves witches were really just the flighty types who had gone to Marling's class with her and compared black dresses and shoes and gothic accessories. They wanted to look very dark, and very deep. Girls like that tended to disappear when they finished their classes, because it was a lot less trouble to just buy nice black dresses and accessories than to live life as a witch.

Marling could understand this way of thinking, sometimes, though. Especially when she compared her own choices with those of someone really dedicated like Emma.

And especially since she had all but given up on magic several years ago.

"Perhaps some of them just didn't want to… you know, disappoint us. Maybe they decided to become beauticians or real estate agents and they chose not to tell us," Marling suggested, handing Emma a wine glass. "Maybe I should have a glass of this too. Tomorrow night I have an important work thing to deal with. I have to go to a party."

"You sound so tortured! Your job is a lark, Marling; you just flutter around to parties and ask people if they want to write books. If only life was so easy for all of us!"

Marling sighed. "It's not really that easy. And according to my boss, I probably won't have a job for much longer anyway."

Marling didn't have an official job with Moonhorse Publishing. She'd started off as a temp and had been instructed to go to a party or two, run a few errands, enter some data into a very old and disturbingly slow computer. Eventually she'd been invited to a few more parties with instructions to meet and schmooze with authors, wannabe authors and other publishers and industry professionals. No one liked to talk about her in a direct manner, but everyone had come to accept her existence and take advantage of her people skills.

"You know who I wish you'd talk to? Hmmm, that Russian guy, the one who writes about the fae. He's beautiful!" Emma's voice took on a new quality, one that sounded suspiciously fangirly and not at all witch-like. "You must have seen him. I mean, the *real* fae are a witch's greatest natural enemy in theory but the way he talks about them, the way he writes them- Oh, it makes them seem so sweet and wonderful! If you see him, you *must* get him to sign something for me. No, wait, actually, you should call me. Can you do that? I want to hear that sexy voice saying my name. Didn't you date a Russian? I bet you died every time he said your name, with that delicious accent."

Ugh, of course Emma had to bring up the Russian ex. As it was, Marling cycled through periods of attempting to remember everything about Viktor and attempting to forget everything about Viktor. For a long time after the breakup she'd been convinced that he'd appear at her door with flowers and tell her how sorry he was for running away. Then she'd decided she'd never see him again and needed to get over him. Then she'd gotten really into trashy romance novels with names like CEO DUDES AND BUSTY BABES.

Most of the last five years had been a desperate race to forget Viktor Kalashnik and his hot accent and killer skills with making delicious coffee from subpar coffee beans. More importantly, it had been a desperate race to forget that Marling had actually been foolish enough to put an unlove spell on herself so she could never fall in love with anyone besides Viktor.

And why had she done it? Because he was crazy hot? Because of his accent and endearingly broken English? Or just because she was really bad at magic?

Okay, it was definitely because she was bad at magic.

Marling had spent a few hours with a bottle of cheap tequila (eww) and a few of her spell books, the night of her breakup with Viktor, attempting to place a love spell on him that would send him running back to her with tears in his eyes and helpless devotion in his veins. Instead, she had messed up some of the words and accidentally placed an unlove spell on herself, which prevented her from ever falling in love with anyone but Viktor.

The unlove spell was considered shameful among witches, and with good reason. It showed a certain weakness of the soul, according to Kyran Gray. Whatever in the hell that meant.

"If you see the Russian writer guy, you really must call me," Emma said, gulping down the rest of her wine as if it was water. "Alright, darling, off I go. I need to visit the rest of the witches on my part of the Witch Chain and warn them about all of this bad news before the snow gets too bad. We're supposed to have a huge storm, like, four feet of snow or something." Emma hugged Marling. "Be careful, will you? There's bad magic in the air right now, I can feel it."

"Like unemployed magic?"

Emma shook her head, a serious expression plastered across her face. She pulled her jacket on and shuffled toward the door. "Good luck with your party and your job and all that, but remember… if you lose your job and want to come back to the NYWS, I'll do my best to talk Lady Grieve into giving you an entry level position. She'll want to know you're more serious about your magic this time, of course. But she adores me, and we could at least have you help with decorating for holiday meetings or filing some paperwork or… or, you know, cleaning or something."

The last thing Marling wanted to do was return to New York Witch School, but then, homelessness didn't sound so appealing either, relative local cautionary fame aside. "I'll think about it," she said at last. "But I really don't want to lose this job. I like working in publishing, and I'm not very good at uhhh… at magic. Or cleaning."

"Oh, darling, you've never done anything TOO awful with your magic. It's all about practice."

"Yeah! It's not like I put an unlove spell on myself!" Marling said, forcing a laugh.

"Aww, no, only idiots do things like that. Ta ta, lovie, I'm off to warn others of the impending danger. If I didn't know any better, I'd say we were at the beginning of the end of all things, but then, I'm not that dramatic." Emma waved goodbye and blew a kiss to Marling and stumbled off mumbling to herself about something, leaving Marling with a sense of unease and an empty wine bottle.

End of all things.

chapter two

W ell, it snowed. And the whole four feet of snow thing wasn't entirely accurate but it also wasn't entirely inaccurate.

About thirty minutes after the party's start time and several terrifying experiences with strangers on the subway later, Marling finally managed to arrive at her destination.

When Marling caught sight of her reflection in the elevator's mirrors, she gasped. Oh wait, wait. She always forgot about the fact that mirrored elevators and hotel bathrooms were built with the most unflattering angles and lighting in existence. Even Hollywood actresses looked like hunchbacks in hotel bathroom mirrors.

Yes. Absolutely. Even the most gorgeous Hollywood actresses of all time.

After pondering if her eyes disappeared whenever she smiled and if her lips really *did* look that chapped- and if that spot on her chin really *was* the size of a pencil eraser- Marling decided that the mirror was warped. She looked amazing.

Her black A-line dress definitely fit a bit snugger than it had when she first bought it, though. Maybe she should cut back a bit on the late night mugs of hot chocolate. Maybe. Probably not.

The doors slid open.

Benjamin Gross, the host of the party, had transformed his rather spacious apartment into a winter wonderland, thanks to twinkling string lights, white and silver accents and a table piled high with holiday themed foods. Marling could smell a combination of dinner items and baked goods, even from the elevator. And really, half of the reason for attending parties was the promise of dinner, right?

"Marling Ellis," she said, to the man at the door.

He looked at his list. "Is your first name Marling or Ellis?"

"Marling. My last name is Ellis."

"Hmmm, I see a... oh wait. Here you are. Alright, yes."

Marling planted a big smile on her face as she pushed by the man at the door, and then dropped it as soon as she had left his sight. People checked invitations for this party? What was this, one of those royal balls from the fairytales? Or were there going to be really great goody bags?

A daydream of goody bags chock full of expensive cosmetics and gift certificates to spas filled her mind, but she forgot about it as soon as she approached the refreshments table.

Working in the book industry, especially in a capacity that didn't include a title or full time job or any security in the future, Marling wasn't rolling in money. She made enough money to cover her rent, but that didn't usually leave her with a lot of extra for things like... well, food. Especially not food in abundant supply.

Oh. Oh, oh, oh. There was a whole platter with Chinese food. Not the kind of Chinese food that was even remotely eaten in China, but the delicious kind of Chinese food that you can buy until 2 am on the corner. The kind you know with absolute certainty is filled with ingredients that weren't made to be consumed by humans. You know, the good stuff.

Marling scooped some crab rangoon and eggrolls onto a plate and then let out a heavy, happy sigh when she noticed the bottles of champagne and wine that cluttered one end of the table. This party was looking quite good right now.

"Don't try that merlot."

Crab rangoon and eggrolls flew as Marling jumped, but she somehow managed to catch them all and reposition them on her plate. She turned slowly, taking in the orange-haired kid behind her.

"Uhhh?"

"The merlot, it's really dry. I almost threw up," the kid said, and Marling realized with another startle that this kid was Patrick Jones-Wiley, the young author that her boss had instructed her to schmooze with. This was it! This was it... she needed to impress him, lure him to Moonhorse Publishing, if she wanted to keep her job.

"I don't usually drink red anyway," Marling said. "It's supposed to be better for you or whatever, but I like white. I like champagne."

"Eh. Enjoying the food?"

She glanced at her plate and realized she had six crab rangoons and three eggrolls sitting atop it quite conspicuously. Did it seem overindulgent of her? "Oh, I suppose I will," she said, a blush creeping up her neck and into her face. "Didn't mean to grab that much food but it sort of just... leaped onto my plate!" She let out a nervous laugh and then plunked her plate down on the table. Time to move into business mode. "You're not Patrick Jones-Wiley by any chance, are you?"

The kid's eyes registered murky surprise. "Yeah," he said, as if testing the answer.

"Well, isn't that fortunate. When Benjamin invited me, all I could think about was how excited I was to meet you. Your last book was just such a breath of fresh air. I mean, the first one was good, especially for your age, but this last one? It was like I could feel you stumble across your authentic voice and then just... own it. You owned your voice in that book. It was beautiful."

Patrick's eyes widened and he perked up, smiling and raising his empty wine glass to Marling. "You're right. You're so right, because I had this moment where I felt as if I'd tripped over the dead body of my old self and found this new self." He nodded. "That's probably the coolest thing anyone's ever said to me."

Marling cleared her throat, a bit thrown by the dead body analogy but determined to keep this moving in the right direction. She was, after all, a professional schmoozer, and she could roll with anything. "Well, I can always hear a confident voice in books. I guess it's my talent." She gave a meek little shrug.

"Are you a reviewer?"

"Oh, well no."

"A blogger? Sometimes I wish I was better at blogging. I know this kid who earns his living off of blogging about tuxedo cats. It's crazy."

"No, I work a bit closer to books, you see. I work for Kim Reese at Moonhorse Publishing." Marling turned away just long enough to pour herself a glass of champagne, and then looked at Patrick in the most casual manner she could manage. "Kim's always on the prowl for the next great book, but I'd like to think I'm the tastemaker at Moonhorse. I found Richard Rum, actually."

Patrick twitched a little at the mention of an author currently living on almost every bestseller list in the country. "Richard Rum? I know about his bestsellers. What did he publish through Moonhorse?"

Ugh. Why did this kid ask so many questions? "He published a small... novel."

"Wait, was it a kids' book?"

"Well, if we're being technical, you could say it was a kids' book, but it was actually quite a lot deeper than just a picture book or something. It was an *allegory*." Marling realized she was leaning closer and closer to the kid and that he was starting to look a bit disturbed. Might be time to back off a little. "But you know, it was a great step for him. Big book deal, movie deal, the whole thing."

"I guess. I mean, Moonhorse is kind of the last thing you want to want to have people associate you with, though. It's like telling people that you had something published through Run Bunny Run or something."

Run Bunny Run. The most embarrassing indie publisher, maybe ever... so embarrassing that they'd been parodied in a famous TV skit but *still* hadn't achieved cool "bad" status. Marling almost spit out her champagne, mid-sip.

Patrick nodded then, looking away from Marling. "I think I'm gonna have more wine."

"How old are you?"

"Uh. Nineteen."

"Maybe you should think about your life choices if you're already drinking at nineteen years old," Marling said, and then turned on her heel, walking away in such a huff that she almost collided with a woman carrying a tray of empty wine glasses.

Ugh, whatever. Marling would just wait for Patrick to stop haunting the refreshments table and then she would make her way back over, fill up her plate, and enjoy the rest of the party. Maybe she could tell Kim that Patrick hadn't even *been* at the party. And then she could apply to Forever 21 immediately.

"Everyone, can I have your attention?" someone called, from the other side of the room. Must be Benjamin Gross. "Tonight we have a special, special guest and I am just honored beyond belief that he would join us. Ladies and gentlemen, could you put your hands together for the expert on all things magical? Viktor Arson."

Ooooh, was this the faerie guy? Marling pushed through the crowd to get closer, because she was a bit (way too) short to see in a crowd like this. She inched forward and sipped at her wine, raising her eyes to the man who stepped out of the shadows to accept the offered microphone. And all at once she realized she was looking at the only person she had never ever ever expected to see again in her entire life.

chapter three

T here were a few things you have to understand about Viktor and they were, in no particular order, the following: He was on the tall side (thanks to long legs that looked great in everything), he had the shiniest black hair (which fell just below his ears), he had the approximate complexion of an airbrushed vampire (Anne Rice variety), and his blue eyes always looked as if someone had lovingly ringed them in kohl (even when he first woke up in the morning).

Viktor glowed with some electric dark energy, and Marling could swear that shadows bent around him, dancing at their wizard's bidding.

Of course, she had always known him as Viktor Kalashnik, not Viktor Arson.

Marling stared at him from her somewhat convenient spot near the front of the crowd, and a wave of memories attempted to overtake her.

The strongest memory was this one time when Marling was drunk and she couldn't open a jar of pickled banana peppers and Viktor opened the jar with such ease that she'd accused him of cheating. Which didn't make sense, now that she thought of it.

Why was that her strongest memory of him, though?

"It's crazy that I managed to get this guy," Benjamin said. "Over in Europe and the U.K. he's more popular than most Hollywood heartthrobs. I discovered him last year when I was, uh, I was visiting some friends in the U.K. and Viktor was at this book signing in a tiny bookstore in London. You'd have thought royalty was visiting! And you can see why. He's handsome, and gracious, and he knows all about magic. I know many of you probably first heard about him a couple weeks ago when he appeared on that morning show. Did any of you see that?"

A flurry of hands waved in the air.

"Yeah, wasn't it great? For those of you who didn't see, Viktor was interviewed by a very pretty young lady. Somewhere along the way, this reporter… well, she just sort of forgot herself and said something like 'God, you're beautiful.' It was a great moment. I checked earlier this afternoon and the video was uploaded to that uh, that website with the videos? Yeah, and it's got probably a zillion hits."

Viktor bowed his head in response, a half smirk tugging at his lips.

"Ladies and gentlemen? Viktor Arson." Benjamin waved his arm, motioning Viktor closer. As soon as Viktor was within reach, Benjamin hugged him and handed over the microphone, then hugged him again, lingering so long that everyone laughed. "Tell them one of your cool stories or something, huh? You're so hot. Okay, I'm gonna go get a drink." Benjamin tripped away, as if he was walking on a boat.

Wow.

"Don't have too much more to drink, Ben," Viktor said, the warmth of his killer hot Russian accent amplified by the microphone, which was wrapped in one of his elegant, slender hands. "Hello everyone, good evening."

Wait, was he wearing leather pants? *Leather. Pants.*

"It was so kind of Ben to invite me, and an honor, too. Don't let him say otherwise." Viktor lowered his gaze, as if thinking, and then said, "Does anyone here believe in magic?"

Was this some kind of joke? Was Marling imagining all of this? Had she fallen asleep back in the hotel and dreamed about Viktor and leather pants and... wait. Wait. Oh no. Was he looking at her? He was looking at her. He was burning holes into her with his eyes.

"You," he said, the microphone deepening his husky whisper into something else altogether. "Do you believe in magic, Marling?"

Marling let out a laugh that didn't really sound like her laughter. In fact, it sounded more like one of those squeaky toys that you buy for dogs.

"Come up here," Viktor said, his eyes still locked on her.

Marling shook her head.

"No? You don't believe?"

An uncomfortable sense of reality crashed over Marling and she glanced to her left and right. It seemed that the eyes of everyone in the apartment had turned on her. She wouldn't have been surprised if everyone started chanting and commanded her to jump into a fire and burn to death for being an unbeliever, at this point. There was no arguing with the crowd.

"Uh, I... I do," Marling said at last.

Viktor nodded, holding one hand out towards her. "Come here then."

Shaky step by shaky step, Marling walked toward Viktor with her champagne glass still clutched in hand. He was taller than she remembered, but maybe that was just because it had been such a long time since she'd seen him. And whoa, had he always smelled like he'd crawled out of a bakery? Oh wait, never mind. That was the huge platter of brownies atop the piano behind him.

But still. Had he always been this unfairly attractive?

"In the world of magic, everyone exist in three categories. They are either a magic user, a nonbeliever or... in most cases... they are just a gray. Undecided. There is a lot of gray in the world. They live among us. Perhaps some of you are gray." Viktor looked around at the crowd, and then at Marling, moving closer and closer until their noses were almost touching. "But occasionally, usually when you least expect it, you can find a magical being."

Finally, finally, finally Marling's brain kicked into gear and she realized exactly what he was saying. Was he trying to out her in front of all of these people? Tell everyone she was a witch?

"Yeah, he's right," she said, taking the microphone from him. "Occasionally you find a magical unicorn. I think we can all agree on one thing… Viktor Arson is the magical unicorn that we never expected to catch a glimpse of. I certainly never expected to catch a glimpse of him again."

Viktor ghosted his fingertip down her cheek, sending a shiver through her. "How can you tell if you've found a magical being?" he asked, his voice carrying even without the microphone. "Is it the fearful look in their eyes when you identify them? Is it the quickening of their pulse when they realize they've been discovered? Or is it the mischief that you know lurks just below their skin?" He smirked at Marling. "Maybe it's the strange buzz you hear in your ears when you stand close to them, or the burning sensation you feel if you touch them. Or maybe the taste of their skin if you're brave enough to test…"

Marling twitched.

"That is, by the way, perhaps the most accurate way to determine if someone is magical being. They all taste of traces of licorice and malevolence." Viktor brushed his lips over Marling's neck and she almost lost her balance. She cleared her throat so loudly that someone probably heard it in the apartment next door, and then she thrashed around, attempting to extract herself from his grip. What if he kissed her and she turned to jelly in his arms? What if he raked his teeth over her skin? She knew from past experience that one of his canine teeth was especially sharp… so sharp, in fact, that it could leave a mark that no amount of expensive department-store concealer could cover up.

Somewhat to Marling's relief, a girl standing close to them dropped her wine glass with a swoony sort of gasp. Marling used this as her chance to escape Viktor's hold.

Viktor smiled at her, the same exact smile that had melted her into a puddle of soup, five years ago, and then he pulled her close against his side. He grinned and posed for someone with a camera.

"Magic people and magic beings are not easy to spot and they are not easy to hold onto. If you do find one, you're already very lucky. If you want to keep one… well, perhaps you should read my books. Thank you for your time, all of you, and if you have any question for me, please feel free to ask. For now, though, please enjoy Benjamin's wonderful party." Viktor released Marling and bowed to the crowd.

"I have a question, I have a question!" a young woman in a green dress said. A small gaggle of girls and boys ringed around Viktor, leaving Marling thoroughly unable to escape.

"Do you think it's possible to see… well, you know. A real faerie? Or an elf or something?" one of the girls asked.

"Is it possible? Yes, it's possible, but by its very nature, it's also improbable. There aren't many magic folk left among us, unfortunately. And the ones that remain, they clever at hiding. They have to be."

"Your book was sooo good," one of the boys said.

"Oh, oh, where can I get your book?" an older woman asked, and the group exploded into conversation, and interchanges, and questions, and laughter.

Marling inched to the side but found she was trapped by a few more of Viktor's enthusiastic fans.

"Is it true that you can taste magic on someone?" one of the women asked. "I mean, because, I've always wondered if I had some magic…"

Viktor raised an eyebrow and nodded. "It's possible. I would suggest you draw yourself a bath with lavender and jasmine, soak in it for a few hours, and then ask someone very close and special to you if they might give a little test," he said, reaching up and pushing strands of his black hair behind his ears.

"Ahhh, that sounds heavenly." The woman blew him a kiss and then wandered off, mercifully prompting most of the crowd of fangirls and fanboys to flee with her. After all, free booze and food was enough to draw people away from anything, even sexy Russians with shiny hair and leather pants.

Marling, for her part, concentrated on doing anything other than staring at said Russian. And, after several long and burning seconds, Marling realized she had failed this attempt. Then, just as slowly as she had realized that, she realized Viktor had caught her staring.

"What are you doing here?" he asked, in an undertone.

"I'm here for work. What are *you* doing here?"

"Benjamin invited me," Viktor said.

"The Gross guy?"

"Yes, his surname is Gross."

Marling raised her chin. "I know that. I wasn't making a comment on his appearance. I was just… clarifying. And you have to admit, his last name is kind of funny."

Viktor's mouth quirked into a smile, as if he was struggling to hold back laughter.

A short woman approached Viktor then, staring up at him with wide eyes and an open mouth, adoration nearly dripping off of her. "Someone told me that you got your scar during an encounter with a real fae. Is that true?" she asked, and Marling stepped away from Viktor.

"I'll leave you to your fans. Goodbye," Marling said, her stomach plummeting to her feet from old memories and something else, a tug stronger than anything she'd ever felt. Oh no. No, no, no, no. No! The unlove spell. She'd almost forgotten about it, after all of these years of minding her own business and living entirely without worry about love or romance.

No.

Marling walked away from Viktor, dropping her empty champagne glass in a trashcan along the way. She had to get away from him, and she didn't care where she went.

"Marling?"

Had he called her name? No, no, no, no. A silly and incredibly naïve young girl had placed a spell on herself, five years ago, but that girl was gone now. Marling lowered her head, afraid to meet anyone's eyes as she pushed through the crowd and headed for the door.

There were three things that Marling was not particularly pleased about in regards to herself. One, her nose was crooked. Two, her voice was a bit deeper than she'd like it to be. Third, even after two consecutive years of French tutoring as a child, Marling could only remember about a dozen French words. Of course, there were also three things that she was terribly proud of. One, she'd never dyed her chestnut-brown hair (well, maybe once she'd dyed it with a spray can of sparkly pink stuff but it had mostly washed out after five weeks). Two, she had always maintained a comfortable size 12 (petite). Third, thanks to her mother's Indian heritage, she always looked tan, even in the dead of winter, when her whiter friends were desperately scrubbing lotion into their skin to look less ghostly.

Her ability to perceive magic didn't fall into either the embarrassment or pride category, though. It fell somewhere in the middle, along with her ability to cook, and her three attempts at driving stick-shift. She wanted to feel and understand magic, but she wasn't a natural talent at it.

But, just as she reached the door, Marling felt a shiver of something distinctly, powerfully magical.

chapter four

M agic, real magic.

Marling winced as another wave of warm, tingling energy danced through her insides, all the way to her head. She had only ever felt magic like this a few times in her life, and all of those times had been during her lessons with Lady Grieve, witch extraordinaire. Lady Grieve liked to say that sensing magic out in the real world was highly unusual, and she encouraged her students to enjoy the sensations if ever given the opportunity.

After all, the witch liked to say, *there are almost no magical beings left. And you know what flakes humans are, even the ones who practice magic.*

But this was certainly stronger than anything Marling had ever felt, even in her classes. And despite all of Lady Grieve's insistence that magical creatures existed, Marling had never so much as seen a photograph of one.

Where was it coming from?

Closing her eyes, Marling reached out with her senses, whispering silently to the noises in the room to reorganize themselves around her so that she could hear through the laughter, shouting, conversation, and pounding music. Finally, Marling caught the strands of magic. Good, good, now to follow it.

It turned out that Benjamin Gross' swanky apartment situation came with an equally swanky set-up of things like a fitness room, a "greenery room," and an indoor swimming pool. It was the swimming pool that Marling felt herself drawn to, without any explanation or promise of discovery.

"Alright," Marling muttered, looking around the empty pool room. She'd half expected to see a unicorn or something, considering how powerful the tingly sensation had grown, but she didn't see anyone. Not even fat old guys or skimpy-clad girls or children that should be supervised. All she saw was a stack of neatly folded towels on one of the poolside tables, and something that looked like a discarded black dress or cover-up.

Weird.

Marling turned to walk away, but she heard a splash and whirled back around.

"Hello?" she called, her eyes dancing around the darkened pool room. She saw no sign of life, no bubbles in the water, no wet footprints around the edge of the pool. Marling crept closer to the pool, kneeling when she reached the edge. She dropped her purse and then peered down into the water. "Hello?"

A hand extended out of the water so quickly that Marling barely saw it. It wrapped around the back of her neck before she could stop it. With a gasp, she felt herself tumbling forward, into the water, and then she was under water, flopping and fighting against the firm grip that had taken hold of her.

Thrashing about, Marling realized somewhere in the back of her mind that it felt like arms holding her... but far stronger arms than she'd ever come into contact with. Finally, as if her captor had changed his or her mind, the arms fell away and Marling was able to kick her way upward, toward the surface. She broke water and let out a gasp.

Fingers laced around her ankle, slow and graceful, and someone tugged on her. Marling barely kept her head above water. "Leave me alone! Let go! Help!"

"Shhh, darling, don't be so loud," a voice said, from just behind Marling. "You'll wake the dead."

Marling kicked, as hard as she could, and felt the hand release her ankle. She spun around, hands slapping desperately at the water, determined to keep herself from getting dragged under again.

Eyes peered back at her, the approximate color of dirty emeralds, and the smile that accompanied the eyes sent a shiver through Marling. "Who are you?"

"You don't know me, so don't worry," the stranger said, gracefully gliding closer and closer to Marling. She was female, that much was obvious both from the delicate bone structure and the pale, ample breasts that were half visible above the surface of the water. But something about her didn't strike Marling as human, starting with the pointed teeth that flashed between full, pink lips. "But I'd love to know who you are."

"I'm lost," Marling said, before she could think of anything else. "I'm... I was trying to leave the party and I got lost."

The creature cocked her head to the side, sliding her tongue out between her teeth and slowly licking her upper lip. "Mmm, lost? Are you sure?"

"Yes!" Marling said, kicking away from her. "And you've probably ruined my dress. And definitely my hair."

"Did I? Well, I suppose I'd be sorrier if it was a nice dress. I did you a favor as far as I can tell," the stranger said, and grinned.

Rude! "What are you?" Marling demanded. "Are you a mermaid?"

The green eyed creature smiled again. With an elegant but dangerously fast movement, she seized hold of Marling's arm and pulled her close. "A mermaid? You're going to have to be a bit more creative than that. A lady of the elements who happens to sometimes prefer the water? Getting closer," she said, in Marling's ear. "But don't worry, little girl. I know you're just ignorant." With one last smirk, the creature released Marling and swam to the shallow end of the pool. Pearlescent purple fins splashed behind her as she pulled herself out of the water.

Marling's mouth fell open.

The creature's magnificent tail evaporated, a few scales at a time, revealing shapely white legs and wide hips.

"You like to stare, don't you?" the woman asked, standing and reaching up to straighten her short hair. Her frame was small but exaggerated, and the skin of her face might have belonged to a young child for how clear and smooth it was. Her walk was inherently sassy as she sauntered to the neatly folded towels and wrapped one around her tiny waist. "Please don't tell me that this is your first time seeing something magical, little witch."

With a great deal less grace than the mermaid, Marling managed to climb out of the pool. She shivered, wrapped her arms around herself, and tried to keep her teeth from chattering. "How do you know that?" she demanded.

"Know what? That you're a witch?"

Marling nodded.

"Simple enough. You felt that something was a bit off, so you explored and poked about until you found me, didn't you? Hardly the calling card of a normal girl. Plus, you're surprised, but not as surprised as most would be." The strange lady picked up the crumpled black dress from where Marling had earlier spotted it. "My kind and your kind tend to know each other in a crowd."

"Isn't it just a little bit dangerous for you to be... to be swimming around down here with a *tail*?" Marling could think of a lot of places that a mermaid could go for a swim, and the indoor pool in Benjamin Gross' swanky apartment building was not one of them.

The woman slipped into her black dress and patted delicately at her short hair. "Dangerous? No. Daring? Maybe a little. But that party was oh so boring and I wanted to take a swim. It's not too much to ask, really, just a few moments away to regain my sanity after listening to everyone fawn over Viktor Arson and tell him their favorite party stories." She shrugged. "My name is Petra. What's your name, little witch?"

"Marling Ellis."

Petra's eyes turned up with her smile. "What a strange name. I like it. Come along now, let's return you to the party before someone misses you. A boyfriend perhaps? Your mother? Professor? Your favorite warlock?" Petra walked away then, with the ease of a runway model.

And, eventually, after Marling had patted at her hair and dress with a towel, muttering all the while, she realized she should probably follow Petra.

After all, she had a lot more questions now than she had fifteen minutes ago.

chapter five

Marling caught up with Petra just as the other woman reached the elevator. When the door chimed and opened at the correct floor, Petra simply held her arm out for Marling to go first.

"If you're not a mermaid, what are you?" Marling demanded, but Petra rolled her eyes and walked away. In seconds, Marling lost sight of the other woman as she was swallowed into Benjamin's party.

"Are you okay?" someone asked Marling, eyeing her up and down in horror. "You're... Is it snowing that hard out there?"

Marling shook her head. "No! No, I uh, I... I fell in the pool." When this answer was met with only a stony faced expression, Marling added, "You know how it is. Too much champagne."

Suddenly the other person smiled and nodded and walked away.

Still shivering, Marling worked her way across the room, intent on snagging something to eat and then making a hasty exit. After all, nothing about this party had gone right. She'd embarrassed herself in front of Patrick Jones-Wiley, run into the only man she never wanted to see again, discovered a mermaid, and trashed her dress. And her hair. How much worse could things get?

Well, considering Marling's luck, things could get much, much worse, and a long history of "much, much worse" had taught her not to push it in these situations.

And, as bad luck would have it, the crab rangoon was long gone, as were the egg rolls. The only thing left on the once laden tray of Chinese food were a few pieces of skewered chicken that looked as if they'd seen better days. Marling let out a disappointed sigh usually reserved for more important things, like empty bags of Lindt chocolate, and considered the table's other options. The soup appeared to be roughly the color and consistency of something that came out of your nose when you're sick. Worse, when Marling leaned closer, she spotted several unidentifiable vegetables floating in it. They smelled vaguely onionish but for all Marling knew, they might be leeks or something.

And leeks were *not* real onions, no matter what anyone tried to say.

Marling felt someone standing behind her and groaned, closing her eyes. It would be Patrick, all buggy-eyed and annoying, probably ready to pounce on her with rude words in exchange for their conversation earlier. Normally she would take a deep, cleansing breath and act professional, saying all sorts of cute, funny and complimentary things to Patrick Jones-Wiley until he melted at her feet and begged her to publish his next book. But there was a mermaid on the loose and Marling was hungry. She would just ignore him, and hopefully he would go away.

"What happened to you?"

"What?" Marling said, turning around. "Oh. Viktor."

"You're soaking wet!"

"It's not as bad as it looks, I guess." She shrugged and took a step back from him, wishing for the millionth time that she hadn't put that unlove spell on herself. Every instinct begged her to get closer to him, to hug him and kiss him all over his face. But she couldn't do that, and she shouldn't even talk to him. If she talked to him, she might tell him about the mermaid and receive an invitation to investigate or, worse, a look of disbelief. "Uh, I'm just getting something to eat and then I'm leaving."

Viktor offered Marling his plate, which was topped with an eggroll and a few pieces of Crab rangoon. "I thought maybe you were looking for these. I know how much you like Chinese."

Oh, he knew alright. They'd once made a disastrous journey together for Chinese food, which they'd dubbed The Great Eggroll Crisis as soon as they'd finally sat stuffing their faces with sweet and sour chicken. The Great Eggroll Crisis had taken place on the fourth day of their romance, and late that night, bellies full of MSG, they'd wandered together along 5th Avenue. Halfway into their leisurely stroll, Viktor had gotten the phone call that signaled the end of something Marling had never planned to begin in the first place.

Even now, she would hold fast to the claim that his cell phone had accidentally fallen into the street, causing it to be run over by all of those taxis. Even now she couldn't quite admit that seeing his face crumble from bad news, hearing him raggedly announce that he had to leave, had prompted her to use magic to take some childish revenge on the bearer of his bad news.

"Uhhh..." Deflect and deny? Nah, her stomach was threatening to gnaw itself inside out. "Yeah, thanks," she said at last, accepting the plate. "Shouldn't you be running around meeting your fans?"

"I like running, but not indoors. It's easy to catch your foot on something and fall face-first into a coffee table."

"You're pretty graceful."

"Ah, that's what I'd like you to think." Viktor's eyes worked over her. "What happen to you? You look like you fall in a pool."

"You're not far off. Someone pulled me into a pool."

"What were you doing near a pool in first place?"

Marling turned her face up, meeting his eyes. She couldn't tell him the truth, of course, because mermaids were generally not real, and when they were real, they weren't real in swimming pools inside New York City apartment buildings. "I was lost," she said, stepping away from the table and leaning casually against a wall.

"Lost?"

"Yes. I was trying to leave and I… got lost."

"And someone pull you into a pool? On purpose or on accident? I can speak to Benjamin about this if you'd like."

"No!" Marling startled herself as much as Viktor with the volume of her reply. "Benjamin doesn't need to worry about it. It was an accident."

Viktor's eyes narrowed. "You're lying to me."

"Uh, no I'm not. Why would I lie about something like that? You make it sound like some monster pulled me into the pool and tried to drown me, and I just don't want to tell you or something, ha ha ha." Marling took a too-big bite of food and chewed, trying to ignore the confused and suspicious expression on Viktor's face.

"A monster?"

"See how crazy that sounds? A monster, ha. It was an accident Viktor, don't make it into… you know, one of your fairytale books."

As if speaking about monsters had summoned her, Petra showed up just then, cradling a tall flute of champagne in one delicate hand.

"Petra, there you are," Viktor said, holding his arm out to her. Petra pressed against him and leaned in for a kiss. This wasn't some friendly Eastern European traditional peck on the cheek kiss between old friends. This was a full on open mouth kiss that made Marling feel as if she might burst into flames just from observing it. She was the exact kind of cool, effortless woman that Marling had always desperately wished she could be. Just observing her made long-buried jealousy rise in Marling's stomach, if only because the other woman was so... suave.

"Aw, Viktor, you found my new friend," Petra said, releasing Viktor and casting a sinister half smile at Marling. "Isn't she cute? I found her wandering by the pool." Petra took a long sip of her champagne and then patted Viktor on the shoulder with one hand. "Keep a close eye on her, though. I think she's a bit more troublesome than she looks."

Petra sauntered away as easily as she'd appeared, and Marling turned immediately to Viktor. "Do you know her?"

"Yes, she's one of my oldest friends."

Marling opened her mouth to say something but found the thought interrupted by a more important inquiry. "Do you greet all of your friends like that? Is that why Benjamin likes you so much?"

"No, Petra and I are close."

"Close like she's your girlfriend?"

Viktor frowned. "Girlfriend? No, no not at all. I told you, we're very good friends. I know Petra since I'm a little boy."

Oh. Well, that complicated things. Marling didn't feel it would be polite to say, *Well, are you aware of the fact that your very good childhood friend is actually a mermaid?* Marling said, "Okay," and then couldn't think of anything else to say, so she returned to eating her Chinese food. But she did so in a very pensive manner.

"Viktor! Viktor, Viktor, would you mind signing these? For the silent auction?" Benjamin asked, crashing past a few of his guests to reach Viktor. He shoved two books into Viktor's hands. "Do you need a pen? I can get a pen."

"It's alright, Ben, I have one." Viktor reached inside his jacket and withdrew a fancy silver pen that looked vaguely familiar to Marling for some reason. He signed his name with a flourish in each of the books and then smiled, handing them back to Benjamin. A light flashed and Viktor raised his head to smile for the camera.

"You've read his books, right?" Benjamin asked, nudging Marling.

"Err, no."

"Oh, you should. You have to! This guy makes you feel like you could reach out and touch a magical being." Benjamin nudged Marling again. "If you told me he had a unicorn and an elf chained up in his backyard, I wouldn't be surprised, you know?" Benjamin laughed and Marling caught sight of Viktor's rather horrified expression. "That's how familiar he is with it. He writes about these things like he knows them."

Marling thought again of Petra the not-really-a-mermaid.

"You're too kind, Benjamin. It's just lot of research. Extensive research in fae history. And of course, also overactive imagination," Viktor said, his lips curling up in a manner that didn't convey any happiness to his eyes.

What was wrong with him?

"Naaaah, you have a talent that borders on the obscene. I think you're hiding something, Viktor! I bet you're actually an elf or something." Benjamin slapped Viktor on the back, a bit too hard, and laughed heartily before walking away.

"Benjamin. He's so weird," Viktor said.

Marling just stared at Viktor, though, questions lining up in her head and demanding answers. "Can we talk?"

Viktor shook his head and opened his mouth to say something, but he was interrupted for a second time, this time by a woman wearing a baggy green sweater. She was a bit braver than some of the fans from earlier, going so far as to reach out and pat him on the back until he pulled back from Marling and turned around. "Darling, do you write about vampires?"

"Vampires? I don't know very much about vampires."

"Really? My daughter's such a vampire fanatic, she reads any book about vampires. Aren't vampires almost the same thing as faeries? I mean, none of them are real, of course, but..."

Viktor offered a closed-eyed, tight-lipped smile that Marling had long ago realized meant he would rather be tongue kissing an iguana than smiling and nodding. "Well, you see, no. It's different. Just a little."

"Leetle," Marling said. "Leetle! I love his accent. Don't you love his accent?"

The green sweater lady politely cleared her throat and patted her chest a few times. "Yes, yes, it's a lovely accent. You know, I spent eleven years in various parts of Russia. You know how it is when you're young, you just want to see everything! And anyway, it's gall darn weird but I just... I can't place your accent." She patted her chest again. "Where exactly in Russia are you from, Viktor?"

"Yeah, Viktor, what part of Russia are you from?" Marling asked, in a mocking voice. Maybe she could distract him from the whole mermaid issue until she could successfully escape.

Viktor looked as if he might actually turn into a vampire and bite the woman's neck, more so to kill her than to pacify her. After a long and increasingly tense pause, he said, "My mother live in St. Petersburg when she was young and then she meet my father in Moscow. I was born in Moscow but I grow up in a very small town that you likely never hear of."

"Ohhh, Moscow!"

"Travel will chip away at your accent too," Viktor said, his tone becoming a little more serious as he fixed his gaze on the woman.

The green sweater lady blushed a little, stepping away from Viktor. "Well, cheerio. I'll have to uh, tell my daughter I met you. I think she's a fan. I'll see if she wants me to buy one of your books for her."

"Do you want me to sign something for her?"

The green sweater lady coughed, shaking her head. "No, no. No, but thank you. Interesting talking to you. Enjoy the party!" She made a hasty exit, muttering under her breath, and Marling just stared after her.

"Wow. You really do have a power bordering on the obscene. You just terrified that woman."

"Not really. People are not accustomed to eye contact like mine."

And didn't she know it? Viktor's eye contact had been a huge factor in why she'd fallen for him in the first place. But no, stop it. Leave it alone.

"Did you say you wanted to talk?"

"No, I… no. I've gotta get out of here. I was supposed to talk Patrick Jones-Wiley into signing a book with my company and not only did that not happen but I think I offended him for life. And I don't really care because he's kind of a pretentious little jerk. Plus he's a teenager or something. He looks twelve. Tops. But I'm definitely going to lose my job, and end up homeless so I should go put some job applications in at that mall near Macy's." Marling tugged at her ear. "Hey, thanks for the Chinese food, really. Thank you."

She walked away, every fiber of her body calming as she put distance between herself and Viktor. *Keep walking, keep walking, hurry or you'll change your mind. Keep walking! Keep walking.*

chapter six

Outside, the temperature seemed to have dropped and the snow had taken on a new monster-like appearance, as if marshmallows and malevolent angels had combined forces. Marling shivered and tugged the hood of her jacket down to hide her face from the wind.

"Marling! Marling, wait." Viktor darted toward her, his feet slipping on the icy sidewalk as he approached her. "Wait."

"Don't fall! And get back inside; you're not even wearing a coat!" Marling said.

Viktor motioned at his dressy jacket. "I am."

"That's not a real coat." She shivered. "It's freezing out here. Go back inside before you catch a cold or something."

Viktor shook his head, half a smile lifting his lips. "You're so bossy."

Powerful forces pushed her closer and closer to him, begging and commanding her to touch his face… or shove him into the wall and get them both in trouble for inappropriate behavior in public. But she forced her chin up and met his gaze. His eyes were so pretty...

No, no, stop it! Focus, Marling!

"You should go back to your party. Your fans probably miss you," she said, her words coming out a bit more sulky than she'd intended them to be.

"You're certainly very concern about my fans."

A giggled escaped Marling before she could stop herself. "Very concern."

"Yeah! You keep throwing me back to them. What do you want me to do? Take off my shirt and... crowdsurf or something?"

Marling shook her head, laughing even harder. "That's not why I'm laughing. I'm sorry, it's not nice of me at all. It's just... the things you say. You say phrases wrong, and it still cracks me up. It's cute."

"I mean, sometimes I think I'm rock star too, but probably not at a party like this. Maybe in Berlin. Or Tokyo or something." Viktor shrugged. "Why do you have to leave?"

Before Marling could answer, some idiot in a puffy bright orange coat barreled through, knocking into her and sending Marling's sense of balance into the outer stratosphere. She reached for anything to grab hold of and Viktor was the closest tall, steady object. She attempted to steady herself with him but then he slipped too and both of them slid around on the sidewalk, dangerously close to falling. Finally, Viktor wrapped his arms around Marling and held her completely still.

"Calm down," he whispered. "The easiest way to fall is to panic."

Marling groaned, tipping her face up to look at him. "You can let me go, really. I'll be okay. The newborn deer on unsteady legs act is over, I promise."

"That's too bad, it was kinda funny to watch."

"I'm glad it was so amusing for you." Marling gave up squirming and allowed herself a few seconds of contented cuddling against the unusual warmth of his body. "Do you have a fever or something? You feel really warm."

His arms tightened around her a little. "I'm always warm."

Actually, now that she thought about it that was true. During their four days together, she'd never found him to be particularly susceptible to the cold weather, not even when she was buried under a scarf, mittens, a sweater and thick coat.

"Please don't tell me you're a werewolf or something," she mumbled against him.

"I promise I am not a werewolf."

Of course, that just sent her mind back to the pool and the mermaid who may or may not be Viktor's best friend/future wife. Marling sighed and pushed away from Viktor.

"You said you wanted to talk about something in there," Viktor said. "What was it? I think there's no way we ran into each other again just by accident."

"By accident? I don't know about that."

"It's been really, really long time, and we end up at the same party together. Seems like fate to me. You said you're here for work? Is it the same place you worked when we were together? No, wait, you'd just gotten fired..."

Marling pressed her lips together. "Mmm hmmm."

"Just gotten fired by 'evil, red haired Medusa from Hades', I think that's what you called your boss." Viktor chuckled, his gaze becoming a little unfocused and introspective. "And you were rather please with yourself because getting fired mean you had the holiday off. Please enough to tell this entire story to some old homeless woman."

"Hey now, I didn't mean to tell her anything. That was bad whiskey."

"Bad whiskey, yeah. Like when I have a lot of bad whiskey at that party. The reason we met."

For a long time, neither of them spoke, until Marling became aware of the fact that her fingers felt like they might freeze and fall off. "You sure remember a lot of what happened, Viktor," she said, and his smile fell away slowly.

"It was good time."

"Was it, really? Because the part I remember most clearly was how you got a phone call and suddenly had to leave. And then yeah, I said some mean things to you. But you couldn't take it and you left. And nothing I said made it better. Oh and then I never heard from you again."

Viktor let out a huge sigh, his breath floating visibly around him like a cartoon cloud. "You tell me, 'I hope I never see you again. I wish I'd never met you. Why don't you just go away?' That's what you say."

"Yeah, it was dumb," Marling said with a helpless shrug. "But we were always saying dumb things to each other and squabbling from the beginning, so I didn't think it would matter."

"Saying you wish you'd never met me? That's not squabbling, Marling."

"I was angry! I say stupid things when I'm angry! And then I told you I was sorry."

"You swore at me in French."

"I called you a *pineapple!*" Marling exclaimed. "I don't know any swear words in French, okay? I know like ten words and most of them are the names of fruit."

Viktor frowned. "You call me a... pineapple?"

"Yeah, well, there you go. All this time you thought I called you something awful and really I called you a pineapple." Marling's face warmed to an unbearable temperature. "But you just had to walk away and leave me."

"My mother died."

Marling had a whole speech in mind, which would have probably been delivered sloppily but with a great deal of self-righteous passion. But those mumbled words from Viktor sent her plan crashing into a hundred pieces.

"That's what the phone call was. Her best friend call to tell me that my mother die and I need to come home as soon as possible." Viktor shrugged one of his shoulders, locking eyes with her.

"You should have told me."

"I didn't know what to say, because I hadn't known you that long and it seem like an unfair burden to place on your shoulders."

"But if you'd said… if you'd told me that's why you were leaving… Well, maybe things could have been different. I wouldn't have said those things. I'm so sorry, Viktor. I had no idea. I thought it was some business thing maybe, or just something stupid." Marling stepped toward him, hugging her arms tight around her chest. "I'm sorry."

"It doesn't matter. Look, what I'm saying is, it was a long time ago and no matter what happened, there must be some reason why I would run into you again. There's always a reason."

The wisest thing, of course, would be for Marling to say her goodbyes and continue back to her hotel as planned. After all, it was dangerously cold out and the snow was piling up. Cars were barely moving from the storm, and who knew how bad the subway stations would be? On top of all of that, everything Marling had built up inside herself, the determination never to be foolish and naïve and lovestruck again, felt as if it was shaky for the first time in five years. Escape was the only choice, really.

"It might not be some glorious act of fate," she said, her voice nearly breaking. Marling cleared her throat and tried again. "You and I meeting might not really be anything more than my stupidity. I- I accidentally put an unlove spell on myself when you left, something that stops me from being able to love anyone else but you. And I don't know if there's a way to reverse it but as far as I can tell, I'm stuck with it. I was an idiot. And I live with that every day." She cleared her throat again as tears burned her eyes. "All of this might just be…well, nothing more than my spell at work. It's trying to bring us back together."

Viktor shook his head.

"It was so stupid of me but I was a lot younger, and I guess I thought it was noble at the time. Or maybe cinematic, I don't know. Like romance movies! But it was stupid, let's be honest,"

Marling said, stepping backward, away from him. "And I think tonight was just some part of that spell."

For every step Marling took backward, Viktor took another toward her, until finally he reached out and took hold of her arm.

"Just let it go, Viktor, please. It doesn't mean anything."

"No, no. You were about to walk over the curb." He motioned behind her and Marling slowly turned her head. Sure enough, she'd been about to step over the curb, at which time she likely would have fallen to her death.

"Oh. Thanks."

He dipped his head in response and then frowned. "So you weren't kidding about being a...?"

Marling's mouth dropped open. "Really? Really, that's all you can ask right now? If I'm really a witch? I *told* you I was!"

"Calm down, yes you did. But you also tell me you're professional tennis player from Sweden, with a collection of expensive cars in your mansion. You tell the homeless person that too."

Wait, was he laughing? He was. Viktor was laughing at her. Jerk. "It's not funny!" she said.

"I'm sorry for laughing at you. But really, you can do spells?"

"Yes I can do spells and you know what? If I wanted to, right now, I could turn you into something. I could turn you into a..." She searched her mind for something even slightly plausible, but nothing came to her. Marling and pretty much every other witch that had ever come into contact with her knew that she couldn't turn a human into anything. Not even a decent cook. She knew that one in particular because she'd tried to turn herself into a decent cook.

"Yes?" Viktor prompted. "Into what?"

"I could turn you into something that hasn't been invented yet," she said, in the most cryptic tone she could manage. "You won't even know that I did anything to you at first, the change will be so subtle."

"Ah."

"I happen to have been trained under one of the most famous witches in all of America," Marling said.

Viktor nodded, visibly fighting against a smile. "I never doubted your credentials, don't worry. I was just unsure if you could cast spells. It's not as easy as people make it look in the movies."

"Who told you that, your mermaid friend?" Marling demanded, and then realized what she'd just said.

Oooops.

chapter seven

Viktor clapped his hand over Marling's mouth, yanking her full against himself and looking around frantically. He heard a muffled protest and realized what he'd just done. He removed his hand from Marling's mouth but continued to hold her close. "We need to talk," he muttered.

"Don't you dare try to like, kidnap me or something!" Marling attempted to push away from him and then wiggled a little when she was unsuccessful. "I swear I'll turn you into something. Let me go right now, Viktor Arson, or I will turn you into something really, really bad."

Viktor rolled his eyes. "You can't heat a cup of coffee with your magic. Now be quiet until we find some place private to talk."

Earlier, Viktor had taken a short walk, clearing his head and preparing himself for the party. He wasn't an introvert, certainly, but neither was he a flaming extrovert. There was a part of him that loved posing for pictures and acting hammy for a crowd. Who didn't like the attention? Especially when you'd grown up second best to a more popular sibling, a flamboyant mother, and a thousand hallways of ancient history that you could never fully comprehend?

But he still always felt a nervous sensation deep in the pit of his belly before he was forced into a large crowd in a small space, so he liked to walk it out if possible. During the walk, he'd noticed a coffee shop two blocks down that looked rather comfortable and cozy.

"Where are you taking me?" Marling demanded, as Viktor all but dragged her away. "If you're trying to kidnap me, you're going to be sorry. I eat a lot. And I think I snore."

"You don't snore."

"Well maybe I snore now! My roommate said the other night she got worried about the sounds coming from my room." Marling cleared her throat. "I think it was their cat, but who knows. Maybe it was me. Maybe I have sleep apnea. That would be really annoying."

"You don't need sleep apnea to be annoying."

Marling attempted to elbow him, but that only caused her to lose her balance. Viktor caught her, barely, and steadied her before continuing on.

"What is this? What is this place?" Marling demanded, as Viktor opened the door to the coffee shop.

"Your lips are turn blue from the cold. I thought we could talk somewhere warm, but if you want to go back outside, we can do that."

With a quick glance over her shoulder, Marling let out a little sigh. "Fine. Fine!"

Viktor hooked arms with Marling, leading her toward the counter. "We'll take a plain latte and hot chocolate with extra whipped cream," he said, reaching for his wallet.

"You're buying me something?"

"Is that alright?"

"I'm just surprised, since you're kidnapping me." Marling tapped one finger on the glass over the food display. "While you're at it, you should buy one of those brownies. Those look good."

The man behind the counter shot Viktor a quizzical look, his hands hovering over the register. "Do I know you from somewhere?"

"I don't think so. We'll take one of the brownies too," Viktor said. "For here."

Normally he didn't mind running into fans or curious types, but right now he had something vitally important to discuss, namely the fact that his cover might have been fully blown by Petra. She'd always been reckless, but lately it had reached a new level that could land one or both of them in a dark cell somewhere, iron chains on their ankles, cords hooked up to their veins, drained of their lifeblood...

Marling elbowed Viktor so hard that it hurt.

"Ow!"

"Thanks for the hot chocolate."

"You're intent on breaking my ribs, aren't you?" Viktor rubbed his side and then led Marling to an empty table in the back corner of the shop. He perched on the edge of a chair, waving a hand rather antagonistically at Marling. "Now sit down and tell me exactly what you know about Petra."

Marling sat down and took a long sip of her hot chocolate. "She's a mermaid. Did you collect her in your research travels? Or was she some kind of super special edition mail order magical bride? I mean, I know you Russians are into that kind of thing."

"Do you even hear the words coming out of your mouth right now? God."

"What's the big deal? I'd just like to know how you found her. I mean, it's pretty cool that she can turn into a mermaid. My teacher always said there were magical beings out there but after a while you kind of stop believing it. I mean, even Kyran said he didn't think there's much of anything left of elves or dragons." Marling took another long sip. "This is delicious."

Viktor leaned across the table, as close to Marling as he could manage. "You saw her transform?" If Marling had seen Petra transform, who else might have? A hunter?

"Yeah. Do you know any faeries? I've always wanted to meet one of those."

Warmth flooded Viktor's face, his hands, the insides of his arms and the top of his chest. Fire fought to escape him, but he silently commanded it to calm, to cool down, to dissipate. He took a few long, slow breaths.

"Why are you doing that with your mouth?"

"What?"

"You had your mouth in an 'o' shape. Are you going to throw up? I hate when people throw up. I always remember this time when-"

"Your mother threw up in front of you, yes, I know. Listen to me, Marling, this is very important. You have to swear to me, right here and right now that you will never, ever tell anyone else about Petra. Do you understand? Not your mother, not your father, not your best friend, not your boss, not your teacher. Swear it to me."

Marling stared back at him, her eyes reflecting only a shade of fear and that stubborn curiosity that maddened and intrigued Viktor. "Okay."

"No, it's not okay." Viktor reached across the table, snatching hold of one of her wrists. "Swear it. Swear it like you... swear it on the unlove spell."

"I won't tell anyone, geez."

Viktor pulled his chair closer to Marling, still holding her arm. He leaned his forehead against hers. "If someone is discovered as fae, they're carried off in chains made of iron and hidden somewhere, away from light, away from chance of rescue, and their captors take knives and slice their skin open and drain their blood, a little at a time. Fae blood is worth a fortune."

For the millionth time, he thought of his brother. Was Haven hauled into some dingy basement and drained of every drop of his blood, left to turn to ash while rich fools drooled over vials of his fae blood?

Viktor had grown up hearing stories about the Missing Ones but it wasn't until Haven disappeared that it really meant anything. The elder fae prince, the mischievous favorite had been kidnapped, and suddenly their mother looked Viktor in the face and said, *Your brother is gone. Your brother is gone and now I just have you, my sad little beauty.*

Marling shuddered against him. "You... you're one of them too, aren't you?" she whispered.

"Swear you'll never tell anyone, Marling."

"I won't, I won't. You know I won't."

Viktor released his hold on her arm. "I'm sorry. I didn't mean to do that."

Marling took his face in her hands, stared at him as if she'd never seen him before. She brushed her thumb over his cheek, raked her fingers gently through his hair, brushed a fingertip over his bottom lip. "Why didn't I see that before? I should have known. You're so weird and I found you in a crowd." She shook her head. "Well, a crowd of drunken idiots, but still. I should have known."

"No, the idea is that no one knows."

"But I should have known, Viktor. Remember when you said we know each other in some weird way, like we were lovers in a past life?"

Viktor sighed. "I think you're the one who said that."

"No, you said it. And you're right, we do know each other. And I should have known." Marling brushed her fingers across his face again. "Are you a... a... a mermaid too?" Even as she asked it, her face twisted into a smile, as if she was trying to hold back a laugh.

"No, no. I'm only half fae, and not the same bloodline as Petra. Please listen to me, Marling. It's crucial that you understand that you can't tell anyone. You not only put Petra in danger, but you also put my life in danger. And those people out there, those hunters, they don't want to kill a captive fae, not all at once. Better a slow bleed, because then they have some left for next buyer, next season."

Marling's face blanched visibly. "I won't tell anyone, I promise. I just wish you'd told me, before."

Someone cleared his throat, loudly, and Viktor and Marling both jumped, turning their heads to find the employee who had earlier helped them. "Did you even want this brownie?" he asked, in an unnecessarily gruff tone.

Silently, Viktor stood up, accepted the brownie and placed it in front of Marling before returning to his own seat. He flashed a look at the employee that sent the man scrambling.

"Whoa, you did that again," Marling whispered.

"Did what?"

"You gave him the evil eyes. You did that with the vampire question woman back at the party. Is that because you're a..." Marling glanced around before leaning closer and whispering, "Is it because you're fae?"

"More likely because I'm very frustrate right now."

Marling giggled and it almost felt like old times again, with Viktor trying to get an important message across and Marling snickering and smiling up at him sweetly, and telling him that his English had come out hysterically wrong. He'd never known anyone as ridiculous, and silly, and carefree as Marling. Despite Viktor's best efforts, he found himself smiling and shaking his head.

"You're impossible, Marling."

"I missed you," she said, and for once, he knew she meant it.

"You too."

"Is there anything else I should know about you? I mean, I just feel like I never really knew anything about you at all."

Viktor sat back in his chair, commanding the warmth in his fingers to fade away, calming himself as much as possible. He picked up his coffee and took a few long sips. "We only knew each other four days. It's not much time."

"Well, I mean… do you have any rich cousins? Are you royalty? Did you like to dress up in red fringe dresses and high heels and sing Patsy Cline songs in high school?"

Viktor choked on his coffee and coughed so hard that Marling got up and hit him a couple times on the back. "Red fringe dress, Marling?"

"I guess the high heels part was a bit much, considering you're already taller than 75% of humans but you never know. And if a guy can secretly turn out to be a magical creature, he can also have a few fringe dresses or Cher records in his closet, if you know what I mean."

"No," Viktor said, as he regained his breath. "I attended very stuffy boys' school, so that kind of thing wouldn't go over well."

"You attended a boys' school? You never told me that either! Please tell me you're the heir to some huge oil fortune or something. Or one of your great aunts was actually Anastasia Romanov."

Viktor had grown up in a cold environment, literally and figuratively. Someone like Marling wouldn't have fit into any part of his childhood home. Her laughter was too uncontrolled, her jokes too wince-worthy, her questions too direct and unfiltered. A part of him warned that Marling was dangerous to his sanity, because she was a candy coated drug that he would never be allowed to make a habit of.

But he was going home tomorrow, wasn't he? He would take up the responsibilities that someone as innocent and happy as Marling would never have to understand. He would fall or fly under the dead eyes of generations of magical beings that would never know his name or his heart.

"You're all quiet. Did I get it right? Your great aunt was Anastasia? Because I always really wanted to meet Anastasia. I wrote her a letter when I was 8, for this school thing. The teacher said it was really impressive because I worked time travel into my letter," Marling said, still standing beside Viktor and tracing her hand across his back. "I don't remember the time travel thing, but then, my logic has always been a bit weird."

Viktor turned his eyes up to meet her gaze. "No, I'm afraid I'm not related to her."

"Well, you were really quiet, like more than usual. I must have gotten something right, so just tell me."

Tomorrow. He was leaving tomorrow, so why not tell her? It wouldn't matter after tonight anyway.

"I'm from a royal family, yes. And I will inherit a great deal of money from my father someday." Too much money, of course, just the way his mother had planned it. Money that would fund the fae cause for decades. "It's not as exciting as it sounds," he said, his gaze falling from hers again.

Marling gasped. "So you're a... you're a prince? Like Prince Harry?"

"I'm actually not a prince."

"You don't have to be humble about it. It's not like I'm going to reverse-judge you or something."

"No, I'm not being humble." Viktor sighed. "I'm King now. I should have been crowned five years ago when my mother died, but in Surki you're allowed five years of mourning before you must take the throne. I've given myself as long as possible but I'll have to allow the ceremony when I return home."

Marling stared at him for a long time.

"You don't have anything to say, Marling? I find it a little disconcerting."

"I'm taking it all in, give me a second. Somehow, the part about you being... you know what... was easier to digest than the second part." Marling sat in his lap, propped her hands on his shoulders. "My mom used to tell me that I'd marry a prince someday. It might have been because I was obsessed with Anastasia for a while but who knows. But then my teacher said the same thing, when I started training under her. She said

I was going to marry a prince or a king or at least someone with a 'lot of acres'."

Guilt bubbled in Viktor, stronger even than the fire earlier. "I don't doubt they're right, little one, but I also know that it won't be me."

"Why, because of Petra?"

"No, not Petra. I was born with the rest of my life plotted out for me already. When I meet you, I still think perhaps I can escape it, but my writing is only escape I'm allowed. You would be nothing but a flower pressed into a heavy book if you marry me. I'm leaving tomorrow and... you have to promise to forget about what I told you, and forget me forever, if possible. No more of this unlove spell."

"That's the trouble with the unlove spell. It can't be undone," Marling whispered, with a little shrug. She ran her hand through his hair.

"There must be some way to reverse it. Ask your teacher maybe."

"Ha, no. She never returns my calls, and I wouldn't want to tell her about that anyway. It's a little embarrassing, to be honest."

"I wish I can take it away from you. You have so many exciting options in life, and many adventures. You shouldn't let anything hold you back."

Marling leaned in and kissed him, more gently than she ever had, and Viktor closed his eyes until Marling pulled away again. "You were right," she whispered. "You do taste a bit like licorice and mischief."

"Malevolence."

"Close enough." Marling stood up and straightened her clothes. "Thanks for the hot chocolate. It was good to, uh, to see you again. I should really get home, though, and call my boss. Good luck with... you know, all of that stuff you told me about. And don't say it again, Viktor. I won't tell anyone. I'm actually really good at keeping secrets." Marling shrugged. "I haven't told anyone but you about the unlove spell. So there… we both own each other's secrets now."

Marling snatched up her purse and walked away without another word, and Viktor couldn't help thinking he much preferred walking away to being left behind.

chapter eight

Marling made it all the way out of the coffee shop before she burst into tears, but she only made it three more steps before she slipped on the icy sidewalk and flailed around, desperately trying to regain her balance.

As soon as she found her balance again, Marling sniffled and continued on her way. More accurately, she attempted to continue on her way, but someone barreled into her. At first she thought maybe it was Viktor, chasing her down, but no. No, this was some big guy who smelled remarkably like wet, moldy newspaper. And he was considerably wider than Viktor.

"Errr, excuse me?" Marling said, trying to wrangle her way out of meaty, smelly arms. "I'm not in a very good mood right now, so you'd better let go."

"Sorry, he wants to talk to you."

"What...?" Marling's feet left the ground at the exact instant that the meaty arms lifted her up, up. After a bit of shuffling and nervous movement, Marling was tossed into the backseat of a vehicle.

Really.

If it weren't for the possibility of danger, Marling might have appreciated the novelty of having been pushed into the backseat of a car, but as it was, she sat up and straightened her hair and tried to look as cross as possible.

"What is going on?" she demanded, expecting to see a tall guy in a suit, or maybe some shady looking gangster from the streets, complete with fingerless gloves and a smudge of soot over one eyebrow. Instead, when she looked across the car, she saw a familiar face with fluffy hair atop it, and a soft looking beard. Wait a minute. "Kyran...?"

"Marling."

Marling opened her mouth to say something, but wet newspaper guy leaned into the car. "You need anything else from me?"

"No, that's good. Thank you," Kyran said, flashing a smile. "I'll see you at practice next weekend, same time as usual. Close the door, would you?" Kyran raised one hand and waved, then turned his attention back to Marling. "Terrible weather, right? Snow's fun when you're a kid and you get to stay home from school, but then you're an adult and you have to go to work in it. Or ride the subway in it, yuck."

"I'm... so confused right now."

"Oh, yeah, sorry about that. It was a little crazy, I admit, but I didn't feel like jumping out of the car and chasing you down. These shoes are terrible in the snow." Kyran lifted one of them and twirled his foot at the ankle. "I didn't realize he was going to toss you, though, that was a bit much."

"A bit much?" Marling cleared her throat as the car pulled into traffic. "You could have just rolled the window down and called my name."

Kyran's smile faded a little. "Really? Most witches don't like to be seen in public with me."

"Oh. Well, why would I care? I'm not much of a witch."

"You mess up one potion, even just one little potion, and suddenly you're shipped back to Manhattan. And Lady Grieve is screaming in your face that you're a disgrace, that no witch with any sense or decency will ever talk to you again." Kyran tugged at his scarf, his big gray eyes dark and heavy with memories that Marling was unlucky enough to have witnessed.

"Being blacklisted doesn't just make it difficult to buy movie tickets for a bargain price or something, Marling."

Marling had always liked Kyran. His work ethic was almost overwhelming, considering he'd once told Marling's class of newbie witches that he'd gotten three tattoos of difficult spells, so he'd never forget them. But he'd made up for his type-A personality with snarky comments when he thought no one was listening. More than once he'd made Marling laugh so hard that it hurt. He was a crazy powerful witch and he'd saved the lives of at least a dozen people right in front of Marling's eyes. Plus he wore a lot of cool scarves.

"Well, you know I'm not like those people. I don't mind being seen with you," Marling said. "Like that time I ran into you at Starbucks, when you were wearing the maroon scarf."

"That was the first time anyone from the community had spoken to me in seven months and three weeks. Well, Janet spoke to me once, but she called me a leper." Kyran tugged at his scarf again, harder this time. "You probably saved my life that day, because I'd gone to a very, very dark place. Very dark."

"Ah."

"No, I mean, very dark. I'd called my brother and told him that I didn't want to see Kings of Leon. And I bought boxed wine. I was borderline suicidal, Marling, and for you to look me in the face, and say my name, and act so cheerful... You pulled me back from the brink. I can never thank you enough for that."

In Marling's mind, she'd bumped into Kyran outside of Starbucks and had spilled some of his very hot chai latte on his shirt and had profusely apologized and then complimented his maroon scarf and asked how he was holding up. Then she'd received a call from her boss and ran away without giving it a second thought.

This whole suicidal thing certainly brought a new level of memorability to their encounter.

"I'm glad to hear that!" Marling said at last, trying to sound chipper. "And I'm sorry you were in such a dark place. I've been in dark places before too. Though maybe not boxed wine dark."

"It was very dark."

"That's really sad, Kyran," she said. "Um, is that why you pulled me into the car...?"

"Lady Grieve yelled at me in front of all of those kids, all of those new people. God, it was the most embarrassing thing that ever happened to me." He shifted in his seat, his eyes taking on the quality of someone who has lost themselves in a bad memory. "If you'd seen it, you'd understand how terrible it was."

Marling cleared her throat. "I, uh, I *did* see it. I was one of the new people. I was the one eating the apple, actually." Suddenly she wished she was wearing a scarf too, because it seemed to be a helpful tool for moments of uncomfortable fidgeting. "But look... it was terrible, that's true, and I always thought it was ridiculous for her to get that angry, especially with all of us helplessly sitting there with no choice but to listen. And I mean, what did you even do? Make someone's hair the wrong color or something?"

"It doesn't matter!" Kyran said, his voice suddenly much louder than before. He seemed as startled by the change in volume as Marling was, so he blinked a few times and then his lips curved upward. "Anyway, I heard Viktor Kalashnik would be here for one of his book appearances, so I staked the place out. I saw you show up earlier and then I saw you LEAVE with him. Luckily Robert back there knows someone who got me this car. Pretty gangster of me, right?"

He looked more like one of those hot hipsters with sweet indie tunes on car commercials than a gangster, but Marling sighed and shook her head.

"Spill, Marling. Did you interrogate him?"

"I met Viktor a long time ago and we ran into each other tonight at the party, so I... so we decided to catch up a little."

"Wait, you know him?" Kyran demanded, his voice dropping to a stage whisper.

"Yeah, we sort of dated. I guess. Well, a long time ago."

"Oh, that changes everything." Kyran tapped his finger against his chin. "What matters right now is that you're the only witch that has been kind to me, and you saved my life. I like you, and I trust you... plus it sounds like you have some useful links to Viktor. You, my dear, are going to help me rescue Lady Grieve and the other missing witches."

Only moments ago Marling had found out that Viktor was not only fae but fae royalty, and it seemed appropriate for her to be given at least ten or fifteen minutes to digest that before being forced to go on to the next thing. Especially a thing like missing witches. "Lady Grieve is missing?"

Kyran gasped. "Oh, you didn't know? Marling! You didn't know about *Lady Grieve*?"

"I... no?"

"Marling, Marling, Marling."

"Okay, saying my name three times in a row doesn't help me understand what's going on any faster."

"You've heard about the missing witches, of course?" Kyran asked.

"Yeah, yeah, Emma told me, and I hear about it in those emails we get sometimes. I mean, come on, they're probably not even missing, strictly speaking. Maybe they just decided they don't want to be witches anymore. That happens all the time."

"Really? You think Pebble and Francine would just skip town?" Kyran uncrossed his legs and leaned forward, his gaze intensifying. "Do you really think Lady Grieve would just up and abandon her studio, leave behind her students? Fall out of contact with everyone?"

"She disappears all the time for missions. Or vacations. I'm not sure of if they're actually missions, because it's a little weird for a mistress of magic to have so much business in the Bahamas, but that's none of my business."

Kyran slapped his hands on his knees. "I'm actually happy that you're questioning this, Marling. You're smarter than the others, so that's good. I *knew* I liked you." Kyran wiggled a cell phone from the pocket of his dark wash jeans, and punched some buttons on it. "Here, put this to your ear and tell me what sounds wrong."

Marling caught the phone and held it to her ear. At first she heard only static and crackling, but then she heard Lady Grieve's hoarse, commanding voice.

"IF YOU GET THIS MESSAGE YOU BETTER COME GET ME! I have been taken. DO YOU HEAR ME? ...have TAKEN me and I'll be in... TUNDRA for all I know. Surki. It's called Surki."

The message ended abruptly and Marling sat frozen to her seat, unable to speak. It really did sound bad. Maybe Emma had been right for once...

"She, like so many other witches, has fallen prey to good old prince Viktor and his sweet, sweet mother, the Queen of the fae."

At this, Marling laughed. "Okay, this is really, really funny Kyran. Really funny. Did Viktor put you up to this? Is this some kind of joke?" Marling asked, her voice coming out a bit higher and more strained than she'd meant it to. "Like, a super, super elaborate joke?"

"I wish it was a joke," Kyran said. "Actually, no, I don't. It's better that it's not a joke, because you and I are gonna save Lady Grieve and all of the others! And then everyone is going to realize that making one mistake doesn't mean anything. And no one deserves to be, you know, ostracized. Or called a leper." Kyran's mouth turned down into a pout.

Marling turned her head to the right, noting that the car was still inching along in traffic. "Where did you get this car?"

"I told you, I rented it."

"Okay, let me out."

"No, no, I need your help! Well. I don't *need* your help, but I want your help. Aren't you excited about this? I mean, it's a bit dangerous, obviously, since the fae hate witches. And the Skyler bloodline in particular, I think they hate us more than the other fae do, but it's okay."

"Kyran, look at me and don't even think about lying. Is this some kind of prank?"

"No. You know about the great witch and fae rivalry, of course, and the Silent Wars? Well--"

"I don't know. Stop, rewind, explain."

Kyran shot Marling a look, the exact sort of look that usually melted the hearts of the little newbie witches in Lady Grieve's classrooms. It was a gray-eyed, smoldering, and slightly disappointed sneer, but Marling found herself wholly unimpressed. "Sounds like someone didn't pay much attention to her history lessons. I memorized all of this stuff by my third week under Lady Grieve. And by my second month? I'd recited the Plea of St. Christoph, word for word, before the elder council."

"Whatever," Marling said, almost embarrassed by the level of nerdiness she'd just personally witnessed. "What's the Silent War?"

"Rasputin, remember him? Well, he was one of us, but that was sort of on the DL. The down low, if you know what I mean. And of course, it got really ugly in Russia with the revolution and all that. Rasputin turned on the wealthy, and most of the pointy eared freaks are megarich. So they yelled traitor, and boom! Silent War. Fae blood is worth a lot of money, so captured fae would usually get sold to Collectors. And witches? Who knows what happens to captive witches, when the fae get their hands on them. Some of them end up…

well, this is horrifying, but I've heard that about 50 years ago, a whole bunch of witches were found in this lavish fae home. They'd been turned into taxidermies." Kyran paused, glanced again at Marling for her reaction.

"Taxidermies."

"Yeah, but I'm hoping that sort of thing was just old fashioned brutality. The tips I got said that Queen Gloriana has been holding the witches over there in 'Mother Russia.'" Kyran mocked an embarrassingly bad Russian accent. "Which means that we just go there, we bust them out, and everything's cool." He smirked.

"We can't just jump on a plane and putter over to Russia. I don't have my passport with me, I don't have any clothes. And, of course, that's assuming that anything you're telling me is true. You don't just get on a plane and *go to Russia*!" Marling said.

Kyran nodded.

"I have some super good contacts in Russia, people that still talk to me. You know how it is, the Eastern European witches are much quicker to forgive mistakes, since they take part in so much shady business of their own." He paused then. "So, I've gotten the flights arranged. They won't mind me bringing you along, especially not when they find out you have a line directly to Viktor Kalashnik."

"You don't even know Viktor!"

"No, but it sounds like you do. That'll make everything soooo much easier than I pictured it."

"Viktor told me his mother is dead. So that kind of busts up your theory about what he and his family are up to."

"Dead? No way is she dead. She might be in some other form, but she's still kicking around. That woman won't die any time soon."

Marling grabbed the door handle to her right and tried in vain to open it.

"It's locked, Marling," Kyran muttered, in a flat tone.

"Let me out of here!"

"You're gonna like Surki, I think. I mean, aside from the unfortunate fact that a bunch of pointy eared monsters live there, it's actually a beautiful place."

chapter nine

Viktor couldn't think of anywhere uglier than Surki.

He and Petra had been whisked from the airport by a palace car and had endured the too-familiar two hour trip through the snow-engulfed countryside, with very little entertainment besides the driver's occasional off-key humming. Petra passed the time by pulling up a website called "MARRY ME VIKTOR ARSON (100 Reasons I Should Be Your Wife)".

"You have a lot of marriage proposals," Petra said. "Ooooh, one of the 100 reasons on this site is 'I can cook a variety of traditional Russian dishes... while wearing lingerie.' Is that a skill? Really? She should try riding a firehorse or something that's actually impressive." Petra tapped at her phone. "10,000 people have Liked this page. All of this just because of that TV appearance a couple weeks ago?"

"Well, it's helping me break the American market finally."

"You should see this, it's crazy. You're so popular, Vik." She tapped at her phone. "Oh, you're trending on this social media site, under the tag, I'M FAE, VIKTOR, COME STUDY ME. How clever."

"I'll thank them on Twitter later." Viktor had never expected so much positive response from his work, but it certainly gave him a little something to smile about.

Even with that good news, though, nothing prepared him for the stomach-sinking sensation of arrival at the main entry of the palace. Or the circle of black robed women awaiting his return.

Petra leaned closer to Viktor, eyeing the shrouded women. "Who are they?"

"They look like mourners."

"Aw, your mother is so cheerful. Her son's returning to take the throne and she has mourners waiting for him." Petra slid her hand over Viktor's knee and patted his leg. "I'm sure your crowning ceremony will be a complete *party*, if this is any indication."

One of the black robed women rushed forward and opened Viktor's door for him, raising her voice in a depressing manner that sounded vaguely song-like. Viktor gathered his backpack and travel bag and climbed out of the car, wincing as the rest of the women joined in with the song.

The grand doors of the palace opened before Viktor could reach them, and a host of servants rushed him on either side, grabbing for his bags and greeting him in Russian, in English, in French. Wait, French? "I'll keep my bags!" he said, pulling his travel bag close against his chest.

"Welcome home, Master Kalashnik. Her highness has requested your presence in the tea room as soon as you've settled in," someone said. "Feel free to settle in first!"

"Yes, yes, I'll try to do that."

The black robed women had dialed their song up to a wail, which Viktor was almost certain would have broken the windows of the palace, had they not been made thick enough to withstand Russian winters.

Viktor managed to reach the grand staircase finally, phantom memories gripping at his ankles as he jogged up the stairs for the first time in a few years. He'd run up these stairs a thousand times, intent only on escaping the watchful eye of his mother, and when he was a child, his tutors. He'd fallen down these stairs once and cut open his face. He'd promised himself six years ago that he'd never set foot on these stairs again.

Ha.

As soon as he'd reached the top of the staircase, Viktor turned right and ducked into the less crowded hallway that led to his mother's gown room, her history room, the library, and the study room where Viktor had spent countless childhood days. He barreled his way into the dark study room, closing the door behind himself and letting out a sigh of relief.

Viktor snapped his fingers once, twice, a third time, and a tiny flame crept into existence, hovering over his fingertips. He held his hand out like a candle to light his way across the spacious study room, past outdated maps, faded charts and photographs as old as Viktor. Old habits returned as he swayed slightly to the right, avoiding the sharp corner of his childhood desk, and stepped wide over the space in the middle of the floor, to avoid the horrific creaking he knew it would make.

He jiggled the doorknob of the door set against the back wall of the room, twisting it just so, and smiled when he heard the familiar click. Viktor pushed into the secret passageway that his older brother Haven had shown him ages ago, padding on silent feet through cobwebs until he'd found his way to the other end. It would seem that no one had used the passageway since he'd left, which didn't surprise him.

In theory, Queen Gloriana might know every hall, every corner in her family's palace, but Haven, Viktor, and Petra understood it on a different and more physical level.

The passageway dumped out into a mostly forgotten room that had once housed seasonal decorations and paintings. Someone had removed the decorations, and had draped the paintings in dust-thickened white blankets. Viktor sneezed and shivered as he crossed the room and entered the hallway that led to his bedroom and, just before it, Haven's.

Some sad curiosity led him to open the door to Haven's room and peer inside. Everything stood exactly as it had been, twenty one years ago. Haven's stuffed animals, many of them gifts from important fae dignitaries around the world, still snuggled each other atop his bed. A book of legends lay sprawled face down on the carpet, and without a doubt, Viktor knew it was still open to page 32 and 33.

"We dust it every day," a voice whispered, and Viktor started with a gasp, turning around. The fire that had before barely danced over his fingers now raged into a flame. Viktor struggled to extinguish it. "Aww, my poor little firedancer. You still miss your brother, don't you?"

"Mother." Viktor flicked his wrist a few times and the flame disappeared, revealing the fluid, hazy outline of his mother's ghost.

"It's alright to miss him, we all do," she whispered, her words distorted by the gentlest of wavers. In the five years since her death, Viktor had visited home exactly 3 times, and he still hadn't become accustomed to seeing her in this form. Her English had improved considerably, too, to the point that it was almost flawlessly accented. "How was your journey?"

Viktor turned away from her, closing the door to Haven's room and walking down to the hall to his own room. "Tiring. I need to sleep before you throw official business at me." Viktor pushed into his bedroom and tossed his bags on his bed.

"You've grown into such a handsome man, Viktor." Gloriana appeared in front of Viktor, floating along the edge of his bed as if she'd perched there. She folded her translucent hands in her lap, cocked her head to the side. "Your brother would be so proud to have you in his place."

He dug into his backpack, withdrawing his laptop and notebooks. "Petra tell me you're angry about my writing."

"You have to understand that I'm a mother and I lost so many of my children, ages ago. And then, in my old age, I had these two wonderful little boys, one of which I've lost now." Gloriana's delicate chin lowered and her long, dark eyelashes swept down so that she seemed to be in a state of meditation. "If I lost you, I would have nothing left. The bargain I made with the Elders, ages ago, allowed me to continue on this way once my physical body wore out. But I can no longer have children, can I? I can't have another heir. You're all I have left."

"My writing doesn't put me in danger. In fact, it's the only thing I've ever enjoyed. I love to write."

"Of course, of course, but you write about us."

"No, I write about what everyone thinks we are," Viktor corrected.

"But, my dear, I just don't know how you expect to continue a writing career. You take the throne in a few days!"

Viktor paused in putting away his belongings. He straightened slowly, turned to look at his mother. "A few days?"

"I think that should be quite enough time for your fittings, and to go over the lines for the ceremony. It's a very long ceremony, but most of what's said is said by the Elder in attendance." Gloriana flickered from view, reappeared beside Viktor. "You've lost some weight, little firedancer. But no matter, our tailors will take care of it in no time. You'll be a sight in your royal finery." She paused then. "So much better than those awful things you're wearing. Are those... 'jeans'?"

"Yes, Rock & Republic, don't you like them?" Viktor asked. He rolled his eyes and turned away from her again.

"They're so *human*."

"I'm half human, I suppose it's in my blood."

"That's a wonderful point, Viktor. And that reminds me... I've been curious about why you've told everyone that your name is Viktor Arson, when you have such an honorable name like Kalashnik."

"In human world, names carry connotations. My name carries money and my father's history. I'd like my books to belong to me." Viktor unbuttoned his jacket, but Gloriana held up her hands.

"Wait, don't take your jacket off yet. There's something I need to show you."

"Can't it wait until tomorrow? I haven't slept in 32 hours."

"No, it's terribly important." Gloriana flickered from sight, reappeared by the door, then flickered again and appeared just in front of Viktor. She brushed her hand against his hand and he shivered.

"Alright," Viktor said at last, and followed her out of his room. "I've asked my agent to send me list of media appearances for the next three months. I have to make those appearances. I want to break the American market."

"Of course, darling."

"There won't be any negotiating. This is my priority," Viktor said, and much to his surprise, Gloriana didn't correct him. "It's possible that I'll have three, four of them a month."

Gloriana led Viktor down the grand staircase, silent and glimmering with a darker energy than usual. Mercifully, most of the crowd, including the wailing women, had disappeared. Though a few servants remained, they scattered and disappeared as the queen approached.

It felt as if the temperature outside had plummeted in the time since Viktor had arrived in Surki. Snow fell in depressing clumps around them as they left the palace and continued into the Frozen Gardens.

"Watch your step, Viktor," Gloriana said, her voice ringing in Viktor's ear, even though she floated on and on before him, out of reach. "One of the new servant boys fell and dashed his head on a rock. Oh the mess! Please don't break your head, my sad little beauty."

The palace grounds were not particularly ornate in the fashion of so many of the palaces of the past. A simple walking maze inhabited the west side of the palace, and a frozen pond stretched across the south. But the palace's Frozen Gardens made up for any minimalism, thanks to its miniature forest of frozen flowers, vines, and magically modified fruit trees.

Passing a cluster of frozen pink trees, Viktor wondered if Haven had been in the Frozen Gardens when he was snatched away, as the family legend claimed. According to the eye witness account of one servant, the fae prince had been sitting encircled by the golden birdberry trees when a group of five or six dark figures had grasped him by the limbs and dragged him away from sight. That servant had died an untimely and somewhat suspicious death soon after recounting what he'd seen.

"Viktor?"

Viktor blinked away memories of his brother's disappearance and focused instead on the misty shape of his mother.

"Through the gate, hurry. Make sure no one's following you."

"It's too cold for anyone to follow us," Viktor said, but he glanced over his shoulder anyway, and then at the gate in question. "I thought you say, it's dangerous to walk through there."

"Gravely dangerous, yes. Follow me." Gloriana pressed her insubstantial fingers against the tall wooden door of the gate situated along the darkest and coldest corner of the Frozen Gardens. The gate swung open, soundlessly, and a bitter wind hit Viktor in the face, colder than the air, and considerably sadder.

"What's back there?" he whispered, hesitating.

Gloriana flickered in and out of view, pressing a thin finger to her lips. "Hurry, hurry. Hurry!"

With a sense of foot-dragging doom, Viktor obeyed. His fingers ticked at his sides as he walked through the gateway and ducked his head under vines. He found himself facing an array of stationary, ice-tinged bodies.

Viktor's eyes caught on a short woman, her hands outstretched in desperation and her feet bare against the snow. She stood arched forward, as if she'd been crying for help, a long time ago. Even under the thin layer of ice, her eyes shone sad and helpless.

"What is this?" Viktor said, when at last he regained his voice.

"They're witches."

Viktor raised his arm, cautiously, and brushed his fingertips against the outstretched hand of the ice woman. "What have you done to them? How long have they been here?"

"There are so many things I hoped I'd never have to tell you. After all, you were the second son... it should have been Haven here today, not my sad little beauty. But you're heir and this is yours now," Gloriana said, her words a sigh on the wind. "The war, the witches, the blood, it's all yours now. These are our prisoners."

"Prisoners."

"For generations they've taken ours and we've taken theirs. I knew my time would be up soon, so I struck at their heart. See this one? Here?" Gloriana flickered here and there, swaying between the frozen bodies, until she reached an older woman with close-cropped black hair. "Lady Grieve, they called her. I've very recently acquired her." Gloriana peered at her prisoner, and then motioned for Viktor with one finger. "They are our natural enemy, Viktor. They want to see every single one of us drained to nothing but ash. You must swear to me that you'll take up the fight. For all of us. For your brother."

"But what did they do? What did this Lady Grieve do?"

Gloriana's gaze fell to the snow covered ground. "Do you remember Rasputin?"

Viktor thought of Marling's insistent questions back at the coffee shop. "The adviser to the Romanov family...?"

"He manipulated magic and though he wasn't called a witch, it's common knowledge that he was. He created a list with our names and sold it to protect himself. I was still very young then, with only a few children of my own. The fires and the paranoia were terrifying. So many of our kind were murdered, even children, Viktor! Even children. Many of us fled, far and wide. I took my children to Iceland for a few years before we dared return. But the repercussions spread. And they thought they killed him. Ha! They merely did away with a part of him. It was only a few years later that his followers murdered my babies, my children. *All* of my children! And then it took decades for me to find a safe home again, to start over and have your brother, and you."

"And what does that have to do with these people?" Viktor said, turning around again and looking at all of them. "They're not old like you."

"Not all of them follow his ways." Gloriana floated away, invisible fingertips brushing here and there. "But Grieve took my son away from me. She sold him to a man named Gorey Billings. And do you know what Gorey Billings did to your brother?"

Viktor felt as if all breath had left his chest.

"He sold him like a golden goose, for the exact value of the blood in his body." Gloriana disappeared completely, but her voice whispered against Viktor's ear. "I will have my revenge on them, and you will help me."

chapter ten

Twenty-one years ago...

It was against the rules for a young prince to escape early from his lessons and run through the halls of the palace, especially through passageways that the queen had deemed unsafe. But Viktor wanted to catch a glimpse of preparations for the night's festivities, even at the risk of his mother's wrath.

Viktor's older brother, Haven Skyler, Grand Prince of the fae, would turn 13 years old at midnight, and that meant that the palace's spectacular Mordvu Ballroom would be opened, decorated from top to bottom, and allowed a night of glitter and excess.

Viktor arrived at the end of his favorite passageway, the creepy one that Haven had long ago shown him, and he creaked the door open as quietly as possible. After a glance to the right and to the left, Viktor padded on bare feet across the hall and to the entrance of the Mordvu Ballroom. It was by far the best part of the house in Viktor's opinion. Perfect, from the black, gold, and glass chandeliers that hung high above, to the row of tall windows along one wall, each complete with a window seat for reading or staring out at the snow-covered world. Of course, that said nothing of the murals on one wall, full color representations of scenes that Viktor wished were in his history books: battles, feasts, strange animals, and beautiful fae women perched atop fluffy clouds.

Haven liked to say that the pictures were made up stories, but Viktor preferred to think they were all true.

Dozens of servants scurried across the room, carrying decorations, and climbing ladders, and dusting things, and laying out tables. Viktor worked his way through the room, dodging the harried servants and focusing all of his attention on only one thing… someone had placed a gold chair in the center of the room, a chair that was instantly recognizable to Viktor as a throne.

Now, the queen's throne was a fancy affair, with massive glass wings attached to the top of it, as if it might fly away at any moment, and rubies set into each of the four legs of the chair. Viktor had always felt intimidated by it. But this throne was child-sized, with a navy blue cushion, and gold feet speckled with sparkling stones of all colors. Viktor had never seen a throne so small except in a picture in his history book, of the young princess Olya, who had become queen at 14 years old.

"Dontcha like it?"

Viktor wheeled around to find his older brother standing behind him, a smirk on his face. The Grand Prince stood the same height as his younger brother, though they were three years different in age. And Haven had atrocious posture, according to their mother.

"It's for you?" Viktor looked at the throne again. "Because of your birthday?"

"Because I'm gonna be king." Haven said this with the same offhand quality that he talked about anything vaguely related to responsibility. "Last night Petra said she saw a firehorse in the Frozen Gardens."

"She told me too."

"Don't you want to go see?"

A wave of excitement nearly overwhelmed the younger prince. His brother rarely asked him along on adventures, both because of their mother's insistence that Viktor study and behave himself, and the fact that Viktor wasn't very good with adventuring. He could potentially get in the way or make himself into a nuisance. Or get hurt again.

"I could," Viktor said, as casually as possible.

Haven shrugged. "I'm just surprised you haven't already gone to look. I saw the tracks earlier. Tomorrow morning I bet I can find it." Haven's lips curved up into a smile. "Maybe I'll ride it!"

If anyone could ride a firehorse, it was Haven. Even Petra had said that, though begrudgingly.

"Be careful if you do. You know Mother won't like it if you get hurt."

"Nothing can hurt me, dummy. And nothing can hurt you either. You've got Skyler blood in you, and that can get you through almost anything."

Most people dropped a hint here and there, in conversation, that Viktor was only half Skyler. Even the queen mentioned it often. Haven, though, seemed eternally unfussed by that fact.

Moments later, Petra's mother stormed up to the boys and grasped both of them by the hand, muttering about how badly behaved Viktor was these days, and how his tutor had been so worried, and how Haven wasn't even *dressed* for his party, and there were only *six hours* until the party started... Viktor and Haven exchanged glances from either side of Petra's mother as she tugged them along from the Mordvu Ballroom.

"Now, both of you need to run along to your rooms. Haven, the tailor is waiting there to finish your measurements. You've kept him waiting long enough. And you, Viktor." She released Haven's hand but held to Viktor's, turning so she could face him. "It was terribly disrespectful of you to leave your lessons. You're old enough to know better than that! A prince should not behave himself so irresponsibly. What do you think your father would say?"

Viktor's cheeks burned pink and he felt his hands warm up. "How do I know, I don't know him," he said, before he could stop himself.

Petra's mother raged at him for a few seconds in her fancy English accent, but Viktor barely heard her. His attention was on his brother, who shot him a triumphant smile, as if he was proud at Viktor for being contrary. By the time Viktor took stock of what Petra's mother was saying, she'd quieted anyway.

"There now, it's not my place to be cross with you. We'll let your mother do that," she said, "Later, though. After your brother's party. It's his big night tonight." She paused. "What's wrong with your hands?"

Viktor turned his palms up and stared at them. He whispered silently to the fire to go away, go away! But it rose from his skin, phantom flames, and he could only clap his hands together in a vain attempt to displace it.

"You need to learn to control your temper," Petra's mother said, though her voice seemed less angry now. "And stop trying to steal attention from your brother. Go on, go to your room and get ready for tonight. The tailor will be along for you, too, soon enough."

Viktor walked away with his head still as high as he could manage, determined not to show his embarrassment, and he ducked into his room without hesitation. As soon as the door was shut, though, he felt the burn of angry tears in his eyes.

Why did they have to yell at *him*? He studied and studied and studied and took his dancing lessons (dancing with *Petra* even, eww) and took the boring lessons in manners that his mother insisted on. He was quiet and got up at dawn and went to bed when he was told and honestly, except for today, he hadn't done anything even slightly naughty since... well, since two weeks ago when he stole a pastry from the kitchens, carried it back to his room, and then felt so guilty that he returned it to the kitchen and told the head chef what he'd done.

Stomping across the room, Viktor flung himself onto his bed and lay face down for a long time. After his rage had passed, Viktor sat up and caught sight of his reflection in the mirror near his bed. His hair stuck up in every direction, and just like always, even his best attempts at straightening it did little to remedy the situation.

Whatever. When Viktor was older, he was either going to cut his hair all the way off or grow it out… out to his chin! Like a rock star.

A noise in the closet made Viktor jump. He scurried off his bed and ran towards the closet, swinging open the secret door in the back. "Haven?"

"That tailor took forever," Haven muttered in Russian. As soon as Petra's mother was out of sight, the boys always conversed in their native language. And sometimes, just to frustrate Lady Marsh, Haven would pretend he couldn't remember English at all. But it was a lie… Haven had a knack for languages that left all of his tutors terribly impressed, and Viktor a little envious. English was difficult for Viktor. "I don't think he's ever taken measurements before. I had to help him!"

"Aren't you going to get in trouble?"

Haven stood up to his full height and propped his hands on his hips. He looked remarkably like their mother when he did that, all the way down to the long eyelashes and full lips.

"You need to stop worrying about getting in trouble, Viktor. Trouble is the best thing to get into." He marched forward then, glancing around the room as if he'd never been there before. "You still got all those figurines?" He pointed at the array of animal figurines that their mother had given Viktor when he was very sick with the flu a few years ago.

"I lost one."

"Oh. Which one?"

"The tiger."

Haven clicked his tongue, perusing the offering of figurines. "That's too bad; the tiger was the best one."

"The giraffe is my favorite," Viktor said.

"That's a funny choice." Haven poked at the giraffe. "Good job with Lady Marsh, by the way. You watch, she'll run crying back to England in no time." He snickered. "Petra would like that, wouldn't she?"

Petra was always glad when her mother went to England, and very sad when she returned to Surki. Viktor shrugged.

"You're getting pretty good with that fire thing, too."

"No I'm not. I can't make it stop when I want it to," Viktor said.

"Then don't stop it! Make a big fireball next time. Everyone will call you... errr, Viktor the Firethrower!"

Viktor pulled a face. Their mother called him 'firedancer', but somehow, it never sounded like a compliment.

A noise in the distance alerted the boys that a search had been called for the Grand Prince.

"Here," Haven said, reaching into his pocket and slipping something from it. He pressed the gift into Viktor's hand and then stepped back, grinning so wide that his sharp, pointy teeth gleamed in the light.

Viktor opened his hand to find a small key. "What is it? It's not iron, is it?"

Fae were allergic to iron. Viktor knew this because his mother reminded him of it constantly, and yelled at any servant that might be foolish enough to bring anything iron-related near her precious elder son.

"Don't be stupid, of course it's not iron. It's made from something else. I found it." Haven nudged his brother. "It used to belong to a Russian tsar. I thought you'd like it."

Viktor turned the key over and over and then raised his head to look at his brother.

"You like it?"

"Yes, thank you." Without thinking, Viktor threw his arms around his brother for a hug. Haven wiggled a little in his grip, letting out a sort of groaning noise, but then he finally relaxed and patted Viktor's back.

"I should get back before Mother calls out the guards," Haven said, heading for the secret door in the closet.

Viktor followed him. "Happy almost birthday."

"Yeah, yeah. There'll be time for that tonight. And for you to have to dance with Petra again!" Haven laughed and disappeared through the doorway. After a few seconds, Viktor realized he wanted to say something else to Haven, to thank him, but speaking through doorways was bad luck.

Viktor stared at the key for a long time, listening to the distant roar of adult voices as some relieved servant yelled that the Grand Prince had been found, in his room, and he was just fine. Viktor could thank his brother later. There would be time for everything, later.

chapter eleven

Present day

One thing was for sure... not all kidnappings were equal. There were kidnappings that involved hot chocolate, brownies, and kisses. And then there was Kyran.

Marling preferred the hot chocolate approach.

"Why is it so *cold*," Kyran demanded, for maybe the 20th time in five minutes. His face was mostly hidden behind gigantic sunglasses and his black scarf, but his voice was certainly not muffled. "This isn't human. No wonder all of those nasty beasties live here." Kyran let out a dramatic sigh. "I shouldn't have brought so many bags."

The bags in question numbered approximately half a dozen, all of which hung off Kyran's arms and hands. He stumbled forward a few steps and then held one heavy laden arm out toward Marling.

Marling shrugged. "What?"

"Well, help me! Just because I didn't need to bring all of this doesn't mean you shouldn't help me carry it. You only have three bags." Kyran pawned off two of his bags, and then fished a piece of paper from the pocket of his jeans. He stared at it. "Alright, well, our escort should be here to pick us up any minute. And she speaks English, thank God."

"What if I tell her that you kidnapped me?"

"Oh, she already knows," Kyran said, with a casual wave of his hand. "I told her you were coming along, somewhat reluctantly. They don't frown on that kind of thing here like they do back home."

Marling grumbled and shivered. Kyran had allowed her ten minutes to gather essentials from her apartment, instructing her to pack light. Then he'd proceeded to bring along six bags of his own. And, stupidly, Marling had grabbed her stylish navy blue peacoat and a hat as defense against the cold of Moscow. Now that the sun was down, Marling was fairly certain that she was going to die from cold exposure.

Brilliant.

Kyran stepped closer to Marling. "Do you know they say Moscow is the most unfriendly city in the world? I mean, it makes sense. It's probably because it's so damned cold."

"I still don't know how you got us on that plane," Marling said.

"Would you like to know? Really? Would you like the hear the details?" Kyran asked, and something in his voice answered the question for Marling.

10 hours on a nonstop flight from New York City to Moscow wasn't exactly how Marling had envisioned spending one of the few days left before Christmas, but then, Kyran hadn't really been part of her plans for the future either. "How far are we from Surrey?" she asked, with a labored sigh.

"Surrey? Like, Surrey, England? Marling, we're going to Surki, not Surrey. Get your countries right. And it's a long trip, so you'd better have something to read."

"I don't have anything to read, because you kidnapped me, remember? Choosing books and magazines for the trip wasn't exactly part of the deal."

Thankfully, their contact showed up just then. Marling had expected her to be tall and blonde, and to look like a Bond girl, but she turned out to be a bit dumpy, and mousy, and shifty-eyed. She didn't even demand that they know some kind of password. Even more disappointingly, she didn't have any cool gadgets or weapons in her car.

And the ride to Surki was projected to be five hours.

Somehow, this whole kidnapping business just kept getting worse.

Marling attempted to entertain herself by staring out the window and envisioning herself as the heroine of an action movie, whisked away to Russia by a mobster. She cast a particularly agonized frown on her face, lowering her gaze, and leaning her forehead against the cold window, imagining a melancholy theme playing in the background. Kyran elbowed her and asked if she was going to puke or something.

After that, she tried to appreciate the fact that she'd just gotten a free trip to the other side of the world, but that positive attitude was dulled by Kyran reading aloud from the Village Idiot's Guide to Russia. He'd removed his jacket but his scarf and sunglasses were still firmly in place.

"Wow, the meals here are crazy expensive. This is nothing like Mexico," Kyran said. "Ugh, well at least it looks like the whole vodka thing isn't an urban myth. They're heavy on the vodka. I like vodka."

"Better than boxed wine?" Marling muttered.

"Thanks for mentioning that. You really know how to bring a conversation down." Kyran flipped through pages of the book and then sighed. "We shouldn't be fighting. We need to be a unified front in this endeavor."

"You kidnapped me."

"No, I drafted you for an assignment that you didn't know you wanted to take."

"My boss doesn't know about this assignment either. Maybe you should fill her in on it."

Kyran closed his book and gave Marling a long suffering look. "I told you that you're not allowed to call your boss or your mom or anyone else until we're done with this. You're not trying to go back on the promise you made me, are you?"

"I never promised you anything."

"We had a silent understanding, Marling. That's powerful. Especially among witches," Kyran said, shaking his head.

"Or, especially powerful for someone with three tattoos of spells?"

With a haughty frown, Kyran sat up a bit taller in his seat. "I have four tattoos of spells. And I'm going to get a fifth, because the Canyon Curse has evaded me for… for months. At this point it's just humiliating to have trouble memorizing a spell as simple as the Canyon Curse. I'm thinking of getting it on my calf." Kyran peeled back the right sleeve of his long sleeved black shirt and held his forearm out for Marling to see. "That's the last one I got."

Most of the inside of Kyran's forearm was decorated by a spell, written out in a flowery script. Marling just stared at it for a few seconds and then raised her gaze to Kyran's. "I think that's the most skin I've ever seen on you, especially since Emma said…" Marling stopped, and cleared her throat. "Errr, but yeah, nice."

"Who's Emma?"

"Uh, Primrose."

"Oh! Primrose!" Kyran cleared his throat. "Primrose said what?"

"Nothing."

"What did Primrose say?"

Emma had said a lot of things about Kyran (in her weird faux-English accent). One of the highlights had been that Kyran was actually a vampire's lover and was in the process of being turned, but that he was clinging to humanity a little longer because he had a powerful aversion to blood. And then there was the slightly less exciting theory that Kyran had actually covered his entire body in tattoos of spells and didn't want to admit it to anyone.

But really, Marling though Emma just liked imagining Kyran without his clothes on.

"She said you seemed a little shy," Marling said at last.

"She said she thinks I'm a vampire, didn't she?"

Marling nervously twirled a strand of hair around her finger. "No…"

"You're twirling hair around your finger, Marling, don't you know that's a dead giveaway that you're lying? She said I'm a vampire!"

"Actually, I'm not lying, because she said you were a vampire's *lover* and that you haven't been turned yet. *There.*" Marling scowled at him.

Kyran considered this. "Hmm, well that's kinda cool I guess."

"Why, though? I mean, if we're talking about it. Why do you always wear like six hundred layers? Did you used to be fat or something?"

Kyran's mouth fell open and he turned his head toward her. The sunglasses made it a bit hard for Marling to take him serious, but she attempted to look suitably sorry anyway. "Yeah, I used to be fat. *Yes, Marling, I was fat.*"

The air crackled with heavy static and Marling jumped in her seat from the charge. Well, there was an unexpected turn of events.

"Sorry. I wouldn't have said it if I thought it was actually… well, you know. I wouldn't have… It's like how you'd say, 'What, because a rabid kangaroo bit your ankle once?' or something. Because it doesn't seem likely to be the real reason. Sorry."

"I'm beginning to question your appropriateness for this mission," Kyran said, and the air crackled again, this time zapping Marling's fingertips, toes and… forehead?

"I've been questioning that since you first had me tossed into your scary black car! Now stop with the weird static stuff, you're hurting me."

They sat in silence for a long time, until Marling realized that their escort was peering at her judgmentally in the rearview mirror.

Great.

Marling cleared her throat. "I'm sorry," she whispered, but Kyran ignored her and picked up his Village Idiot's Guide to Russia, burying his nose in it.

After a long time, Marling gave up and dug through her purse for her phone. After a few rather anxious seconds, she located it in the very bottom of her purse. "Good thing I have an international phone," she said, but Kyran continued to flip through his book. "My boss, Kim, wanted me to have one, just in case. You know. Like if I needed to fly to London and meet someone important author or spend a weekend in Paris." She shrugged. "Or get kidnapped."

Kyran turned another page in his book.

Marling plugged the name 'Viktor Arson' into a search engine on her phone and squinted at the results. Whoa. That Gross guy hadn't been kidding… Viktor *was* popular. As Marling scrolled through the results, she had to pause on a few. "There's a website with 100 reasons why Viktor should marry this girl."

"She's an idiot. He's not even that attractive," Kyran said, and then cleared his throat, as if remembering he wasn't supposed to say anything to her. "I mean, as Russians go. Also, he's fae. And I'm pretty sure he's burned a couple people to death."

"He has not burned anyone to death."

"How do you know? People don't tell each other everything when they're dating. Some people are actually cannibals and they don't mention it until they've invited you over to their place for a late night dinner for one."

"That's disgusting," Marling muttered.

"Just because he's a fae prince doesn't mean he's your shining fairytale prince. If you looked him in the eye and asked him what happened to Lady Grieve and the other witches, he'd lie and say he has no idea. And if you asked him why witches hate the fae so much, he'd just tell you some sugary crap about how there was a little misunderstanding in the past. Oh, and he'd say there's nothing to worry about anymore. I've had a run in with one of his kind, and it was not a pleasant experience. I have an impressive scar on my ribcage to prove it."

"Great. I don't need to see it."

"I wasn't inviting you to see it, Marling Ellis."

Marling couldn't think of any adequate comeback for that remark so she scrolled through more search results. "I think this is a picture of Viktor and Sting. Sting like singer, not wrestler." Marling scrolled further. "You know, I heard people say the name 'Viktor Arson' but I never realized it was connected to Viktor Kalashnik." She checked her Tumblr page and found that she had a stack of questions waiting to be answered.

Maybe she could tell her Tumblr friends that she'd been kidnapped!

Typing and Marling's phone didn't mix very well, so it took her all of five minutes to draft up a reasonably detailed explanation of her absence, and a complaint about her situation. Marling's finger hovered over the send button when Kyran snatched her phone away.

"I suppose we're going to have to consider this a mission of mistrust," he said, his sunglasses still firmly fixed on his face. It seemed like he was scowling at her though. "I'm disappointed with you, Marling. You really should think about the 8th article of the Witch's Beginner Manual of Manners and Customs pamphlet." Kyran dropped the phone into one of his bags. "Tomorrow we go to the Skyler house. This is going to be a long, long trip for you."

chapter twelve

Five years ago, three days before New Year's Day

"Wait, how do you say it? Say it again," Marling requested, and Viktor repeated his last name. "Kalayshnik? Did I say that right?"

Viktor grinned, and though sunglasses covered his eyes, Marling could tell the smile was genuine. "Close."

They'd met last night and had a sloppy but somewhat magical alcohol-fueled quickie, before migrating their way from their friend's house together in the morning. After a short debate on whether or not they should wait in line at Mac's Cafe for coffee, they'd trudged their way through the cold morning streets back to Marling's apartment. The agreement had been that Marling would make them each a cup of black coffee, but a search of her kitchen had provided no clues as to where her wayard bag of coffee beans had gone.

"I guess I just assumed all Russians had last names that end with 'ov'. I went to school with a girl whose last name was like... Navinov or something. That might not have been in it but it sounded like it." Marling shugged, opening her cabinet for the third time and looking around for the coffee beans. "I always thought that was cool."

"Marling. Top of the fridge."

"What? Is that a Russian phrase...?"

"Look on top of your fridge, Marling."

She glanced up, even though moving her head made the headache worse, and spotted a half-used bag of coffee beans. Success!

After a bit of struggle, she managed to remove the bag from its perch.

"Oh great. These are the gross coffee beans," she said. "I had these fancy ones that were supposed to be gourmet and they had vanilla and hazelnut and cheesecake flavor in them. They tasted like a disappointing birthday cake, but let's be honest. Even a disappointing birthday cake is more delicious than drinking plain black coffee."

Marling was fairly convinced that bad coffee beans wouldn't be considered a crisis by most of the population. But there was a hot Eastern European guy in her apartment and so far he hadn't tried to murder, maim or steal anything from her, and he hadn't mentioned being a Jehovah's Witness, so that upped the stakes. After all, her last boyfriend had been cute but crazy. The one before that was cute but had turned out to be living in a tent in Central Park. The one before that had a really hairy back, so he'd only been her boyfriend for two weeks. Actually, a week and four days.

"Do you want me to make it?" Viktor asked, stepping closer and leaning against the counter. There was approximately enough room in Marling's 'kitchen' for two people to stand. Normally this frustrated her but right now it was kinda nice, because it meant she was very close to a total babe. "The coffee, Marling. I can make the coffee."

Marling handed over the bag of coffee beans. If he made terrible coffee, he would have to blame it on himself rather than Marling. And if he managed to make it taste alright, neither of them would suffer. Win-win situation right there.

Viktor worked silently but with a certain grace and fluidity that Marling had never seen before, as if his movements were choreographed. Marling never felt graceful, but certainly not during a hangover that could win an award for Worst Hangover of All Time. "Where are your mugs?" Viktor asked, without turning around.

"Oh! Uh…" Marling opened the cabinet and searched through the disorganized contents before finally discovering two coffee mugs. One of them had been a joke gift from Marling's mother that said OVARIES ARE A GIRL'S BEST FRIEND, so she kept that one for herself. "Here you are!" Marling sniffed at the coffee as he poured it. "That smells pretty good."

Viktor cradled his coffee cup between his slender hands and glanced at Marling. "Try it."

To be honest, it tasted like Marling had been sent to coffee heaven. She wasn't sure what he'd done, but the coffee was smooth and velvety and delicious in that robust coffee sort of way, and Marling let out a long groan and closed her eyes. "This is… this is delicious."

"I know some magic too."

Marling burned her mouth with a too-big sip. "Oh, um. Magic. What do you mean?"

Viktor smiled behind his sunglasses. "I have three magic trick. I can set things on fire. I can make really good coffee. And my third trick, I think you learn that last night."

"Oh." Marling shuddered and her legs went a bit wobbly just remembering how great that third trick had been. "Please remind me?"

"Right now? I thought you have headache."

"I do." Marling slurped a bit more of her coffee. "But I'm always up for learning magic tricks. And you know, they say sex is really good for curing headaches."

Viktor set his coffee cup on the counter and leaned over Marling, taking hold of her in an alarmingly strong grip. He lowered his mouth to her ear and whispered, "I can teach you, if you want," and then he bit her neck with just enough pressure to make her drop her coffee cup.

And that was how Marling cut open her leg, burned her foot, and broke her OVARIES ARE A GIRL'S BEST FRIEND mug.

Fifteen or so minutes later the mess had been cleaned up, Marling had bandaged her leg, placed a bag of frozen peas on her foot, and settled next to Viktor on her apartment's tiny couch. Normally she would be quite miserable considering the injuries, but snuggling next to a Russian hottie makes pain marginally less unpleasant. He had even taken off his sunglasses finally so she was reminded every 2.4 seconds that his eyes were crazy pretty blue.

"This coffee really is delicious," Marling said.

"I know, your foot seemed to enjoy it."

Marling giggled.

"What's this?" Viktor asked, shifting around on the couch and then retrieving a book from seemingly nowhere. He flipped through it for a few seconds. "Hmmm… 'Village Idiot's Guide to Ghosts' huh? You have a ghost, Marling?"

"Oh, I don't know. You never know if you do! I mean, I was just watching *Ghost* and got to thinking that maybe everyone has a Patrick Swayze in their house. You know?"

Viktor blinked. "I don't understand."

"Well, but then you have to consider that there could be a dangerous ghost too. It might *not* be Patrick Swayze. And we were talking about ghosts in my class, so I got the book." Marling snatched the book away from Viktor. "I just thought it might be smart to learn how to talk to them. Or get rid of them, if needed. I had a boyfriend once who could get rid of ghosts, but he moved to France and stopped emailing me."

"To get rid of ghost, you must know their true name and call them into being," Viktor said.

"Wow. That was poetic!"

"Poetic? Not really. The most important thing is, if you need to get rid of it, believe in yourself. They thrive on fear and disbelief."

Marling glanced at the book and then back at Viktor. "Really? I don't need salt? Or a crossbow with silver bullets?"

Viktor gave her a strange look, so Marling changed the subject to something intelligent. "So you're not really a Russian spy, right?"

"Maybe? I'll never tell you, Marling Julianna Ellis."

Marling almost dropped her second cup of coffee in her lap. "How- how did you know my middle name?" she asked, as casually as possible. Inside she was screaming and pondering just how he'd known, and what would happen if he really *was* a Russian spy and how she would feel about it… especially if some kind of interrogation scene ended up being involved.

Maybe it was weird, but Marling had always been curious about what it felt like to be kidnapped. And tied to a chair. But she was only curious about the latter if the person who tied her to a chair was insanely attractive and stern.

"I know all kind of things about you," Viktor whispered.

Oh boy.

"But how did you know my middle name…?"

Viktor laughed then and shook his head. "Your name is in the ghost book. On the first page."

"Okay, but you're not really a Russian spy, right? I mean, that would be silly."

"Would it?" Viktor murmured.

"Well, who's really a Russian spy? No one's *really* a Russian spy."

"Here, I'll tell you a secret." Viktor lowered his voice to a husky, quiet timbre that made Marling feel all weak again. "When I was a boy, I was in the circus. I perform for hundreds, thousands! I do… handsprings and rolls and leap through ring of fire. And then, one day when I am nineteen years old, they scout me."

"Who?" Marling whispered, enraptured.

"Russia's Third Elite, of course! Secret organization. They say, you join us or we kill you. So I join them and they teach me how to kill people and make it look like accident. They teach me to seduce beautiful women, and leave them helpless at my feet. Leave them unable to do anything but follow my every command."

"Uh. Oh. Really?"

Viktor placed the book on the floor and shifted positions on the couch so he was kneeling beside her, all but towering over her. "I learn where to touch, where to caress and kiss, for any reaction I want. I learn domination." He traced one finger over her jaw, down her throat. "I learn how to coax truth out of any woman, no matter how stubborn."

Marling was pretty sure she was on fire.

"And then, they give me fake passport and fake name and they send me to England, where I make my first kill. And then they send me to United States." Viktor brushed his lips against Marling's neck. "They send me here to find someone and seduce her, find her apartment and then..." His hand had migrated up her leg and Marling felt powerless to stop him. "And then I defect. And they're out to kill me now, but I manage to evade them for two years. And now I meet you, and everything change."

She was supposed to be upset about this turn of events, but she could only bring herself to gulp. "Is that really true?" she demanded finally, and Viktor threw his head back and laughed so hard that his face tinged pink and he coughed a little.

"Do you really think a Russian spy would tell you all of that, Marling?"

"I don't know! I mean, it sounded kinda legit. Like the thing about the Fifth Elite. Who's the Fifth Elite?"

"It was Third Elite, and I made that up."

Marling felt disappointed, but that probably wasn't the correct reaction to have. "Were you really in the circus?"

"No."

"You're flexible, though."

"Yeah? Thank you."

"Can you do handsprings?" Marling asked, leaning closer.

"I'll let that remain a mystery for now. Along with whether or not I really did kill someone in England."

"What are you *really*, though?"

"Viktor Kalashnik."

Somehow, despite everything, Marling felt this was the most satisfying answer he could have ever given her. And then he checked on her foot and she thanked him, and he kissed her and, well, there went the rest of the afternoon.

chapter thirteen

P resent day

"I always knew she had something back there," Petra said, climbing onto her bed and crawling across it until she could lean against the headboard beside Viktor. "I just supposed she'd gotten herself another child to replace Haven, and she didn't want you to know."

Viktor shook his head, remembering the frozen faces and the crushing sensation of helplessness on the wind of that hidden prison.

"But it's a bunch of witches, Vik," Petra said.

"She's had three of them out there for twenty years!"

"Since Haven disappeared?"

"What if that's why he disappeared?" Viktor exclaimed. "What if what happened to him was only payback for something that she'd done?"

Petra opened a small bottle and poured oil into her hands. She warmed it between her hands and then smoothed it onto her legs with the precision of an expert. For a long time she didn't say anything, but then she raised her eyes to Viktor's. "Haven disappeared 21 years ago. If witches took him, it had no connection to your mother's collection of ice cubes. It's because they hate us, and they've hated us for generations."

"Not all of them do."

"Is that right? Unless they're playing with magic for fun, like that silly girl at Benjamin's party, they hate us." Petra turned, shifted her position on the bed so she faced Viktor. She tugged at the neck of her night dress until it fell from her shoulder and draped down her arm. "Do you remember my thirteenth birthday? Your mother threw that ridiculous party for me with all of the balloons and the little sock animals."

Viktor traced his finger over the familiar faint outline of a scar on her pale neck. "Of course I remember."

He could see that day in movie reel flashes: the colorfully dressed performers, and a cake smothered in magical candles, Petra scowling because she wanted to wear a different dress to her party, Queen Gloriana insisting that Viktor dance with Petra during her official birthday dance, to a professional Russian orchestra, no less.

But later, in the evening of Petra's thirteenth birthday? Oh, that was forever clear in Viktor's mind, down to the details. Petra had asked him if he'd join her outside, because her mother would be angry if she went outside alone, especially in her fancy high collared, lacy white dress. Viktor and Petra had wandered past the palace grounds, past Dybru Lake and into the woods, in search of some fox-like creature that Petra thought she'd spotted in the distance, earlier in the day. *"Silver, he was silver like the miniature ornaments your mother hangs on the tree in her sewing room!"*

Somewhere along the way, Viktor had felt as if cold fingers walked up his bare spine and he'd grabbed Petra's hand to stop her from wandering any deeper into the woods. And then, as if he'd materialized from out of the mist, a tall human form had appeared in front of them. The man had cruel, deep set eyes but otherwise he'd been rather bland in appearance, and held no outward sign of danger.

For whatever reason, the man had targeted Petra first, snatched her away from Viktor and danced a glistening blade across her skin, across her throat.

Viktor could still remember the way his throat constricted and his heart pounded as he said, *You don't want her. I'm the prince.*

"You have one too, don't you?" Petra whispered, drawing her fingers up his neck and tracing along his jawline. "Because you saved my life. You saved me from a man who meant to bleed me like a fish." Petra smiled, her teeth gleaming sharp in the candlelit room. "That story feels appropriate tonight, since the man who tried to murder us was a witch. And he probably would have succeeded in hacking you to pieces while I watched, and then sliced me up too, if it wasn't for you kicking him so hard. We held him off until my mama took care of him."

Yes, Petra's mother, full of righteous fury and explosive magic. She'd left behind a bloodied mess against the clear white of the snow and Petra had whispered to Viktor, *so that's what the inside of a witch looks like.*

"I'd always thought he attacked us because we were connected to the royal family. That maybe he was..." Viktor hesitated "Maybe he was the one who took Haven."

Petra leaned forward and smiled in his face. "That's a nice revenge fantasy, but I don't think so. Witches hate fae and they always have. It's in our blood. Don't worry so much about it. You saved my life; I've saved your life. And I'll always save you when you need it, even if it's from yourself."

A noise at the door caught Petra's attention and she bounded away to open the door, scoop up the majestic white Persian on the other side, and carry her to the bed.

"I think Queen Mab finally realized you were home," Petra said, dropping the white cat onto Viktor's arms. "She was so unhappy when you left. I thought she might run away. I told her that you had to go to New York City, and that this time I would join you. I told her I wouldn't let you fall in love with any American girls that kept you away."

Viktor's mind returned to Marling for the millionth time that evening. "It's not just witches that mean to bleed us," he said, stroking Mab's head until she relaxed against him and purred. "It's anyone. It is humans and the light people in the north and the old ones in South America. It's everyone who knows what we are."

Petra sighed. "Oh, Viktor. You have such a generous nature." She pressed one fingertip against his chest, nearly drawing blood with her nail. "But your heart can't rule your head anymore, no matter how much you want it to. We survived to adulthood, we thrived in the world despite everything. It wasn't Haven, it was you, and me."

"And what if I free them?"

"Go on and free your captive witches, if you so desire, or burn them into ash! But know that if you rescue them, one might turn and stab you right in your gentle, foolish heart. And then what? Will I take your place? You know I'd love to wear your mother's jewels, but I hardly think her life would suit me very well. There's so many rules..."

Viktor laughed, despite himself, and shook his head. "Are you sure? I think if you were queen, you'd revitalize the winter ball. It's gotten a bit...rustic."

"Rustic? You really are generous." Petra bit her lower lip against a smile. "Anyway, King Viktor, you'll be crowned just in time for the aforementioned winter ball. Maybe you can liven it up a bit. Your mother's away for a few days to prepare for your coronation, so who says we can't invite dancers, and cover everything in tacky glitter?"

Even with his mother packing herself into the royal palanquin and ordering servants to transport her to Moscow for a few days, there was little chance of the winter party turning into anything other than overdressed middle aged fae making grim attempts at dancing to depressing orchestral pieces.

"Maybe you should ask them to play that sugar plum fairy thing. I know how much you used to love the Nutcracker music as a kid," Petra said.

Viktor stood up from the bed then, keeping Mab tucked against his chest. "I still like it."

"Then tell them to play it, King Viktor! Just think, you can do anything you want now."

"If that was true, I'd still be in Manhattan, writing in my hotel room."

"And visiting your little witch girl?" Petra's eyes widened and she tapped her fingertips over her lips in mock surprise. "Oh, sorry. That girl was the American you fell for, wasn't she? Marling?"

Marling, Marling, Marling. Drunk Marling tripping over Viktor at a party and asked him, in a deeply serious whisper if Russia and America were still at war with each other. Marling insisting that they hunt Manhattan for Chinese food. Marling bickering with him for twenty minutes outside a theater because she didn't agree with his movie choice. Marling chasing him down in Times Square before he could return to his hotel room, pack his things and leave.

"Yes."

"So bring her here! Tell her what you are, tell her what your mother is, explain to her your family's history. Tell her about Haven! Oh, Viktor, bring her here and let me tell her about the time you fell through the ice and saved yourself with your magic! Tell her about the time you burned down your friend's home."

"I didn't burn it down. It was... I set fire to the furniture. No one was hurt."

"Of course. It's not that I'm afraid that she'll do something to you, considering that she's not even a real witch. It's just that she might not like it. You know how people respond when they find out what we are. They get knives. Or they get lost."

Viktor shifted Mab in his arms, standing up a bit taller. "I told her."

"I knew it! I knew you told her! And she ran away from you, didn't she?"

A smile lifted the corners of Viktor's mouth. "No, Petra. She'd be here with me right now if I'd given her half the chance."

"If she likes you so much, bloodline and all, I'm sure she'll find her way here." Petra shrugged her slim shoulders and leaned her head to one side. "She'll arrive at the door and throw her arms around your neck and say, 'Oh Viktor, I love you and I can't stand spending my life away from you! Even though we only knew each other for five minutes, a million years ago, I just can't be away from you.' And then you'll get married and it'll be a beautiful little storybook romance."

chapter fourteen

"Wwhat am I supposed to do? Just knock on the door and say, 'Hey, it's Marling! Do you mind if I come in? Oh, and by the way, this is my new friend, Kyran. He kidnapped me'?" Marling demanded, shivering and trudging through the snow toward the rather ominous entrance to the Skyler home. Late afternoon certainly hadn't made Russian weather any more pleasant.

Kyran let out some noise similar to a 'hmmmph' and snatched for her hand. "I almost slipped. Can we pay more attention to not dying, right now?"

"You shouldn't have worn those shoes."

"I didn't have any others that would match these pants!"

Marling sighed. "I told you that you could borrow my boots."

"Ewww."

"Well, why didn't your weird Russian friend drop us at the *door*? The gate's like, six miles away or something. If she got us through the gate, she could have brought us to the door."

"Nah, she's superstitious. The Skyler palace has a reputation around here. I mean, no one knows it's actually a *palace*, because they keep that part under wraps." Kyran froze, looked around as if trying to determine where he should step next, and then hesitantly took a few more steps. "People just think these guys are a weird rich family with a big house and an ungodly amount of land. But there's superstition about it."

"What, they can't drive too close to it or their car might break down? You could have talked her into it, Kyran. You had her totally mesmerized last night with your air ripple trick." To be honest, Kyran had even had Marling rather mesmerized by his air ripple trick, which involved small items floating around the room on invisible tides, but she didn't want to admit something like that out loud.

"Everyone thinks the place is haunted, so they stay away," Kyran said.

Together they picked their way to the doors, Marling holding Kyran's hand against her will. As soon as they reached their destination, though, Kyran released Marling. He straightened his black and gray scarf, adjusted his round sunglasses, and patted himself down.

Marling eyed him. "Gonna fix your hair too?"

"Oh my gosh, does it look bad?" he demanded, suddenly sounding far more desperate than she'd ever heard him.

With a snicker, Marling shook her head. "No, it's fine. You're just so fussy."

"Well, maybe *you* should be. Your hair looks awful. You have *visible* split ends." Kyran reached over, threading some of her hair between his fingers and shaking his head. "Don't you know the spell for that?"

Marling had never heard of a spell for split ends, but somehow, she knew that admitting such a thing to Kyran would be a very, very bad idea. Of course, she also wasn't certain that she knew a lot about the normal fixes for split ends, things like fancy conditioners or leave-in sprays.

But that REALLY didn't need to be revealed.

Kyran sighed. "This bag is so heavy."

"Your murse?"

"It's not a murse," Kyran said, through clenched teeth. "It's a messenger bag. And it has sixteen pockets, plus a hidden zippered section. And it's waterproof."

They didn't speak to each other again for a few seconds, both staring up at the giant doors.

"So what are we going to do? Knock?" Marling asked finally.

Kyran let out another exasperated sigh and motioned at the door. "Do I have to do everything? You're the one who used to date him."

"You kidnapped me!"

"Shhhh. Unified front, Marling, unified front. Just knock on the door."

Marling knocked on one of the doors.

After what felt like two eternities, the doors swung open and an older woman stood before them, her mouth pressed into a thin line. She studied Marling, and then Kyran, and then brought her gaze back to Marling. She asked something in Russian, and Marling just stared back at her.

"Uhhh, I don't... Uhhh. English? American?" she said, reaching over to smack Kyran's arm. "Do you know any Russian?"

"What take you so long?" the woman asked then, in heavily accented English. "She say, 'I have girls here for party' and then you take fifteen minute to arrive at door. Are you always this slow? Gloriana no like slow servants."

"Servants," Marling repeated, reaching over and smacking Kyran again. Harder.

"I'm not a girl, by the way," Kyran said.

The woman looked him up and down, wrinkling her nose. "No. No, you're not."

Kyran pushed his sunglasses up so they sat on top of his hair. "We're here to help with the party," he said. "Natasha sent us. She dropped us off at the gate, actually, and we walked. I'm sorry it took so long."

"He didn't wear the right shoes," Marling added, bit of petty but satisfying revenge against her kidnapper. It would seem that insulting his shoes or hair was near the top of the list of worst things she could do to him.

After a long few seconds, the woman stepped aside. "The last girls were prettier," she muttered as they walked by. Marling just smiled and nodded and plotted more revenge tactics against Kyran.

Now, if the outside of the Skyler home was intimidating, the inside was far more so. The ceiling curved in and out in ways that made it feel vaguely cave-like. The curtains on the windows were jewel-tone blue, the walls were almost entirely gold, and the chandeliers looked as if they might be taller than Marling.

Stranger still, though, was the indefinable sensation Marling felt that someone was not only watching her, but attempting to wipe all memories of this place from her mind the second she blinked or looked away.

As soon as their host walked far enough ahead that she was out of earshot, Marling grabbed Kyran's shoulder. "Servants? That was your idea? What are we going to do? Put on aprons and serve dinner tonight?"

"No! Well, I hope not. I don't look good in aprons."

"Don't you think Viktor might recognize me? Or were you counting on him not making eye contact with servants?"

Kyran raised his chin. "When he sees you, we can drop the act. Obviously."

"And then explain to him that we tricked our way into his house? That makes sense. You are the *worst* kidnapper ever."

"Oh please. What was your idea? Just show up at the door and tell that scary woman you're Viktor's ex-girlfriend?"

"Actually, my idea was to go home and call my boss, tell her that I failed my mission, and then eat a lot of junk food. And call my parents on Christmas Eve. And *forget Viktor ever existed!*"

"Marling?"

Oh. Oh, Viktor.

Marling turned around very slowly, attempting to rearrange her expression so she didn't look as if she'd just lied to break into his home. "Hello, Viktor," she said, managing a smile. It vanished almost as soon as she met his gaze, though, because he looked as if someone had wrung him out a few times like a wet towel. Was he sleeping enough? Was he eating enough?

"Ah, your Highness." The woman who had escorted them inside stood up taller when she faced Viktor, and smiled. "Your mother bring these witches here?"

Viktor's eyes hadn't left Marling's. "What are you doing here, Marling?"

Okay, so here were the facts as Marling could see them... First of all, witches and fae hated each other, right? And taxidermy was involved. Secondly, Kyran had already screwed everything up with his plan/lack of plan. Thirdly, something in Viktor's voice hinted at the fact that he was quite happy to see Marling, despite the downturn of his lips, and the way his eyebrows were knitted together.

Also, the woman who had escorted them inside knew they were witches, and she might be plotting to make them into the newest part of the Skyler taxidermy collection.

Brilliant.

"I came to see you," Marling said. She prayed for strength, and a steady voice. "I came here, all the way here to Russia, because I... because of the unlove spell."

Kyran cleared his throat.

"I decided," Marling went on, "that I'd come here and spend a week with you. At the end of the week, if we decide that we can't make it work... then I'll have him remove the unlove spell from me." She pointed at Kyran.

"But you say, it can't be undone."

Marling nodded. "There's a way. It's just... unpleasant."

A long pause followed. Viktor stared into Marling's eyes until she felt like her knees might give way, both from nerves and swooning. Just when Marling couldn't take it any longer, the servant woman shouted something in Russian. Whatever it was, it caught Viktor's attention immediately, and he stepped in front of Marling in a protective manner.

"Do you have any idea how dangerous it is for you to be here?" he demanded of her, his eyes flashing between hers and the servant's.

Marling knew that any admission of knowledge about the fae/witch ugliness would only add suspicion to her current situation, so she plastered a fake smile on her face. "What do you mean?" she whispered, hoping she sounded convincing. "And why is that woman yelling at us?"

Viktor glanced up and said something in Russian to the servant woman that sent her scurrying away.

"She's like one of those super angry German housewives in the movies," Marling said, trying to smile. Viktor didn't return the smile. "I'm sorry. That was probably rude of me. Is she a friend of yours? Your childhood nanny? Your grandmother? Aunt?"

"How did you find me?" Viktor asked, lowering his voice so much that Marling could barely hear him.

"Oh, uh, you know me. I'm resourceful. One time I tracked down Robert Rum on his vacation and reminded him that he needed to get his manuscript to us before deadline. He was in Hawaii. He threatened me with legal action." Marling waved one hand. "It all comes down to uh, asking the right person."

Viktor glanced at Kyran. "Who is he?"

"He's one of my magic teachers," she said, before thinking. "You know, kinda high up in the chain of command."

The slight twitch in Viktor's cheek warned that she might have said something wrong, but he nodded and studied Kyran for a few seconds.

"Just a week, Viktor," Marling said. "Please? Just a week. If it doesn't work out, I'll leave you alone forever."

A door opened in the distance and Marling heard clattering and voices as a group of servants pushed a huge cart inside.

The procession made its way past Viktor, Marling, and Kyran and then continued down a hall, out of sight. Marling couldn't help noticing something that looked suspiciously like a jeweled scepter poking out of one of the many boxes on the cart. Hadn't Viktor mentioned he was about to become King?

"Oh, I'm sorry. Have you had your, uh… your coronation thing yet?" Marling asked.

"Not yet. Soon." Viktor shot another glance around before letting out a heavy sigh. "Come on then. If you must stay, I'll give you rooms."

"We'd better share a room," Kyran said, stepping toward Marling. He opened his mouth to say something else but Viktor cut him off by leaning closer and pointing his index finger in Kyran's face. His eyes flashed with intimidating power, and Kyran backed down immediately.

"You'll stay in room I put you in," Viktor growled.

Kyran's eye widened and he didn't let out another peep.

Viktor turned on his heel and walked away, leaving Marling no choice but to rush after him and try to keep up with his long legged strides. She could hear Kyran behind her, but didn't dare take her eyes off of Viktor. He led them up a grand staircase and down a hall, walking with purpose. "Here," he said, swinging open a door. He winced and waved his hands. "It's a bit dusty, but it should work." Viktor whipped a sheet off of a maroon-cushioned couch, and after fumbling about a bit, he flicked on a lamp.

"Is this… her room?" Kyran asked, distaste dripping from every word.

"No. Yours." Viktor shrugged. "Make sure to lock the door at night. And don't open the closet."

"What's in the closet?"

"Don't open it, or you'll find out." Viktor turned back to Marling. "Stay here for a few minutes. I'll be back as soon as I can."

He hesitated and then leaned down to kiss her cheek before rushing away. Marling watched him until he disappeared from sight.

"Do you have any idea how creepy this room is? It's Jane Eyre level creepy, Marling!" Kyran said. "We are not staying here a week. Are you crazy?"

"We're staying."

Kyran grabbed hold of Marling's arm, shuddering. "Did you hear that? It sounds like someone's clawing through the walls. New plan: we find the witches, and then we leave. I've got all the spells prepared, so we can face anything." Kyran paused. "Except fire. I... left the anti-fire spell in my other bags. Well, I can't deal with spiders either. Not yet."

"I don't think Viktor knows anything about the missing witches."

Kyran stepped forward and put his hands on Marling's shoulders. "Look, I get it that you like this guy and you dated and all that. I mean, I don't *get* why but whatever. But listen, he was raised to hate us and there's a huge damn chance he's planning to add you to his collection of captive witches." Kyran shrugged. "Also, I'd like to point out that he just put me in a creepy room with a haunted closet. *Hello.* We can't trust this man."

"Give me a couple days," Marling said. "Viktor will help me, if I ask him to. I'll- I'll find out where Lady Grieve and the others are, and then we can free them. And you can go home a hero."

"Uh huh, and what happens to you? I suppose you'll stay here with the pointy eared freaks?"

Marling pulled away from Kyran. "Maybe. I don't know yet."

"Wait. Wait, wait, wait. I forgot about something that I meant to ask you," Kyran's eyes widened. "You didn't *really* put an unlove spell on yourself, did you? That was just for dramatic effect, right? You're not actually dumb enough to do something like that to yourself."

Marling tried not to look guilty. Then Kyran let out a theatrical gasp, and Marling gave up on the guilt and pondered slapping him. "Anyway, the important thing," she said, with a great deal of emphasis on *important*, "is that Viktor doesn't know about Lady Grieve. He's a really nice guy, even if sometimes he's a little bit of a know-it-all. I already feel guilty for lying to him about why we're here, so the last thing I want to think about right now is abandoning him." She cleared her throat. "Even when we're done with your kidnap-and-rescue plot."

"You need to listen to yourself for a minute. We're here because we have an obligation to witchkind. All that nonsense you just said? That's the unlove spell talking, Marling, nothing more. You don't have real feelings for Viktor, trust me."

Marling shot him an ugly look and stomped out of the room, slamming the door behind herself before realizing that Viktor had told her to wait there for him.

Ooops. Oh well, Viktor probably wouldn't mind her waiting in the hallway for him, right? It wasn't like there were werewolves wandering the halls and waiting to eat interlopers. Hopefully.

To Marling's great relief, she only had to wait a few moments before Viktor reappeared like some kind of hot Russian ghost. "Is that the only jacket you brought?" he said, motioning at her.

Marling dropped her gaze downward. Did her attire look that bad? Was it offensive to wear a peacoat in Russia? Did he hate the color? Had she spilled something on herself? "Is there something wrong with it...?"

"It's not very warm."

"I live in Manhattan, Viktor. My wardrobe was chosen to be chic and cheap, not to withstand a Russian winter."

Viktor motioned for her to follow. After a moment of hesitation, Marling chased after him.

Now, castles in movies have tons of fabulous rooms. The library. The ball room. The kitchens. But as Marling followed Viktor through the house, she caught glimpses of rooms she'd never pictured existing. One of them seemed to be entirely devoted to a collection of small knives in tall glass cases, and another room was filled with mirrors of all sizes. One seemed purposefully empty. Another one had only a wheelbarrow in it, for some reason.

"Here," Viktor said, throwing open two heavy doors and revealing a room stuffed high and low with… clothes. Beautiful clothes. Magnificent dresses, full skirts, handsome military jackets, plump fur coats, cute fur hats and luxurious fur stoles fought for Marling's attention. It was a bit like one of those really great vintage pop-up stores in Manhattan, but stocked by someone with a time machine linked directly to Imperial Russia.

"Can I… I just… Can I touch something?" Marling said, her voice barely over a loud whisper. "Please, Viktor, tell me I can touch something." She reached out and patted one of the fur coats.

Viktor crossed the room and snatched one of the particularly amazing fur coats down from its rack. He worked his way back to Marling through armies of beautiful clothes.

"Wait, wait, wait. This one, this one! It's almost exactly the color of the Tiffany's box," Marling said. "I had a dream when I was like nine and I swear, I still remember it like it was last night, and *this dress was in the dream*." Marling pointed at it. "It's my dream dress. Literally a dream dress." She paused. "What are the chances of me getting to try that on?"

"Right now? Not good." Viktor held the fur coat out in offering. "You can wear this, though."

Marling mentally took note of a new rule for her life. When a Russian prince offers you a fur coat, you take it.

"We should hurry and get outside," Viktor said, helping Marling into the jacket. "There are too many listening spirits in this house."

Even with the jacket, Marling shivered. Since the moment she'd walked into the Skyler home, she'd felt as if someone was watching her. And the mystery presence wasn't happy.

chapter fifteen

One thing was for certain- Russian winters are a lot easier to deal with when you're wrapped up in a fabulous fur coat formerly worn by royalty. As Marling followed Viktor further and further from the house, through the gardens and toward the woods, she couldn't help wishing everything was taking place under slightly different circumstances, because she'd really like to snap a picture and send it to all of her friends and family. *ME, JUST BEFORE CHRISTMAS, IN RUSSIA. Xoxo. PS- THAT FUR JACKET WAS WORN BY ROYALTY.*

The most confusing aspect of the whole cold Russian winter thing, though, was how Viktor was wearing only jeans, boots and a long sleeved gunmetal-colored sweater. Marling stared at his back, noting that his shirt was thin enough for her to see his shoulderblades through the material. How was he not freezing? Also wow, did his shoulders ever look good...

Viktor slowed down gradually and then stopped altogether, turning to face Marling. "Listen, Marling, this is very important. I need you to tell me the truth about something."

Oh no, he knew. He had to know. Viktor had this weird ability to see through everything she said and did, like that time she'd yelled at him that she wasn't drunk, and he'd wisely stopped her just before she tipped over and almost crashed her head into a glass table.

With a wince, she nodded. "Alright."

"Did you really come here just to see me?"

Marling searched her mind for the spell that Lady Grieve had taught her for persuasion. When her memory failed to kick anything back, she just forced her face not to tremble, and stared him square in the eye. "I did," she whispered, finding an edge in her voice that she'd never heard before. "I came here to see you. I couldn't let you run away like you did before."

"Why?"

Because you stayed up with me until 4am so I could talk to that fortune teller. Because you joined me on the Great Eggroll Crisis. Because you gave me your jacket when I was cold, even though I told you not to. Because you laughed so hard at my dumb joke that your tears actually started stinging your eyes and you started crying for real. Because you look uber hot in leather pants. Because you brew really amazing coffee even with lame coffee beans. Because you wrote a phone number on the back of your hand and saved the day. Because one time you said "mine God" instead of "my God," and it was so adorable. Because you kiss like a love god.

Because you said you thought I was lonely, when no one else ever bothered to notice.

Marling opened her mouth, trying to sort through all of her thoughts, and catch just one accurate answer. She should go with something deep and heartfelt. "Leather pants," she said and then realized what she'd said. "I mean, you know. You look really good in leather pants."

Thankfully, she was saved by a giant white horse with a fiery red mane crashing through the woods just about then.

"What… is that?" Marling demanded, leaping as close to Viktor as possible. The horse seemed to notice their existence and circled back, stomping toward them. "Is that a unicorn? No, wait, it doesn't have a horn. Is it a… Pegasus? Wait, those have wings. Do they have wings?"

Viktor laughed, and Marling had a feeling he wasn't laughing with her. "It's a firehorse!"

"Firehorse?"

"Yeah, there's only a few of them left in the world."

Marling had never paid enough attention to things like math or history. Or geography. But she was almost completely certain that in all of her years, she'd never heard of a firehorse. "Is it a… Russian thing?" she whispered, somewhat concerned that the horse might hear her and feel offended.

"No, no. There used to be many of them in Iceland."

"Iceland?"

"Yeah, most of our kind come from Iceland, originally."

The horse walked closer to them, letting out a loud "HMMMPH" sort of noise that convinced Marling that she should stand behind Viktor.

"She won't hurt you. They're wild but they're not, uh, what's word?- malicious." Viktor held his hand out to the firehorse, clicking his tongue. "Petra will be jealous."

Even the impending scary horse situation couldn't keep Marling from wrinkling her nose. Mermaid lady. "Oh. Of course Petra likes horses."

Viktor glanced back at her. "What do you mean?"

"Oh, you know. Everyone knows the weird horse girl, the one who draws pictures of horses in their notebooks, and has a horse calendar every year." Marling might have continued ranting about horse girls, but Viktor pulled away from her and hesitantly placed his hand on the firehorse's nose. "Should you be touching it? Don't people sometimes get their hands bitten off by horses?"

"Wanna test?" Viktor asked, moving so quickly that Marling couldn't stop him from grabbing hold of her and tugging her close to the firehorse. She was too freaked out to fight as he grasped her hand and dangled it dangerously close to the horse's mouth.

"It's gonna bite me!"

Viktor laughed. "She's very gentle, Marling. Just pet her."

Marling rubbed the firehorse's nose and then yanked her hand away. "There. Happy?" Even as she shot Viktor an ugly look, though, she couldn't help admitting to herself that the horse had been awfully soft. She raised her hand and petted the firehorse again, quickly, and then gave in and petted it in earnest. This monster was one of the softest things she'd ever touched, so why not?

Viktor reached out and stroked the horse's neck. "I haven't seen one for years. Petra always sees them when I'm gone."

"So… what's the deal with Petra anyway? Who *is* she? Was she supposed to grow up and be your arranged marriage or something?"

Viktor laughed. "Petra wouldn't marry me, even for the throne and all of my father's money. I'm not…" he waved his hands and took on a silly, deep voice, "Not daring adventure. Not the action movie hero. I was made more for…" Viktor paused for a long time, thinking, and then said, "I think I am better made for movie like uh, like *Toy Story*."

"I like *Toy Story*."

"Petra, she likes men to be more dangerous."

"Well, Petra can go screw herself."

The horse bucked and stomped a little, in the most terrifying way possible, and Marling backed away immediately. Maybe it didn't like her talking that way about Petra.

"See, you're still standing next to that thing," Marling said, when Viktor returned to petting the firehorse. "That's dangerous enough for me. Action movie dangerous, even."

"Do you like me, you beautiful beast? You know the fire like I do," Viktor muttered, and it took Marling a few seconds to realize he was talking to the firehorse and not to her. "I wish you could take my fire away. It looks better on you."

With another loud HMMMPHHHH noise, the horse finally ran away from them. It galloped into the woods, joining a fiery shape that Marling could barely make out in the distance. "Is that another one?" she asked, hoping they weren't planning a murderous stampede.

"There's three of them, I think. My brother used to say, 'There's only one left! When it die, they'll all be gone and you'll never see one!' but I think he was just trying to make me sneak outside with him."

"Wait, you have a brother?"

Viktor's smile faded away. "I did," he said, and something in his tone and the glint of his eye warned her to be careful.

Marling decided to change the subject to something safer. "So is your mom really dead or what? I mean… You said she died but then everyone's talking about her like she's alive. I'm confused."

"She did die, but she has… certain amount of time to exist in a new form."

"Oh." That *totally* cleared things up. But thinking of the queen reminded Marling that she'd been kidnapped for a reason. Yes, yes, captive witches, that's right. Captive witches! "You said that I'm in danger. What exactly did you mean by that?"

"My mother, she hates witches," Viktor said, shrugging.

"Oh. Hates like, she's going to call me rude names over dinner? Or hates like she's gonna stuff me and hang me on the wall of her living room as a taxidermy decoration?" Marling asked and held her breath while she waited for his answer.

"Taxidermy? Marling."

"I'm just trying to get a good handle on the level of danger we're talking about here. Why does your mom hate us so much?" Maybe he'd tell her everything, tell her about the 'Silent War' and about Lady Grieve and the captive witches, and Marling could convince him to let the witches go, and Kyran would have to admit that he was wrong about Viktor.

Say it, say it.

"It's… it's old rivalry. I don't know the full history, but it can get pretty ugly." He let out a long sigh, and pressed a kiss to her forehead. He kissed her cheekbone and the corner of her mouth.

And just like always, she responded to him without even meaning to, grasping his face between her hands and guiding her lips to his. Viktor had always impressed her on the kissing level because he had a good handle on the whole tongue vs no tongue balance. And he gave her time for a breath here and there. And he liked to gently bite her lower lip, which... well, until someone's done that to you, you don't understand how awesome it is.

Of course, impressive kissing also tends to lead to other things, and Marling realized a bit too late that one of Viktor's hands had journeyed to the general area of her butt, and the other one was wrapped tight around the back of her neck to hold her in place. And that he had answered her question about the witches in exactly the manner that Kyran had predicted he would, which was with vagueness and distraction.

Marling broke their kiss, though with a great deal of reluctance. Viktor bit her neck. Marling removed her neck from his teeth. "Viktor."

"I'm sorry."

"No, it's okay, don't be sorry. That was nice."

Viktor nodded, stepping away from her and rubbing a hand over his face. "You have a power, Marling. Always."

"You do too. And like, if we weren't standing in the snow near the woods with a bunch of wild mythical animals close by, and your not-dead mother in the house, I'd suggest we continue. But. You know. Wild animals." She paused, seeing his shoulders shake. "Are you laughing at me?"

"You say everything you think. I've never known anyone else who does that."

"Uhhh, yeah. But it's cost me a couple jobs. And a boyfriend in high school," she said, and winced. "And I'm pretty sure Halley Johnson made a voodoo doll of me for our tenth grade craft project, because I told her what I thought of the guy she was dating. I mean, it's not my fault he was a bald weenie."

Viktor laughed, full out, and after a while, he turned and motioned for her to follow him. Marling wasn't sure how she felt about walking into woods that were probably infested with animals that you don't learn about in biology class, but she also didn't like the idea of getting left behind in unknown Russian territory. She chased him down, and they walked for such a long time that Marling wondered if they might be in Siberia. Can you get to Siberia that fast? How do you know when you're in Siberia?

Oh well, even if they were, she couldn't feel the cold from inside the comfort of her huge borrowed fur coat.

Eventually they reached a frozen lake, and Viktor let out a heavy sigh, pushing his hands into his pockets. Marling couldn't help thinking this place must have some kind of significance for him. By the pained look on his face, it wasn't a happy significance.

"I like this fur coat," Marling said, determined not to let him fall into a moody fit. She'd seen him fall into a moody fit once, and it had taken thirty minutes, Nutella, and the removal of several items of clothing to get him out of it. Okay, the Nutella had been for Marling's sake. But whatever.

"It looks good on you."

Marling raised her head, taking on her best runway walk. She tripped over a fallen tree branch and immediately decided against further pursuing a future in runway walking. "So why aren't you cold?" she asked, a handy tactic to distract from her clumsiness. "It's pretty cold out here."

Viktor continued staring at the lake for so long that Marling thought maybe he hadn't heard her. Finally, though, he said, "Most of us have inclination toward one kind of talent or another. The Skyler bloodline is... persuasive."

"Like mind power? Like making people do embarrassing things in public?"

"Uh, well, convincing someone they feel like this, or they feel like this. Maybe you feel happy and they tell you, 'you feel very lonely' and then you're sitting on the floor crying your eyes out, 'I am so lonely!' Does that make sense?"

"Sounds like a pretty typical Thursday night for me," Marling muttered. "Okay, but it's like what you did to that guy in the coffee shop, and that lady at the party? Your evil eyes." Marling caught up to him and walked by his side. "Is that how your family got the throne originally? Bossing everyone around with your minds?"

Viktor bent and picked up a small stray branch and threaded it through his fingers. "I'm not very expert at it, but I'm also not…victim to it, like the others."

"Oh. So they can't make *you* do the embarrassing things in public?"

"They can't make me do a lot of things. My mother, she doesn't like that."

Marling cleared her throat. "So your burning resentment against your telepathic family keeps you warm in the Russian winter? Because your shirt is really, really thin, and I'm finding it hard to believe you're that angry all the time."

"No, my talent is anomaly." Viktor said the word with such force that Marling couldn't help thinking he'd only learned it recently, and was quite proud of himself. "We think my great-grandfather had this too, this fire." Viktor stopped and looked around before wrapping his hand around one end of the stray branch he'd been playing with. When he removed his hand, a tiny flame danced atop the branch… and along his fingers.

Marling thought of Kyran's warning that Viktor had burned people to death. "I see," she said. "Uh, is that just in your hands? Or are you like the Human Torch from Fantastic Four?"

Viktor stared at the growing flame that hovered over his fingers. "Just my hands."

"You've never like… burned anyone, have you?"

The silence was almost unbearable. Marling's mind filled to brim with images of Viktor wearing one of those super stereotypical Russian fur hats and a faded military uniform while he burned down houses with screaming families inside.

She wasn't sure exactly why he would do that, but fear can run rampant in that kind of silence.

"Yes, Marling." His eyes fixed on her, so intense and so dark that she almost backed away from him. "But I'm very careful now. It's been many years since I can't control it. Are you afraid?"

"I'm a little afraid of fire, like most normal people are, but I don't think you've burned anyone… you know, to death, or anything. Right?"

"If you're afraid of me, Marling, then you have answer you need. This is… this won't go away." He held his hand out toward her, the flame dancing over his slender, pale fingers. "You come all the way here from across the world. This is something you need to know, because I can't show you this five years ago."

No, five years ago she'd met a heavily inebriated Russian at a party thrown by a mutual friend. Five years ago the weirdest thing about Viktor was how he dropped words out of sentences and mixed up his tenses.

Five years ago the most confusing thing about Viktor was his utter disbelief in fortune cookies.

"It's not… a deal breaker," Marling said. "As long as you weren't planning to roast me over an open fire and eat me. Cannibalism is actually pretty high on my list of unacceptable qualities in a guy, along with forgetting to shower. And liking that stupid show, *The Big Bang Theory*."

Viktor let out a heavy sigh. "I don't know what that is."

"See? You're fine."

Viktor clapped his hands together a couple times and the flame disappeared. "Come on, it'll be dark soon. We should walk back toward the house." He offered his arm to Marling and she took it immediately. "My mother, she's away for couple of days because of my coronation, but there are many ears. Everything goes back to her. You must be careful what you say there. Also, I have important question. Who is that man who come with you?"

"Oh, Kyran?" Marling tried to think. "Uhh, he's... he's one of my teachers."

"I don't like him."

Marling raised an eyebrow. "Well, don't worry, I think the feeling's mutual." She cleared her throat. "But you're not gonna burn him alive or something, right? This is just one of those stupid boy rivalry things?"

Viktor shrugged. "I might kill him before I burn him."

"Uh, Viktor, after you showed me your Fantastic Four powers, that's not a very good joke to make."

"Says the queen of inappropriate jokes."

Marling bumped her hip into him, a bit too hard, and both of them laughed. "Alright, I'll be careful what I say in your house, and I'll keep Kyran away from you. Anything other important questions?"

Viktor stopped and stepped in front of Marling so he could place his hands on her shoulders and stare directly into her eyes. After what felt like an eternity of hesitation, Viktor wrapped his arms tight around her, hugging her against his chest. Guilt squeezed at Marling's throat, but she relaxed in his hold and settled her arms around him in return, closing her eyes. The thing about Viktor and hugs was that he was always most honest when he was tender. She felt his worry, and tension, and echoes and echoes of gratitude as he lost himself for a few seconds in the comfort Marling could provide.

"Are you alright?" she whispered, rubbing his back.

Viktor pulled back from her a little, though his hands rested on her hips, and he still bowed his head over hers. "You're in a lot of danger here, Marling. I never wanted to put you in danger." He sighed, raising his hand to tuck some of Marling's hair behind her ear. "The only relief I feel is that your manipulation of magic is not so noticeable."

"What! What does that mean?"

"You're not a very good witch, Marling," Viktor said, struggling against a smile. "You're a star at convincing people to do anything you want. And you're very expert at knowing what book or what movie or what song will be a hit. You can charm a room of strangers. You can find Chinese takeout from thirty blocks. And you can trip over someone's legs and say '*Hello*, are you Europe?' and make him want to follow you around a cold city on crazy adventures. Those are your powers, Marling." The smile fell away again, as quickly as it had appeared. "And right now, I'm glad that magic isn't your power."

Marling had never felt this guilty in her life, not even when she'd found Jennifer's lunch money in second grade and used it to buy a soda. Jennifer had later told Marling that she'd gone hungry for the day. It was really awful for both of them. Well, maybe it was worse for Jennifer, since she'd gone hungry. "I-I guess we're a little like Romeo and Juliet," Marling whispered.

"Please don't say that. That was not a happy story."

"Well, yeah, it did have a depressing ending but... hey, it spawned like three hit movies. And a really great soundtrack for the Leonardo DiCaprio version. Radiohead, am I right?"

Viktor shook his head, but at least he was smiling again. Marling's guilt levels dropped a bit.

They returned to the house together and Marling silently promised herself that she would get in better shape soon, because even that little excursion into the woods had left her completely exhausted. And starving.

Viktor took care of the starving part by showing her to the kitchen, and letting her choose from about a zillion delicious looking food items. It felt like something from a foodie's daydream, or a made-for-TV movie about winning the lottery. By the time Marling had finished eating two plates of food and consuming a massive mug of hot chocolate, she felt completely blissful. And like she might fall asleep on her feet.

"Are you going to carry me to my room now?" she asked, and Viktor shot her a confused look. Oh. Well maybe the logistics didn't make that request likely. Especially since Marling was fairly certain Viktor weighed less than her.

"I can show you to your room, but I'm not sure if…"

"Good enough!" Marling said, her face warming up with embarrassment. The last thing she needed to do was get into a conversation with a paramour about whether she was too heavy to be carried.

Viktor led her to a little room with lots of pink things in it… pink pillows, pink blankets, pink teddy bears, dolls wearing pink dresses, rows of pink tea cups, and books with pink spines. Marling stepped just inside, looking around. "Oh, uh, wow. It looks like someone barfed a Pepto Bismal bottle into a room."

"It was supposed to be Petra's room, when she was little, but she didn't like it."

"Not enough horses?"

"She wanted a more, uh, more tough room. Not so girl."

"I really hate to side with Petra about anything, but I think I can see her point."

"You don't like it?"

"Actually, I hate it, but it's nice of you to give me a room so I'll totally sleep here tonight." Marling pushed a few of the particularly scary looking dolls off of the bed. "See? I feel more at home already." She glanced down at the fallen dolls. "I hope I don't regret that later when they come to life and try to stab me in my sleep…"

"Will you be comfortable?"

Marling shrugged. "Hey, whatever. As long as the dolls don't stab me, I'm too tired to care." She leaned up and attempted to kiss his cheek, but he turned his head and she caught his lips instead. After another intense kiss that almost got Marling in trouble, she untangled herself from Viktor and pushed him through the doorway. "I'll see you in the morning," she said.

"It's bad luck to talk through doorways."

"Who told you that?"

"My brother. A long time ago."

Surely there was quite a story there, but Marling was exhausted. She nodded to him and waved. "I'll try not to talk through doorways then."

"You're doing it now."

"So are you, Viktor Kalashnik!"

Viktor walked away and Marling closed the door, threw herself on the bed. She slipped away to sleep almost immediately. Blissful sleep. Blissful, uninterrupted sleep...

chapter sixteen

"Marling. Marling!"

Marling shot up in bed, screeching so loud that she managed to hurt her own ears. She had no weapon to protect herself so she said, "LEAVE ME ALONE OR I'LL HIT YOU!" before realizing the intruder was a sleepy-faced Kyran.

"Marling, calm down. It's just me." Kyran tugged at the ends of his blue scarf so that it tightened around his neck. "You don't have to wake the house up."

"What are you doing in my room?"

"Your room? You've certainly claimed this place fast enough. Did he already ask you to marry him and rule his sparkly fairy kingdom forever and ever as the pretty pretty queen?"

Marling attempted to calm down, but she found that her shaky hands had other plans. "What do you want?"

"Excuse me, Marling, but are you sort of forgetting why we're here? I didn't hire you so you could take long walks with the prince and sleep on a pink cloud." Kyran paused. "This bed *is* kinda comfortable. A lot better than the one in the room he gave me."

"You didn't hire me, you kidnapped me. And I'm allowed to sleep. Do you understand how tiring the last four days of my life have been?"

"Marling. Listen to me, I have to tell you something very important." Kyran kicked his boots off and tugged his legs up on the bed so he was sitting cross-legged, facing her. He took a deep breath and offered Marling a brief smile. "You don't strike me as the most capable witch."

"Why is everyone saying that? You got *exiled*, so I don't really think you have a lot of room to insult me," Marling said, glaring at him.

A muscle twitched in Kyran's cheek. "Do you know why I was exiled?"

"I didn't invite you in here for a slumber party. Get out of my room!"

Kyran let out a heavy sigh and dropped his gaze, playing with the bottom of his long-sleeved black pajama shirt. From his long eyelashes to his old fashioned pjs, he suddenly looked like a sad little boy on Christmas morning, by way of those pencil drawings from the 1950s. He just needed a teddy bear and rosier cheeks.

"Okay, okay," Marling said, groaning. "Why were you exiled?"

"I mixed up a potion."

Marling waited. After a long period of silence, she said, "...and?"

"I mixed up a potion!"

"Yeah, but what happened? Did someone like, turn into a salmon?"

"No, Marling, I put three pinches of cinnamon into the curse potion, and I forgot to put the granite shavings in to balance it out." Kyran's voice fell to a whisper. "Jeremiah August sent the potion to this politician and he... grew body hair. All over. Like... like a gorilla."

"Oh," Marling said, and paused. "Was he able to get rid of the hair...?"

"I'm sure he shaved it off within minutes of the incident, but the transformation took place at a stuffy dinner with a bunch of his friends. And I guess Jeremiah August's wife was there when it happened." Kyran shook his head. "She thought it was funny, but Jeremiah was furious. He called me so many names."

A few times in class, Marling had heard about accidents that involved potions. Usually they resulted in something simple to correct, but occasionally they led to something disastrous like someone turning into a rolling office chair and never being able to turn back again. She had always assumed that Kyran's blunder must be in the latter category, since everyone had treated him like a dangerous outcast. "I'm sorry," Marling said, finally. "I had no idea… everyone always made it seem so serious."

Kyran sniffled. "This is the only thing I've ever wanted to *be*. When I was little, I had this book about England that my mom got from the Goodwill. I'd put it under my pillow and just dream about growing up and moving to England and having a little shop on a cute street called Blueberry Lane. And I'd be a famous magician, and everyone would come to me for their magic problems." Kyran reached up and wiped at his eyes and then hiccuped. He fished a tiny bottle from inside his scarf, poured the contents of the bottle into his mouth, and then hiccuped quietly again.

"Is that alcohol?" Marling asked, her eyes widening. Kyran ignored her question.

"I was going to be a magical investigator. Just without the fedora. Fedoras aren't cool anymore."

Marling moved a bit closer to Kyran and patted him on the back. If he was drinking, the wound of his failure must still be horribly raw. "You don't have to give up that dream."

"Jeremiah said I was worthless as a witch! And Lady Grieve said a lot of very, very rude things." Kyran fished another bottle out of his scarf and opened it. "Just… just be glad you didn't hear them."

"I did hear them, remember? I was there. We've talked about this before."

"Oh, right. Well then, you know it was awful." Kyran downed the other bottle and coughed. "I can't even tell my parents! Do you know how they'd feel? They've always believed in me, no matter what. If I got a B on a test or something, my mom would give me a hug, and tell me how good I did. And then she'd make a cake and we'd roll cookies together, and my sisters would eat the raw dough…" He trailed off.

"That… sounds nice."

"No. If they knew I'd failed, they'd be so disappointed!" Kyran said, and then it happened. Tears. Big tears.

"Aww, Kyran, that's not true. You said your mom made you cakes and stuff. I mean, a B isn't even bad, so it sounds like your family was *really* nice. Maybe they'd just give you a big hug and make you a cake."

Sniffle. "I don't eat sugar or white flour."

"Well, that's weird. But still! Maybe they could make you some… I don't know, steamed vegetables. And the point is, they sound really supportive and loving. You should just tell them! I don't think I could keep anything from my family, even if it was that I lost a job or whatever."

Kyran raised his head. "Did you tell them about the unlove spell?"

"No! But that's… well, that's different."

With another huge sniffle, Kyran wiped his eyes with his scarf. "It's not different. There are some things you don't want to have to tell the people you love. My mom and dad and Nicole and Kate and Karmen and Dusty would be so disappointed."

"But maybe they wouldn't be. You're kinda hard on yourself, I think." Marling tapped a finger on his arm. "You've got tattoos of spells on your skin so you won't forget them. That's pretty hardcore."

"It's my job! It's my dream. Isn't it your dream?"

Marling thought about this for a long time. "I think my only lifelong dream is to have a real and true best friend. And maybe to wear that blue dress that Viktor showed me earlier. And to travel through time. And marry a prince. And get to hire three professional chefs."

"But you're a witch, Marling!"

"Not a very good one, according to you and Viktor." Marling sighed, idly picking up one of the empty raspberry vodka bottles that Kyran had discarded. "I don't think I'm married to the cause like you are. I'm sorry if that's disappointing. I thought being a witch was gonna be this really exciting life... and then I thought working for a theater company would be a really exciting life. And then I thought working for a publishing company would be a really exciting life. And then I knew a guy for four days and tried to put a spell on him, but I messed it up because I'm awful at magic. I dunno. Nothing ever sticks for very long, for me."

"But magic is the best life in the world," Kyran whispered. "Better even than being... Marc Jacobs' personal assistant. And it *is* exciting."

"Well, you kidnapping me and dragging me to Russia certainly upped the excitement factor, I'll admit."

"Whatever. We're going to rescue the witches. I'll be a hero, and I'll open my shop in London. You can marry a prince and eat carbs." Kyran wiped his nose on his sleeve, which Marling couldn't help thinking was probably a sign of a complete mental breakdown on his part. "What did you find out while you were walking with the skinny fairy princess?"

"Viktor?"

"Obviously! What other skinny fairy princesses have you been on a walk with today?"

Marling chose to ignore his snark. She was, after all, a mature and reasonable woman when she wanted to be. "Uh, well, his mom's gone for a few days. And I guess the fae originally came from Iceland, which kind of explains Bjork's existence."

"Anything else? Important information? Juicy details about Viktor's personal life?" Kyran paused, rummaging around in his scarf like he was trying to locate something. "Did he explain his clothing choices? I mean, he *was* wearing that skanky v-neck shirt..."

"So?" Marling demanded, falling back onto her pillow. "Do you feel better now? Because I'd like you to go to your room."

"As if I'm going to sleep in that haunted room with all the weird noises in the walls." Kyran stretched out next to her, on his back, and stared up at the ceiling. "Did you really only know him for four days before you put the unlove spell on yourself?"

"Kyran."

"That's just so impulsive," Kyran muttered.

Marling kicked him. She'd had enough of being mature and reasonable for the night.

"You only knew someone for four days, and that was enough time for you to decide that you wanted to be with him forever," Kyran said. "Then you broke up with him, and didn't see him again for five years. Marling. That's crazy."

"Not crazy. Guys like Viktor don't come along every day."

"Pointy eared freaks with a royal background? Yeah, probably not. But that's not even the point, Marling. You're too impulsive. One of these days you're going to have to make a decision and stick with it."

"You're not my fairy godmother," Marling said. She rolled onto her side so that her back was to Kyran and closed her eyes. Whatever. She had plenty of perfectly valid reasons for falling for Viktor in four days. Like his... kindness? And... well, leather pants!

Dammit, leather pants on the right man were a good enough reason for a girl to do just about anything.

chapter seventeen

Five years ago, two days before New Year's Day

Marling lay stretched on top of Viktor on the couch, listening to the drunken yells from the crazy neighbor in the apartment next door.

"New Year's is our most important holiday in Russia," Viktor whispered, as if a lunatic wasn't making a fuss on the other side of the wall.

"Really?" Marling brushed Viktor's bangs out of his eyes for the millionth time, and danced her fingers over his sleek black hair. He had really, really great hair.

"Yeah, maybe next year I'll show you."

Marling paused in her enthusiastic exploration of his hair so she could plaster an equally enthusiastic kiss on his lips. "Take me to Russia. I wanna see Russia! I wanna wear a big fur coat, and a fancy fur hat, and I want to ride in a sleigh like they did in *Dr. Zhivago*."

Viktor laughed, and then both of them jumped when a crash sounded from the apartment next door. "Sounds like his fridge," Marling whispered.

"Only a fridge? Sounds like quite a party."

"It's just him, you know. And his other personalities. It's no wonder the rent's so cheap, because this guy is loud all the time. Sometimes I think I should have moved to Brooklyn instead, and braved the hipsters."

"Hipsters aren't so bad. Why don't you move?"

"Excuse me, mysterious, possibly insanely wealthy Russian dude, but I can't afford to move, especially to the hipster areas." Marling paused. "Considering that I just got fired, I might be forced to move, though. You know. Out to the curbside, with a jar for donations, and a cardboard sign. Or to Brownsville, where I'll get shot within three days. I guess getting shot would take care of a lot of my problems."

Another crash sounded.

"Excuse me." Viktor untangled himself from Marling gently, pausing to kiss her again, and then he slowly made his way to his feet. He tugged his shirt on, and then his socks, and walked to the door.

"What are you doing?" Marling demanded.

"Talking to the neighbor."

"What? No! Viktor!" Marling snatched up her shorts, tugged them on, and chased after Viktor into the hallway. "You don't want to talk to him. He's crazy!"

Viktor knocked on the door for 516. After another deafening crash, the door swung open.

"What do you want?" Marling's neighbor demanded, glaring at Viktor from behind a thick fringe of uneven, stringy brown hair. He looked almost as bad as he smelled, which was like puke on a summer sidewalk.

"Sir, you've been very, very loud and very inconsiderate. You should quiet down," Viktor said. "Stop yelling and throwing things."

Marling realized that this might go very Stephen King, with her crazy neighbor screaming and stabbing Viktor in the face with a kitchen knife. She reached for Viktor's arm and tried to pull him away.

Viktor, however, continued to stare into Crazy Neighbor's eyes. He repeated his command, "Stop yelling and throwing things."

"Oh. Okay," Crazy Neighbor said, somewhat reluctantly.

Viktor nodded. "You'll be quiet?"

"Yeah, okay. I'll be quiet."

"Good."

Crazy Neighbor glanced at Marling and then slunk back inside his apartment and closed the door. Marling couldn't help thinking he might be retreating to arm himself with an ungodly collection of dangerous weapons, so he could blow her apartment to pieces. She tried not to focus on images of oversize guns and hand grenades.

"He'll be quieter now," Viktor said.

"What did you do to him? Do you have magic too?" Marling demanded. She stared up at Viktor, waiting for his response, but then her phone buzzed in her pocket. Marling gasped. "It's eight!"

Viktor shrugged. "Okay, it's eight."

"No, I mean it's eight o'clock! We're gonna miss her if we don't go *now*."

Marling tore into her apartment, searching for her jacket. After a frantic search, she discovered it in a crumpled pile on the kitchen floor. She had no recollection of how it had gotten there, but she found her scarf close to it. After a bit more frantic searching, she located the sparkly white yarn hat that she'd made during her brief flirtation with learning how to crochet. It had come out halfway decent, so she liked to wear it at every opportunity possible.

"What's going on, Marling?" Viktor asked, still standing exactly where she'd left him.

"On January 30th, every year, Dame Marrow tells 20 people their fortune for the new year," Marling said in a rush. She caught sight of Viktor's raised eyebrow and pinched lips. "You don't know about that? Oh wait, I forgot, you're Russian. You probably don't know about that tradition. Look, just grab your jacket! We have to hurry or we won't be able to get a place in line!"

Viktor gathered his silvery-gray jacket and black scarf from the floor with the gracefulness of a magical creature, and then pulled on his boots while still standing. Despite how impatient Marling felt, she couldn't help staring at him and wondering how she'd managed to find herself a Viktor Kalashnik. She couldn't pronounce his last name, of course, but that didn't matter.

"What's wrong?" Viktor asked, and Marling realized she'd been gawping at him.

"Oh, nothing. You're just really hot, especially for someone who lives in a cold place."

Slowly, Viktor crossed the room to her and slipped his hand around the back of her neck. He leaned down and kissed her until she almost melted into the floor. Marling groaned against his lips, once she managed to recover slightly from the kiss-induced brain fog he'd caused.

"Stop it, we're gonna be late," she whispered. When he tried to pull away, she grabbed his face between her hands and kissed him again.

"I thought we're gonna be late."

With a groan, Marling nodded. "Yes, yes, so stop distracting me. Please." She kissed him again and then grabbed his hand. "Don't even look at me for a little while, okay? You're too attractive, I can't deal with it." She pulled on his hand and led him away before he could say or do anything more.

Outside, Marling led Viktor through the cold streets, worried that she would fail again, like she had last year. She had journeyed to Dame Marrow with Emma at her side. They'd reached the woman too late, and found themselves stuck in a massive line of other curious people bundled up in jackets, hoping for some insight into their lives.

Emma and Marling had spent all of four hours in line, watching with crossed fingers as people tired of waiting, and the line thinned. But in the end they'd been unable to talk to Marrow, and had left in disgrace and disappointment.

"Emma's gonna meet us there," Marling said, staring at her phone.

"Who's Emma?"

"You can't call her Emma. Her name is Emma but she likes to be called Primrose Redhaven. And she's not really English, she just pretends to be. But if you say something about it she'll deny it, and then she'll say she has no idea that she's faking an accent."

"Wait, what do I call her then?"

"Well, I don't call her anything," Marling admitted. "I mean, I try very hard not to refer to her by a name, because she doesn't like being called Emma. And Primrose is embarrassing to say out loud. Unless you're talking to a dog."

"So I should call her Primrose?"

"Man, you're such a nice guy, Viktor, calling her by her preferred name, even though it's dumb." Marling slipped her phone back into her pocket and grabbed Viktor's hand, squeezing it for good luck as they approached their destination. "Look! That must be the line! We'll make it, we'll make it!" Marling let out a shout of triumph and ran toward the half a dozen people standing along the side of a building. We did it, we did it, we did it!" Marling said, jumping up and down.

"Great. What exactly did we do? Someone tell you… your fortune?"

Marling could tell by the tone of his voice that he thought it was a little silly, but then, Russians probably didn't understand. Weren't they super practical about everything? They'd have to be, considering they lived in ice hell. "She's really good," she said, and cleared her throat. "She tells you what your new year will be like. And I talked to this guy who said she told him he was going to take a long journey and like, two days later his boss said he wanted him to move to France for three months." Marling paused. "France, Viktor. *France.*"

"Okay, okay." Viktor laughed and looked at the other people in line. "When do we see her?"

Marling shrugged. "Oh, around midnight. Or one. Maybe two."

"Midnight? Marling! That's... that's hours away!"

"That's just how it works."

"Aren't you going to get hungry?" he demanded, and Marling smacked his arm.

"We'll send Emma to get food. This is important! I want to know what's gonna happen to me next year." Just then Marling's phone buzzed again.

Just got msg from Lady Grieve. Won't be able to attend. Have fun, hope you get to see her!! xox PS- IS HE HOT?! SEND ME A PICTURE!!

"Uh. I guess Emma won't be joining us," Marling muttered, squinting at the text as if it might vanish. Maybe she'd hallucinated it, in her excitement. Surely Emma wouldn't miss out on this important tradition?

"So we're going to stand in line all night with no food?"

"You don't have to stay if you don't want to!" Marling said finally, louder than she meant to. "Just go, if you want. I can stay in line alone."

Viktor sighed, his breath floating visibly around him like a little halo. "No, I'll stay."

The first hour wasn't so bad. And the second hour was interesting because a chatty, cool young couple jumped in line behind Viktor and Marling. By the time it neared 11pm, Marling had, like everyone else, sat down with her back to the cold wall of the building. She didn't notice she was shivering until Viktor leaned closer and whispered in her ear, "Do you want my jacket?"

"No, I'm okay," Marling said. It was a complete lie. She felt like she was going to freeze to death at any moment, but she was too stubborn to admit it.

"Really?" Viktor kissed her ear. "You're shaking all over, Marling."

Pride told her to reject his offer again, especially since he was basically a beanpole in the body density department, but she *was* cold. As Marling turned her head to say something to the couple sitting in line behind them, she felt the weight of Viktor's jacket on her shoulders.

The woman behind them let out a heavy, shivery sigh. "Forget about being cold, man, I'm like *starving.* Does someone have some food hidden up the sleeves of their jacket?"

"We should hit Tavy's after this," her boyfriend said, casually. "They have great food."

Marling looked between them. The girl had a shaved head and impossibly smooth dark skin, and her boyfriend had pink, spiky hair. These were the kind of people that went cool places and did cool things. "What's Tavy's? I've never heard of Tavy's," Marling said, quietly. Maybe she could become friends with them and start hanging out at cool counterculture spots around the city, sipping neon cocktails and wearing impossibly hip clothes made from recycled garbage bags.

Forget being a witch. Marling wanted to be a cool punk.

"They're open 24 hours, and tonight and tomorrow night everything they serve is only a dollar. Like, really," the boyfriend said. "Everything. It's insane."

"Well, what do they serve, a packet of peanuts?" Viktor muttered.

"No man, like... sandwiches, hot dogs. French fries. It's disgusting, but it's insane cheap. It's their big New Year's celebration."

"Are you from Russia?" the girl asked and Viktor nodded. "You look like a model, man." She looked at her boyfriend. "Doesn't he look like a model? He would look great in your sister's boyfriend's magazine."

"Yeah, for sure."

"Or he could be royalty," the cool girl punk said, and turned her heavy lidded gaze back to Viktor. "You could be a prince."

Marling had never felt so proud in her life. "He does look like a model," she said, batting her eyelashes and moving closer to Viktor. She patted his arm, unnecessarily. "And a prince."

"Where is this, uh, one dollar everything place?" Viktor asked, and the girl rattled off an address. Marling made mental note of it, because she knew she'd be hungry later.

"Do you wanna write it down?" Cool Girl Punk asked. "I don't have anything to write on. I try not to use paper anymore. It's so wasteful, you know?"

"No, it's fine. I'm very good at remembering things," Marling said, which was a complete lie. She was actually terrible at remembering almost everything, including her own phone number and her mom's birthday. Once in a while, her own birthday too.

By midnight, Marling was starting to feel antsy. Dame Marrow *should* emerge any moment from the building, open the door and invite the first person to have his or her fortune read. So where was she?

Viktor had rested his head on Marling's shoulder and closed his eyes a while ago. She was pretty convinced that he'd fallen asleep. Similarly, the couple behind them in line had snuggled close together and drifted off to sleep. Marling nervously patted Viktor's head for a long time, eyes darting again and again to the front of the line. Where was Dame Marrow?

Just when Marling was starting to become concerned, the door cracked open and the withered, slumped form of Dame Marrow emerged.

"Viktor. *Viktor!*" Marling whispered. "Viktor, there she is!"

Viktor sat up straight, glancing at Dame Marrow. He let out a quiet scoff. "That's her?"

"Shhh! She's gonna speak!"

It seemed that everything fell silent, and even the passersby froze to stare as Dame Marrow clapped her hands together. "You have all journeyed to see me," she said, pointing a bony finger at the line. "But I will only meet twenty of you so the rest of you might as well bugger off." With those incredibly deep and meaningful words, she took the hand of the first person in line and led him into her little shop.

Dame Marrow only inhabited this tiny shop once a year, on this night… Marling knew this because she'd checked the shop many times, only to be told by the long suffering owner that Dame Marrow would be back January 30th *and don't you want to actually buy something for once?!*

Dame Marrow usually spent about ten or fifteen minutes with each person, so Marling stood up and coaxed Viktor to his feet. She thanked him for sticking it out, kissed him on the cheek. Then she kissed him on the mouth. Then she got a little carried away and kissed him for a very long time, until the man in line in front of them got uncomfortable and cleared his throat in an aggressive manner.

Half an hour later, the door opened again, and the next person in line disappeared inside. The first guy, almost glowing, stumbled into the distance. Before disappearing from sight, he shouted, "Yes. *Yes!* I'm so ready for this year. So ready!"

"He should be careful, not to get hit by a car," Viktor muttered, darkly, narrowing his eyes. "Very dangerous to walk around like that."

Marling just bounced from foot to foot, ignoring his negativity. Everything was going to work out this time. She'd talk to Dame Marrow, and then she'd stumble away, glowing and overflowing with positive energy about her year ahead. "I can't wait to get in there!" she said, rubbing her cold hands together. "We only have to wait a little longer. Soon, soon."

Soon turned out not to be very soon at all. By 2am, Marling felt dizzy with anticipation and low blood sugar. Just before 3am, the couple in line behind Marling and Viktor decided they didn't want to wait anymore, so they left. Marling clung to Viktor, her arms locked around his waist and her face pressed to his chest. It was weird, but he felt so so so so warm, even without a jacket. Hugging him was like hugging a space heater.

"I want hot chocolate," Marling whispered.

"Me too."

"Maybe we shouldn't wait anymore," Marling said, even though it hurt to say it. She was so very close now; there was only one person ahead of them.

"Marling? We've waited this long, we can wait a little longer. You almost there!"

Okay, so maybe he was right. Marling nodded against him and took a few deep breaths, steadied herself. "But hot chocolate after," she said. She tipped her face up to meet his gaze in the dark. "You gonna ask her for your fortune too?"

"Nah."

"Come on, Viktor, don't you want to know what next year will be like?"

"I'll find out next year, won't I?" Viktor asked, with a little half smile. He hugged her to his chest and kept her warm until finally, finally, it was Marling's turn, and Dame Marrow stood before her.

"Get in here," the old woman said, in a voice that sounded even older than she looked. Marling felt so excited and nervous that she thought she might throw up, so she grabbed hold of Viktor's hand extra tight and tugged him along with her.

"Can I bring him with me?" she asked Dame Marrow, pointing in a particularly spastic manner at Viktor. "He doesn't want his fortune told, so I'd just like to bring him with me. You know, to sit with me, or hold my hand or something. Support, you know? Moral support." Marling laughed nervously. "Is that okay?"

Dame Marrow shot them a long-suffering look and rolled her bulgy eyes, but thankfully she let them both enter together.

The shop looked the same as it did at any other time of year: crowded, confused and a little gross. But two chairs and a tiny table had been set up in the middle, the only special additions that the ancient fortune teller brought with her for this special occasion. Dame Marrow lowered herself into one creaky chair and then motioned for Marling to sit in the other one.

Marling sat down, glancing over her shoulder to make sure Viktor was standing behind her, and then faced Dame Marrow again with a nervous smile. "Alright, I'm ready! And really, it's so exciting to meet you finally. An honor, actually..."

"Yeah, yeah." Dame Marrow coughed heavily, like she might keel over and die. After a few seconds of pounding her frail chest with a bony fist, she recovered and sorted through her cards. An eternity later, she reached for Marling's hands. She glanced at them, one hand and then the other, and then returned to her cards for another long period of time. The silence was unbearable. "You're in love," Dame Marrow said finally. She didn't sound enthused about this revelation, or love in general. "And this year you'll get a new job."

"Oooh, nice, yes. I just lost my job actually," Marling said, nodding her head. She waited for a few seconds, expecting more. When Dame Marrow didn't raise her head from her cards or say anything else, Marling leaned across the table. "Love, job. What else?"

"Nothing else. You're done." Dame Marrow pushed herself up out of the chair, her joints creaking almost as audibly as the chair. "Come on, out you go. I need to finish this shit so I can get some sleep."

What.

Marling felt dizzy again, worse than before. No, this wasn't right, this *couldn't* be right. She had no idea how she managed to stand and walk out of the building. She only knew that Viktor put his arm around her shoulders and she leaned against him, heavy with disappointment and shock. She couldn't speak until they'd walked several blocks away.

"That was it?" she whispered. "I thought she was gonna... I thought she was gonna help. I thought she'd *know!*" Marling groaned. "You know, part of why I got into magic in the first place was so I could figure out the future and make better decisions. You know? But that doesn't work at all. And Dame Marrow... I mean, 'You'll get a new job'? Of *course* I'll get a new job." She sniffled mightily. "I'm unemployed. Getting a new job was kind of an obvious goal for this year."

Viktor stopped walking, so Marling had to stop walking too, since she was still basically attached to him. "What did you want to hear from her, Marling?"

"I wanted to hear about myself. I-I want to know things I don't know! I want to know what's gonna happen next, so I can do the right thing."

Maybe it was low blood sugar or the fact that it was 4am, but Viktor seemed taller and more comforting than ever, like some kind of creature from a fairy-tale book. "Marling, you can do the right thing without knowing what will happen. And if there's anything you might need to know about yourself, I think it's that you're lonely."

Ouch. It stung, but only because it was true. Marling's eyes filled with tears. Before she could stop herself, she was sobbing against Viktor's chest and he was patting her back.

"We should go find that... one dollar for sandwich place," he said. "You're hungry."

"I forgot the address!" she admitted, crying even harder. "I forgot it because I'm actually *really bad* at remembering things! One time I forgot my own birthday when I was on the phone to my credit card, and I got so nervous that I hung up, okay?"

Viktor laughed, quietly, and somehow, it made Marling laugh too.

"It's not funny," she mumbled, but at least she wasn't actively crying anymore. "Now we're going to starve. And freeze. And I'll never get my hot chocolate. Dame Marrow should have just told me that was my future... starvation, in the cold streets of Manhattan. Alone, because I can't keep a boyfriend for more than a few days, and I'm terrible at making friends."

"Here, look at this." Viktor rolled his sleeve back and revealed an address messily scribbled on his pale skin with blue ink. "I thought you might forget."

Marling kissed him and kissed him, until Viktor untangled himself from her and politely suggested they actually go get cheap food from this mysterious late night food oasis they'd heard so much about. So they had one dollar sandwiches that night, and hot chocolate. And the sandwiches were as disgusting as promised, but it didn't matter. Dame Marrow had been right about one important thing... Marling was in love.

chapter eighteen

Marling felt something warm and heavy hooked over her waist. She realized after a long moment of confusion that she'd fallen asleep at some point in the night, and Kyran had snuggled close with his arm draped over her. All the way over her. "Kyran."

"Five more minutes."

"Kyran. Your arm."

He mumbled something unintelligable and snuggled a little closer. Then he mumbled Viktor's name in an overly friendly, lovey-dovey tone. Gross. Marling groaned and pushed him away, just before she remembered that he had her cell phone. Could she steal it back, maybe? Would she wake him if she tried? If she woke him, would he turn her into a toilet seat, or make one of her pinkies much smaller than the other one? Marling pulled a face, trying to decide if the risk was worth it.

She examined his sleeping form and spotted what seemed to be the outline of her cell phone in his pants pocket. With extreme precision and more than a little anxiety, she managed to fish her phone out of his pocket without waking him. She let out a heavy sigh of relief, cradling the phone against her chest for a few seconds. Thank God, she had her phone again, everything would be.... wait. Wait, what time did her phone say it was? 1:21pm?

Marling slid off the bed and stumbled across the room, tripping over a few stray dolls and teddy bears along the way. How had she slept this late? Sure, she'd been utterly exhausted, and yes, she'd just flown around the world but *still*. It was 1:21pm. She hadn't slept that late since she had the flu, as a teenager.

A huge pink-framed mirror stood guard beside the door, beckoning for Marling to catch a glimpse of what was sure to be a horrific sight. No thank you, she didn't need to scare herself on top of everything else. She ducked her head and rushed out of the room without looking at her reflection.

Once she'd left the room, though, Marling remembered that she had no idea where she was. She tried to walk with confidence, the way she'd always been instructed to walk in Manhattan when she felt unsafe, but it was difficult in such a strange, winding house. And the only people she came into contact with while wandering just glared at her and hurried away when she tried to speak to them. With an annoyed sigh, she decided to take matters into her own hands, literally.

Marling grabbed the arm of a skinny older guy with an intense, bushy beard. "Where is Prince Viktor?" she demanded, looking him directly in the eyes and trying to give off confident scary-eye-vibes like Viktor did.

"Viktor?"

"Yeah, you know. Tall." She motioned way above her head. "Viktor! Prince Viktor! Black hair, really hot, looks good in leather pants."

The man blinked at her and Marling felt a sinking sensation in her gut. What if he decided to lead her away to a dark room and murder her? She probably should have asked someone else. A woman. Well, a child would be preferable, since they usually didn't have plans for murder at the forefront of their afternoon schedules.

The beardy guy smiled and motioned for her to follow, and after a bit of hesitation, Marling fell into step behind him. He led her up an impressive staircase and down a hallway before stopping abruptly in front of a door. He smiled at Marling again, this time a much creepier smile, and bowed and walked away.

"Is this his room?" Marling asked, but the man had already walked away. With a great sigh, Marling faced the door in question and knocked. She half expected the door to swing open and reveal a torture room full of ghosts, spiders, and discounted Insane Clown Posse merchandise, but instead it swung open and revealed Viktor. Wearing only a pair of loose black sleep pants.

Viktor leaned out of his room to look right and left and then tugged Marling inside his room and shut the door behind them. He walked away from her, to his closet, and sorted through it, probably looking for a shirt. Too bad. But his distraction gave Marling time to look around a little.

Now, Marling had always pictured Viktor living in one of those cozy little apartments in Williamsburg, with a couple ugly paintings hanging over the brick walls. There'd be some stringed lights, too many books, and maybe a collection of vintage Russian dolls that his dear old grandmother had given him. He might have a modest movie collection, and a cute spice rack for cooking. Furthermore, Marling had imagined herself visiting his apartment and feeling instantly at home, hanging her jacket over the back of a tiny couch and thinking, *isn't it strange how comfortable and familiar this place is?* She would instantly know where all of his bowls and plates were, and she'd easily find his one frying pan. She'd borrow a few things from his spice rack and cook up a delicious little meal. Viktor would just shake his head and say he rarely used the spices, but he was *so* happy that someone was finally using them.

They would listen to some of his vinyl records together and decide, without having to actually say anything, that they could make a home together, right there in his cozy apartment.

As it turned out, Viktor's room definitely belonged in a palace, not in Williamsburg.

Viktor's bed was one of those fancy four poster bed deals, and the chandelier hanging in the center of the room looked as if someone had fastened about a zillion diamonds to every square inch of it. A full length gilded mirror stood between a beautiful vintage dresser and a couch with scarlet-colored cushions. A shiny black typewriter sat atop the dresser. Marling found herself itching to touch... well, everything. Including the impressive laptop computer set up at a little desk along the wall. Maybe especially that, since it felt a bit more familiar to her eyes, a drop of modern technology in a room that was drowning in the past.

A collection of glass and gold animal figurines lined up atop the dresser caught her eye, and Marling couldn't help leaning in to get a closer look at them.

"These are beautiful! Where did they come from?" Marling asked, her eyes flicking from the giraffe to the lion, and then the little monkey.

"My mother give them to me when I was seven, because I was very sick with a flu."

"Aww. They're so pretty." Marling traced her fingers over a few of them, and then over an antique key on an aged silver chain.

"Something happen last night," Viktor said, with a heavy sigh. "A friend of Petra's, she tell us that a member of the Marsh family- that's Petra's bloodline- well, she was picked up by a slaver. And when they're done with her, they..." He shuddered. "They leave her in a field. Cut to pieces."

Marling straightened and looked at him, horrified. "Did you know that girl?" she asked, shivering.

Viktor shook his head. "I've spent so long doing what I can to keep us safe. I write these books because people say, 'oh the fae are like pixies, little pixies in your garden!' The slavers and the black market, they know the truth, of course. But everyone else have no idea." He stepped back from her, grinding the palms of his hands into his eyes. "It's better they forget us. It's better forgetting, than what happen to my brother or what happen to that girl or to so many others."

Marling crossed the room to him, and pulled his hands away from his face. "Your brother... is that what happened to him?" she whispered, and winced when she saw the shine of tears in his dark blue eyes. "Slavers?"

"He disappear. It was the morning after his birthday and he disappear. Haven liked to play outside and he always wander away and no one stop him because, oh, he's the Grand Prince! And he's *just like* his mother, he'll be fine! But... but he never came back." Viktor's mouth tightened and he stopped speaking abruptly, looking away from Marling. She held fast to his wrists, though, trying to think of what to say.

"You miss him a lot, don't you?" she whispered finally.

Viktor nodded and when he blinked, a tear rolled down his cheek. He sucked in a deep breath. "He should be here now. He should be King. I don't know what I'm doing! I know... capitals of countries, and I know all the bones in your leg, and the history of Europe, and I know punctuation marks, and-and how to waltz! That's what I learned."

Wow. And all this time, she'd just thought he was a moody Russian writer babe.

Marling wrapped her arms around Viktor, pulling him into a tight hug. "You're gonna be a lot better at it than you think. First of all, you're really good at knowing when people are lying. Secondly, you don't sleep much, which is weird, but also extremely helpful! Third, you can set things on fire if you need to." She rubbed his back. "And also, you're just really warm and fun to be around. Those are your talents, Viktor," she said, recalling his words to her in the woods. "And I guess I'm kinda glad that being a royal snob isn't one of your talents, or I probably wouldn't have met you at that lame after-Christmas party."

Viktor untangled himself from her and bent his head to press a chaste kiss to her mouth. "Thank you. I'm sorry for... I'm sorry."

"Oh please, I've cried because I ran out of breakfast cereal. You have absolutely nothing to feel sorry about." Marling squeezed his arm in what she hoped was a comforting manner. "I'm sorry about your brother. I'm sure he'd be proud of you right now, especially since you weren't prepared for all of this. You didn't go to Russian King School or whatever."

Viktor wiped his eyes with his sleeve and cleared his throat. "I should finish getting ready."

"Do you mind if I use your computer real fast? I just want to check my messages," Marling said, thinking of all of her online friends. They probably thought that she'd gotten a boyfriend, or died. Most likely the latter, given her circumstances over the last few years.

"No, no, please. Use it all you need." Viktor walked away, his head still bowed and his beautiful shoulders slumped. Marling watched him walk away with a nagging sense of guilt. After all, she'd been lying to him since she showed up at the door. How would he feel if he ever found out?

Marling forced the thoughts away and plunked down in front of Viktor's laptop, glad to see it was already turned on and connected to the internet. She wasn't sure how Russia and the internet actually interacted, so it was a relief to find a browser window already opened to Twitter...Whoa. Wait.

This was Viktor's twitter?

Marling stared at the number of unread tweets for so long that her eyes almost blurred together. 198? 198 *unread tweets*?! Since fifteen minutes ago? She glanced in the direction Viktor had disappeared off to. He'd walked through a door and closed it behind him. She'd hear if he opened the door again, right?

With shaking fingers, Marling clicked on the link to read the unread tweets. A cascade of gushing messages filled the screen, stretching far out of sight.

"I LOVE YOUR BOOKS SO MUCH xox"

"Babe, marry me..."

"Yous so Talented you should Be Star msg me for information. I have modelrting agency."

"Viktor, have you gotten to see my site MARRY ME VIKTOR ARSON (100 Reasons I Should Be Your Wife)? I'm still single. ;)"

"You're the best writer ever!!!"

"Viktor, can we interview you on our show, Happy Moms?"

"Thanks to #ViktorArson I found a pixie in my backyard. Trying to catch it now."

"Omg I am totes dressing up like #ViktorArson for Halloween next year!"

"Merry Christmas you SEXY BEAST!"

Marling scrolled down a bit more and spotted at least a dozen marriage invitations. She giggled out loud at some of them and kept scrolling.

"I just watched your interview on CrunchyBugs.com for the 17th time today. Addicted? Yep."

"My womanly parts have fallen for love with you and we should meet soon to make the face. Pls msg me ur address."

Okay, now Marling was full out choking with laughter. She tried to control herself while scrolling down a little further. And then she spotted her name.

I just saw this picture of you with my FAVORITE BLOGGER! Do you know Marling Ellis? I've followed her since forever, she's amazeballs!

With a bit of trepidation, Marling clicked the link and found a picture of herself standing close to Viktor at Benjamin's party. Her face had the confused quality of someone who had no idea where she was… or, of someone who was standing next to leather-pants-clad Viktor Arson.

"You look cute," a voice said, by Marling's ear.

Marling jumped in the chair, so frightened that she squeaked. She turned around slowly and found Viktor leaned down over the back of her chair, an amused smirk on his face.

"I'm sorry!" she said.

Viktor shrugged. "You know which picture is my favorite?"

Okay, good, maybe he wasn't going to murder her for snooping. Marling forced a smile. "Uhh... no. Which one?"

Viktor leaned closer, reaching in front of her to open a drawer on the desk. Right on top of a small stack of papers was a Polaroid photo that Marling knew all too well. She and Viktor had each gotten one of the pictures, and hers was nestled comfortably between some old scrapbook pages in her eternally unfinished scrapbook at home.

"This is my favorite," Viktor whispered.

In Viktor's version of the photo, his arm was wrapped tightly around Marling's shoulders, and his lips were pressed to her cheek with the overly-enthusiastic verve of someone who has had too much to drink. Marling's version of the picture was similar, but in hers, the two of them had their cheeks pressed together, with silly expressions on their faces.

Viktor snorted. "I like how you're winking."

"I wasn't actually winking, something was in my eye. But I guess it does look like a wink." She sighed heavily. "Oh, Viktor, I loved that shirt you were wearing. It was so snuggly. And you look so good in henleys."

"That wasn't even my shirt. I borrowed it from my American friend."

"Well, I liked it."

"You know, that was night of the Great Eggroll Crisis," Viktor said, still folded over her with his chin resting on her shoulder, and his face pressed close to hers. It was like a strange mirror of the picture.

Oh. That's right. About two hours after that picture had been taken, the journey for Chinese food had begun, taking on twists and turns of epic proportion. And Marling had gotten really nervous about her fortune cookie that night, because it had said "*Only the duck knows the pond from above and below the water.*" After a bit of friction between them, Viktor had convinced Marling to switch fortunes with him, promising they could trade back next time they had Chinese together. And when they switched back, he'd promised her, he would determine if her fortune meant anything. She'd begrudgingly agreed.

"I still have your fortune," she admitted, her cheeks growing warm from embarrassment. "It's in a box under my bed somewhere."

Viktor pulled away from her, and Marling's cheeks flamed even hotter. Great. He'd probably forgotten all about that and thought she was some kind of weirdo.

"Funny you say that," Viktor said, returning to her side with his wallet in hand. He opened it and sorted through for a second, and then handed her a tiny piece of paper. It had started to disintegrate around the edges, but sure enough, it said, *Only the duck knows the pond from above and below the water.* "I mean to give it to you at Benjamin's party, but you run away."

Marling stared at the fortune until felt her vision blurred. She blinked, determined not to cry. "You... you kept it?"

"Of course, I told you I would."

"But you don't believe in fortune cookies!"

Viktor crossed his arms over his chest and shook his head at Marling. "No, I don't. But you do, and it belongs to you."

She needed to fix this situation fast, before she got emotional and this mission flew out the window. Marling took a few deep breaths, trying to calm herself. "I... I'd better eat, because my stomach is gnawing itself inside out," she said, forcing a weak smile.

"Are you sure you finish looking at my Twitter account?"

"I won't stalk your twitter account anymore! Honest." Marling scrambled to her feet. "You *do* have a lot of fangirls, I noticed. Is Benjamin Gross jealous? It was pretty obvious he wanted to have your babies."

Viktor laughed at that, a hearty, real laugh that made Marling smile. She loved making him laugh, even if sometimes she didn't do it on purpose. She allowed him to take her hand and lead her from the room, but as they walked away together, Marling felt so guilty and sad that her appetite fled her.

What was she doing to this beautiful, strange, magical man?

chapter nineteen

The kitchen was eerily empty, and Viktor could only surmise it was due to the absence of his mother. While most days the oven would be stuffed with fresh baked goodies, and the counters piled high with choice snacks for the Queen's sweet tooth, today everything was empty and quiet. And instead of the kitchen bustling with people, Viktor found only Eve, the English chef that Gloriana had hired two decades ago for her skill in creating masterpieces in a terribly short amount of time.

Eve turned to watch Viktor and Marling enter the kitchen. She bowed to Viktor, though her eyes betrayed her judgment. "Prince Viktor, the tailor has been looking for you all morning. May I call him..?"

Viktor glanced at Marling. "After we eat," he said. "My friend here is very hungry."

"What does she want to eat?"

Marling walked toward one of the counters, peering at the small selection of cakes from the day before with the intensity of a hungry animal.

"You can ask her, she speak English," Viktor said, motioning at Marling.

"Oh, I'm not picky! A sandwich would be nice," Marling said. "Just something big. These cakes look good. I could eat cake, if you'd rather not make me anything new."

Viktor nodded. "I'll have whatever she has, to make it easy for you, Eve."

Eve cast another judgmental look, this time Marling's way, but busied herself with preparing food for them.

"Oh, Viktor, is this you?" Marling asked suddenly, from across the room. She'd wandered around the counters until she reached the wall with royal portraits hanging on it. Almost every room in the palace had some variety of royal portraits, as if to remind the servants of who the Skyler family was. "I didn't see these last night!"

"Let me see." Viktor crossed the room and peered at the picture Marling was pointing at. Sure enough, his tentative, crooked twelve year old face smiled back at him. "Yeah. The year before I go away to my father."

"You were so *cute.*"

Cute? Viktor remembered feeling awkward and unsure of himself. His legs had suddenly felt too long and his ability to speak in any language besides Russian hadn't yet developed beyond stuttering. Twelve had not been a good year.

"Oh my gosh, is this you as a baby?" Marling demanded, pointing at another picture.

"No, that's my brother."

"Awww. He's adorable. Is this one your Mom? Your brother looks just like your mom. And this one, is this you?" She pointed at the picture of a black haired toddler with big blue eyes. "This has to be you."

"Yes, that's me."

"You don't look very much like your mom." Marling paused. "Why are there family photos in the kitchen?"

"My mother, she wants pictures of us in every room. Well, almost every room."

Marling pointed at a picture of Glorianna. "Your mom looks kinda scary."

Viktor laughed. "Yeah, she is kinda scary."

"So, you must look more like your dad, I assume?"

Anton Kalashnik had always represented an iron will in Viktor's mind. He was an image of strength, emotional winter, and much-earned wrinkles across his forehead. Viktor still saw himself as too gangly and angular to look like his father, despite the fact that they were about the same height and Viktor's given name was Viktor Antonovich Kalashnik. "I dunno."

"Where's the pictures of your dad?"

"My dad? He's not, uh, part of royal family."

Marling twisted around to give him a confused look. "Are your parents divorced?"

"Yeah, when I was a kid."

"So you're a child of divorce." Marling gave a slow nod, peering up at him with a raised eyebrow. "Do you want me to be your therapist and talk about this with you? I can ask about the hole you felt when they told you they were breaking up, and explain that your years of running from confrontation is just a reflection of your helplessness during the divorce." She snickered, but then looked suitably sorry afterward. "Sorry. That wasn't very nice of me. I don't know anything about what happened, so that's not really my place to say."

"I was two, I don't remember them together. My first real memory of my father come from… when I'm thirteen and I move to live with him. He met me at the train station. Didn't send one of his cronies."

"Oh. Well, that's good at least. Is he part of the Russian mafia or something? Does he have cool prison tattoos with hidden meaning? Oh my God. Do you have a family mafia tattoo? That would be really, really, *really* hot." Marling paused. "I mean, I didn't see any last time we… you know. But have you gotten any in the meantime?"

"Marling."

"You could have a crown tattoo over your heart or something, since you're royalty and the son of a Russian mafia boss. You should do that, Viktor, just because."

Despite all of the tension. Viktor had to laugh. "Would you like that?"

"Yeah, I'd really, really like that. Or it could be your family crest. Do fae have family crests?"

Viktor considered her question. "There are fae all over the world, many families, not just in Russia. The Skyler family, my family, has been the ruler for almost a thousand years. Our surname change over the generations but our bloodline goes back very far, back to Iceland. We settle here because it's not so populated, and, later… my mother wanted to meet a wealthy man."

"Yikes. Gold digger," Marling said and then offered a sage nod. "But really. Is your dad part of the Russian mafia?"

"I can't tell you that."

"Oh my God. He is! He is, isn't he? Oh my God."

"Prince Viktor?" Eve called, sounding all too happy to interrupt them. "Your meal is ready."

Eve had been hired after Haven disappeared. In the twenty or so years that Viktor had observed the woman, he'd never seen a look of such disdain cross her face as the look she gave Marling as she placed a plate on the counter for her. Likely, she'd realized that Marling was a witch… and more importantly, that Viktor was allowing her sanctuary in the palace.

"Thank you," Marling said, in a cheerful voice, seemingly unaware of the tension.

Eve placed Viktor's plate on the counter, bowed to him again. "May I be excused?"

"Of course. Thank you, Eve."

As soon as Eve had left the room, Marling leaned closer to Viktor and whispered, "What's wrong with her?" Ah, so maybe she hadn't been unaware of the tension after all.

"She's loyal to my mother." Viktor shrugged. "You're loyal to your teacher, as a witch, aren't you?"

Marling turned her face away, as if she felt guilty. "Yeah, I guess."

"Well, she loyal to my mother. All the fae are. They love my mother."

"Do you think that'll change when you become King?"

"Awww, don't be silly," a voice said. Petra slipped up behind Viktor, pressing a kiss to the side of his head and sliding her hand down his arm. "Everyone's loyal to Gloriana until she gives up her throne finally, and then they'll lick Viktor's shoes if he tells them to." She swayed her hips as she walked around the island counter-space and studied the offerings left by Eve. After a moment of consideration, she picked up a cookie.

Viktor glanced between his best friend and Marling. It felt as if the air had suddenly taken on a dangerous charge.

"Of course, women would already do far more than lick his boots, without needing to know he's royalty," Petra added, casting a smirk in Marling's direction.

Marling moved closer to Viktor. "We saw a firehorse," she said, all at once.

"You did?"

"Yeah, Viktor and I saw it. And I touched it," Marling said, with a proud nod of her head.

"She probably sensed Viktor's talent for fire. Has he showed you that yet?"

For most of Viktor's life, Petra had prodded at him about his magic, encouraged him to flaunt it. In her opinion, it was a great gift rather than a heavy curse, but he still felt somehow betrayed by her mentioning it so casually to Marling.

Maybe she felt this, because she winked at Viktor and sauntered away. "The tailor's looking for you, Vik. A King must be presentable when he's given his kingdom, yes? Especially when the girl he loves is there?" With that, she left the kitchen.

"I don't like her," Marling muttered. "She was trying to make you feel bad! If I could fight, horse girl and I would go at it. And I'd win, not just because I'd pull her hair. I'd do it for myself *and* I would do it for you." Marling stabbed at her plate with her fork, as if she was practicing what she'd do to Petra. "If I could fight, that is. Which, sadly, I can't."

Viktor couldn't help smiling. "Well. Thank you for wanting to defend me."

"I would," Marling said. "I'd rescue you, if you needed it. You know, like in movies, when the princess gets kidnapped? I know you're a prince, but it's pretty close to the same thing."

"If I ever, ever need rescue... I'll count on you."

Marling cast one more withering look in the direction that Petra had disappeared to. "I have a feeling it might be sooner than you think."

A shudder ran through Viktor. He wished that he could ask Marling to take the words back, but there was no changing them now. Yes, it might be soon... but the approaching darkness he sensed wouldn't come in the shape of Petra. "I should find the tailor soon, before they call out the hounds," Viktor said, pushing his plate away.

"Do you think you could show me around?" Marling asked, sitting up straight. "Around the palace, I mean? I've always wanted a tour of a real palace. The closest I've gotten so far is Disneyland, and let me tell you... that place is not as exciting when you're an adult." She paused. "Mostly because you don't have parents to pay for the expensive water bottles and food."

Viktor couldn't help a little smile at her rambling. "I can show you around. Some people, they might not be so happy to see you, though."

Marling shrugged. "It's okay. I just figure if I'm staying in a magical palace in Russia, I might as well see the sights." She shoved the rest of her breakfast into her mouth and jumped down from her chair. "Besides, if the rest of this place is anything like your mom's costume room, I'm in."

"No, no, it's all down the hill from there."

"Down the hill?" Marling repeated and burst into nervous giggles. "Oh, Viktor, I love you."

Even though Viktor knew she'd thrown the phrase out in the casual, easy manner of a joke, he couldn't help wondering if there was something else under it.

"Your... your broken English, I mean," Marling said, as if she was pondering the same thing. "It never stops being funny."

Viktor just forced a smile and motioned for her to follow him.

The palace had felt like a beautiful, sparkling prison for most of Viktor's life, a world that ran parallel to adventure and freedom, but was kept separate from it by birth order and bloodlines. The secret corridors belonged to him and to Haven. The murals in the ballroom offered a glimpse into colors and ideas that Viktor had only dreamed of. Everything else felt like sadness and memories he'd never experienced, lost lives and ancient rules.

But showing Marling the palace changed it, somehow. Her gasps of delight revitalized the dark corners and forgotten rooms, the twinkling chandeliers and heavy, dusty curtains. Her enchantment with the tea room made him laugh, especially when she plunked down in a chair and put on an atrocious posh English accent, reminiscent of Petra's mother. "I feel so English, and I'm not even in England! I'm in *Russia!*" she said, before collapsing into laughter. "Viktor, your mother is very confused about your heritage. I mean, look at this tea set."

"My mother isn't Russian, remember?"

"Whatever, she's confused. I want to steal these tea cups, though. Oh, and the pink ones? Behind the glass up there? I want all of those too."

Eventually Viktor was able to convince Marling to leave the tea room and move on. He showed her the indoor pool and Marling gasped and ran toward it with such fervor that he thought she might jump right in. "Be careful!" he called. "You could slip and hurt yourself."

"Oh, don't worry," Marling said, tossing her dark hair over her shoulder in a suitably dramatic manner. "I'm not like those stupid girls in movies that jump into pools with all of their clothes on."

"No? Take off your clothes and do it."

Marling clapped her hand over her mouth. "Viktor!"

"Why not?"

"Well, for one thing, mermaid horse lady might be in the pool waiting, and then I'd have to hurt her." Marling shrugged, walking around the edge of the pool. "Did you know she tried to drown me at Benjamin's party?"

Viktor frowned. "Tried to drown you? What do you mean?"

"Yeah. That pool wasn't nearly as nice as this one, though. I used to see pictures of pools like this in magazines and I always wondered if they were real. I like the little waterfall. It's great," Marling said, motioning at the decorative waterfall on the far side of the pool. "No big deal, Viktor, your pool has a waterfall. Very normal stuff, I saw them at every Motel 6 my family ever stayed at on vacations, when I was a kid."

"You've never been to the right hotels in Moscow. They put this thing to shame," Viktor said, and Marling laughed. From there, they continued on. The grand tour of the palace ended at the Mordvu Ballroom, which was being aired out in preparation of the upcoming coronation.

"Here, I want you to see this," Viktor said, leading Marling into the darkened ballroom. He searched around until he found the light switch and couldn't help smiling when Marling gasped. "This used to be my favorite, favorite room."

"Was this where everyone danced?"

Viktor's eyes searched out the shadows in the room, imagining for a moment that he and Haven were still young boys, chasing each other between the servants as the room was prepped for a grand party. He could almost hear Haven's peal of laughter as the young Grand Prince snatched a cookie from the refreshments table and wound his way back to Viktor with a triumphant grin.

"Yes. Everyone danced," Viktor whispered. And Haven had been celebrated here, the day before he disappeared.

"Oh, I would give anything to dance here. Anything," Marling said. She twirled around in front of Viktor in the least graceful manner he'd ever seen a human being dance. "It feels so sad here right now, though. I want to see the chandeliers blazing and ladies wearing pretty dresses and masks. I want to hear a waltz... Or maybe we could play Lady Gaga, and everyone could just go nuts, and throw their masks in the air, dance for hours. I want to see someone throw up from drinking too much tequila."

Viktor shook his head and laughed quietly. "I don't know if anyone needs to throw up."

"So, what happened here, Viktor?" Marling asked, abruptly pausing in her ridiculously bad dancing. She held her arms open wide, as if to indicate the whole room. Or maybe the whole palace.

"It isn't what happened here. It's what doesn't happen. My mother close it after my brother disappear," Viktor said.

"So I was right! This room *is* sad!"

Sad? It was worse than sad. It was forgotten. Horribly, irreparably forgotten.

Marling fished her phone from her pocket and hit a bunch of buttons, all the while holding one index finger up, to tell Viktor to wait. Finally, music poured from the tiny speaker on her phone; a pop song that sounded vaguely familiar in the way of any other song in the American Top 40.

"Now come here," Marling said, placing the phone on the floor. She motioned for Viktor and when he didn't move, she marched right up to him and slipped her arm around his waist. "You said you know how to waltz, right?"

"Well, I did. A long time ago."

"Oh, good, because I don't know how to waltz, so you can just throw the fancy dancing crap out the window." Marling glanced at the windows that lined one side of the room. "There's even a lot of windows to choose from. Now come on." She swayed, somewhat unsteady and unschooled, and pulled him with her.

Somehow, before he really knew what was happening, Viktor was dancing with Marling. It wasn't good dancing, of course, and it must have looked absurd. But it was the kind of dancing that starts off slow and awkward and then becomes joyous and silly, the kind of dancing that leaves you breathless from laughing. They'd danced only once before, five years ago, mere hours before they broke up. And then, like now, Viktor had felt convinced that he'd never had such a good time with another person.

After a string of bad pop songs that led them from one end of the ballroom to the other, the phone switched to a bizarre dance song that Viktor was certain he hadn't heard for a decade. Marling dove for the phone, eyes wide.

"Oh, oh. No idea how that got on here!" Marling said, her cheeks red from laughing and from embarrassment. She throbbed with life and reality and modern sensibilities and laughter that echoed throughout her entire body. Viktor wanted to crush her against him and kiss her until he could get a taste of whatever mysterious happiness she encapsulated, but somehow he knew that it would always be just out of his reach.

How difficult would it be for someone to break a spirit like that, a soul so different from Viktor's? Marling had surely bounced back from a million insults, and she'd pulsed her way through all of the confusions of life, with humor and strength still intact.

But how easy it would be for someone to crush her, in every other way.

"Marling," Viktor said, his voice faltering.

She fumbled with the phone, raised her gaze to his. "What's wrong?"

"Marling, you're not safe here." *You need to run away while you can, before they try to ruin you like they ruined me... before they realize they have to turn you to dust.* "My mother, she...she hates witches so much that she's even captured some of them. She hold them hostage outside, behind the house," he said, in a rough whisper. If the wrong person overheard him, word would reach his mother before the night was out.

Marling stared at him, her eyes round with fear, and with something else that he couldn't quite place. "What do you mean, she captured them?"

"They're frozen, Marling, out in a field behind the house, past a gate. And she's killed others, I'm sure of it. It's not safe for you to be here."

"Okay, so it's not safe!" Marling said, though louder than she needed to. "So we don't have to stay here. You're about to become King, right? Can't you do whatever you want? You can say that witches and fae are friends! You can make new laws."

"It's not that easy. This is old, much older than me."

"Then fix it. You make up stories all the time. Why not make up this story for yourself? And for me? Just make it real, Viktor."

Viktor sighed, tearing his eyes from Marling and staring at the murals on the wall. Battles, feasts, strange animals and beautiful fae women perched atop fluffy clouds. In so many ways, he'd spent his years giving life to those images through words, through his books. By connecting those words and books to the minds of anyone who read them.

He'd made stories real, hadn't he?

"Kyran said something to me; he said I needed to make a decision. Well, I'm making one now," Marling said. She took a step closer to him. "I don't want to run away, even if all of this *is* scary. And you know what? I really, really like you, Viktor."

Viktor felt as if his throat might close. "I love you too," he whispered, finally, and Marling's eyes widened again. "I love you, Marling. Sometimes you make no sense, and sometimes you make me so angry, but there's... no other I'd like to argue with so much as you. And you say what you mean, even when you shouldn't. And you're not from here. That is so beautiful and special to me."

Marling started to say something but they were interrupted by Tadya, one of the palace's oldest servants, a woman who had seen Viktor through his baby years to adulthood. She was someone Viktor knew he could trust, even if she would always be loyal to his mother.

"Queen Gloriana has returned," she said, breathlessly. "And she wants to see you immediately, Prince Viktor. Hurry, please."

Viktor's stomach dropped. "Marling, listen to me. Go back to your room and stay there until I find you. Understand? Go now." Marling hesitated, so Viktor kissed her and grasped her by the shoulders. "Go, Marling. I mean it; go back to your room."

With a shaky nod, Marling ran away.

chapter twenty

In all of his years, Viktor had never seen his mother look so pleased with him.

"Are they for me?" she whispered in her newly flawless English, standing at the base of the grand staircase. "You brought the witches here for me, didn't you, my little beauty?"

"They're here as my guests." Viktor crossed the room in long strides, stopping only when he stood beside his mother.

"Your guests? Witches are not guests in the Skyler household." Gloriana's fingers melted through Viktor's hand, once, twice, as if she was desperately trying to take hold of him. Finally she tipped her face up and smiled at him. "Bring them to me, Viktor. Bring them here and we'll destroy them together."

Viktor returned her gaze, unflinching. "Marling Ellis is my guest, as Grand Prince. And day after tomorrow, I'm King."

Gloriana disappeared from sight but her voice fell from above Viktor like drops of rain. "As King, you say? King of what, Viktor? King of the bloodline you deny? The country you abandon, the people you bemoan?"

When Haven had been officially trained by their mother to make royal oaths and decrees, Viktor had been allowed to watch. Gloriana had instructed Haven to turn his palms up and summon his magic until his palms glowed with it, and then to speak the words with conviction. Haven's magic had always tended toward persuasion and charm, so his palms had only glowed with a slight purple tint, but his voice had seemed louder and stronger than ever as he spoke his first royal oath.

Viktor turned his palms up and, after a few seconds of hesitation, he dared to summon his magic, to coax it to dance across his hands. Flames rose from his skin, and he raised his head when he spoke. "As your second son and as heir to the Skyler throne, I claim Marling Ellis as a guest in this home. She's welcome to stay as long as she like and no one will harm her, either in this home or after she leave."

Gloriana appeared in front of Viktor. "Little firedancer, is this really what you want your first royal decree to be? A protection oath over some witch girl?"

"Yes."

"And have you told her what you are? Have you explained to her why you adopted that silly fake name, 'Arson'?" Gloriana's eyes glowed even as the rest of her shimmered from view. "Did you tell her about the time you burned your father's hand? Or when you set fire to your friend's table and almost burned down his apartment? Or maybe about the time that Bruvna School for Boys called and said that you were going to be expelled immediately because you set fire to the commons room?"

"That's not a problem anymore," Viktor said, though the fire in his hands struggled to contradict him.

"Surely if you have feelings for her, you should tell her everything. Tell her that you'll be crowned king soon, and you'll have responsibilities to your people. Tell her that you'll marry Petra within the month. Will your witch accept that?"

"I'm not marrying Petra."

"What you choose to do in your private life is your own business, Viktor, and I would never try to keep you from indulging in whatever pleasure you choose. Even if that pleasure is something as perverse and idiotic as keeping a witch as a lover. But you'll marry Petra Marsh."

"I never agreed to that."

"Agreed? It's not a matter in question! The Marsh bloodline is the purest there is left outside of our own, after what happened to... to our dear friends in Iceland. The old ones, those damned beasts, they've left us broken... We're being driven out on all sides, Viktor! If we're not careful, we'll pass away entirely. It's your responsibility to marry as purely as possible. You're lucky I was able to convince Anne Marsh to move here, to bring Petra for you."

Viktor shuddered with a wave of cold that crept into the room. "You meant for Haven to marry Petra, maybe. I remember you whisper about it to Lady Marsh. But Petra and I are friends, always friends. We're not meant to marry. And I will ask for Marling's hand, the day I'm crowned King."

"I will not let the Skyler bloodline disappear!" Gloriana said, her voice suddenly a cacophony of screams and painful mumblings, clanging bells, ear-piercing whistles. "We have survived wars, famines, disbelief, genocide, betrayal, hatred! We've survived everything, but barely. I will not allow my son to destroy what's left of a thousand year reign." Her voice quieted, which was far more frightening than when it had been loud. "Go on and spend your last day as prince with that girl. She'll run away from you the moment she sees what you really are, you stupid fool. And then you'll take the throne and you'll marry Petra. And you'll give me a grandchild."

In all of his life, Viktor had never felt his mother's wrath. He'd seen servants fall on their knees under her angry words; he'd seen people run from her, and had seen one old man weep pitifully before her fury. But he curled his hands into fists and resisted the impulse to bow to her.

"No. You're wrong about Marling. And you're wrong about me," he said, walking past her toward the stairs.

"I don't need your permission, Viktor. If you cross me, I'll destroy your mind," Gloriana said, her voice echoing in his ear, low and sickly sweet. "Not much of you is needed for my plans, you know."

Viktor continued on his way, though his hands quaked with anger and flame.

"You're unwise to trust a witch, son. Remember what they did to your brother, next time you look at that girl. Remember that they tore Haven apart until they could collect every drop of his precious blood. Remember that you once claimed to love Haven."

Fire rushed to Viktor's hands, begging to be freed, to lick the walls and dance through the hallways, to collapse the roof with a scream of flame and smoke, to burn away every single memory of this place.

"You see?" Gloriana said. "You're dangerous to everyone, even those you claim to love. You'll ruin that girl, if you keep her."

Viktor continued on his way, intent only on calming down and checking on the tailor. Viktor would give him the task of transforming Marling's blue 'dream dress' into something she could actually wear... And he would ask Marling to marry him.

chapter twenty-one

Marling *had* managed to run up the staircase before everything got really crazy with Viktor's lunatic ghost mother. But she'd felt some powerful desire to listen in on whatever happened, so she'd hidden herself just inside a room at the top of the stairs and... well. She'd certainly heard more than she'd expected to hear.

Fear, however, paralyzed her from being able to run back to her room until it quieted downstairs and the coast was clear.

With shaking legs, Marling found her way back to the pink room, opened the door without knocking, and launched herself inside. As she'd expected, Kyran was still inside. He seemed to have changed his clothes at some point, and judging by the pile of protein bar wrappers surrounding him, he'd found food too. Maybe in his sixteen zipper bag, which sat open on the bed. Marling might need to invest in a bag like that, especially if it could hide food and booze bottles.

"Thank God, Marling. Come here, we need to look at this together," Kyran said, leaping off the bed.

"Look at what? And wait, did you change your clothes?"

"Uh, duh. Don't be gross. I change my clothes every day, like a sanitary, respectable person."

"Where did you get a change of clothes, Kyran?"

"My bag! Can you please concentrate for like five seconds? Geez, Marling." Kyran motioned for her. "Now come look at this. I heard the fuss downstairs, so I went out to take a look.

You know what? Gloriana is a half-body, Marling. A legit *half-body*." He sounded entirely too giddy about something that Marling didn't understand.

"Okay, first of all, I was not hiding, just in case you wondered..."

"Marling, focus! Half-body!"

"What's a half-body?"

Kyran's eyes widened. "You don't know what a half-body is?"

"No. No, I don't know what a half-body is, Kyran. I slept through most of my classes and I never got over a 70% on any of my tests," Marling said finally, waving her hands around in the air. "Everything is kinda crazy right now, and I wish I could just have five seconds to process it."

"Whoa, okay, calm down." Kyran picked up his book from the bed and walked to stand beside Marling. "Honestly, you could have just asked what a half-body is."

Marling gave him a withering look. "I did ask."

Kyran ignored her remark, focused on flipping through the book. He stopped on a page featuring an illustration that looked a bit like a floating bedsheet. "This is a half-body."

"A ghost?"

"Well, you could use that cumbersome and frequently misinterpreted word if you want to sound like an ignorant hick."

Marling gave him an even more withering look. "So, she's a ghost."

"Well, ghost or not, something's about to happen, and we'd best not walk into it unprepared." Kyran tapped a finger against the book. "I did some research about how to destroy half-bodies. First of all, most half-bodies can only exist for less than ten years." Kyran turned the page. "They can be transported from place to place if pieces of the house they were transformed in are with them. So remember when we got here, and everyone said she was gone? She was probably being transported around with pieces of this house." Kyran stared at the text on the page for a long few seconds and then gasped. "Wait a minute. Wait, wait… oh no. What edition is this?"

Honestly, Marling had no idea if a book like the one Kyran was holding could even have multiple editions, but she didn't dare voice this. Kyran was already shaking from nerves and excitement, and she didn't want to test his temper. "Um," she said, trying to sound helpful. "I'm not sure." Not very helpful at all, unfortunately.

Muttering to himself, Kyran flipped back to the first page and squinted at a paragraph of tiny text. "This edition is two years old. Marling. We can't use an old edition!" Kyran's face fell. "Any number of things could have changed since then. They get their nasty hands on our books sometimes, and they learn our tricks. And some of the potions could be outdated. We need the new edition! If she hits us with her crazy fae queen power, we're both going to die!" Kyran sunk to one knee and lowered his head.

Really.

"We'll figure something out. Do you know someone with a newer--- *wait*." Marling said, fishing in her pockets until she found her cell phone. "Emma! Emma has every magic book ever."

Kyran raised his head. "Emma? Who is— How did you get your phone back?"

"You fell asleep on me. We're even now." Marling tapped into her contacts and found Emma's number, which she had never labeled in case Emma looked through her phone and realized that Marling didn't call her Primrose Redhaven. "Uh, Emma's one of my friends from class. Lady Grieve loves her." She paused, struggling to force out the words she needed to say. "She calls herself… Primrose…"

"Oh! Primrose! Why do you keep calling her Emma?" Kyran asked, standing up and grinning. "We had a lunch and coffee date one time. She's wonderful. Truly, a delight to the magic community, and her name is so beautiful."

Marling blinked at Kyran and then shook her head and called Emma.

After two rings, the phone clicked. "Marling Ellis, you met Viktor Arson and you didn't tell me? How *cute* do you look with him? He looks so much like that guy you dated for five seconds--"

"Please listen. I'm in Russia and I desperately need your help." Marling paused. "This has to do with something very dangerous and scary," she added, and just as she had guessed, Emma gasped.

"Tell me what to do! Oh, is it a dark witch? Is it Morgana? And why are you in Russia? Is it because of Viktor Arson? Are the rumors *true*?"

Marling frowned. "What rumors?"

"Oh, come on, there's pictures of you two everywhere. Did he take you to Russia?"

"Actually Kyran brought me to Russia," Marling said, still a little confused about what might constitute *rumors.*

"Kyran? Poor exiled Kyran Gray?" Emma asked, sounding almost as dramatic about this as she had about the dangerous and scary news.

"Yep. The very same Kyran."

Emma's voice immediately changed, taking on an even more sickly sweet fake British accent. "Aww, he's so cute and beardy, isn't he? One time Kyran and I had this wonderful little lunch at Category, that place next to our favorite market? And we had the most delicious Americanos. You won't believe how cheap the Americanos are there, Marling, especially considering they put four shots of espresso in each one. I saw more magic that day than I ever have in my life!"

Suddenly, Marling felt as if she understood how Kyran felt when talking to her. "I'm so sorry to interrupt you but I really need to ask you to do me a favor. Kyran's edition of…" Marling grabbed the book from Kyran. "Uhh, 'Witch's Inexhaustible Guide to Defeating Enemies' is a little out of date."

"How out of date, dear?"

"Two years."

"Oh!" Emma said. "That won't do at all! Do you need me to look something up in the new edition?"

"Yes."

"Is it about a dark witch? Or wait, is it a werewolf? I'll bet it's a werewolf."

"No, no. Uh… half-body," Marling said, though the words still felt almost as strange to say as 'Primrose Redhaven' did.

Kyran elbowed Marling. "Tell her it's a half body fae queen," he hissed, and Marling passed along the message.

"Marling, you poor darling! Let me go see if I can find the newest edition…"

"Tell her it's Gloriana," Kyran whispered.

"Did he just say it's Gloriana?" Emma demanded. "Gloriana, like the fae queen? Like *the* fae queen, the one who fled Russia during the revolution when all of her children were murdered, and then returned later to start over?"

Marling sighed. "Yes."

"You're in a lot of trouble," Emma said. "Oh, can you hold? I have to turn down my telly program. It's this new one where people have compulsive collecting habits for weird things. It's better than the ones about hoarders because the collecting is different from hoarding."

"This is kind of important," Marling said, through gritted teeth.

"Oh darling, I really am worried for you. You must remember what I always told you. Do you remember what I always told you? Remain calm! No matter what, remain calm. And do you remember when I taught you about calling something into a solid form? Like genies? Darling, I hope you're listening."

Marling sighed. "I'm listening."

"Don't sigh at me! When dealing with half-bodies, genies, or ghosts or anything like that, you must call them into a solid form."

Marling had never paid much attention to the class about ghosts, but she'd listened very closely to any instruction regarding genies. And why not? She'd always fancied the idea that she would find a genie someday and live a fabulous life with a lot of money, world travel, and hot guys. It just seemed more plausible than winning the lottery, especially for a witch.

Of course, the facts she remembered about genies were the ones that helped you *acquire* one; she remembered nothing about how to destroy one. Who wanted to destroy a genie? They gave you things!

"I... I think I remember how to call them into solid form," Marling said, but it sounded like a lie even to her own ears.

"Honestly, Marling, don't you ever pay attention in class?"

Marling struggled to remember what she'd been told about destroying ghosts and genies. "It was something about... uh, speaking their true name while binding them with their own power...?" Wait, hadn't Viktor said something about this to her once? Maybe?

"So why exactly did Viktor Arson bring you *and* Kyran to Russia? Is he into both of you? That's kinda kinky. But I mean, it's totally okay if that's what you're into," Emma said, and Marling could almost feel the other woman wiggling her eyebrows through the phone.

Kyran motioned to Marling. "Let me talk to her!" He grabbed for the phone and she smacked his hand, but he stole the phone away from her. "Primrose? *Hello.*" A few seconds later he laughed and said, "Yeah, we should. What? No, it's probably near the end of the book. Right? Half-bodies are so weird." He nodded a few times. "Yes, that sounds right. Okay, what does it say about peppermint? No way! How much peppermint? Okay, I'll write it down. What does it say about the eyelashes? Oh? Okay. Well, we'll call you if we have any more questions. Thank you, Primmy."

Wait, did he giggle? Marling stared at Kyran in disbelief.

"No, it's okay now," Kyran continued. "Marling and I are going to save Lady Grieve. Oh, you didn't know about that? I'll have to send you the message! No, no, no! No, don't worry! No, it's okay. We're gonna take good care of it, all of it," Kyran said, and then he grinned a huge, toothy grin. "Awww, no, I'll be careful, I promise. Okay, bye bye, love." He closed the phone and handed it back to Marling.

"Love? Did you just call her love?" Marling demanded, still staring at him.

Kyran turned away from Marling and shoved his face into the book. "I need to study this now, okay?And I really need to get started on this potion. Things are going to get nasty, and we need to be prepared."

"You seemed awfully friendly with Emma," Marling said, and then jumped when someone knocked on the door, mostly because her back was to the door. "Should I open it?" she hissed to Kyran, even as she opened the door anyway.

Oh. Viktor.

Viktor slipped inside and shut the door behind himself, taking Marling by the shoulders. "No one's troubled you, have they?"

"No, no one's even knocked on the door before you." Marling swallowed hard. "Your mom sounded... really angry."

"You heard?"

"Yeah, I uhh, I couldn't... Well, honestly, I wanted to know what she'd say, so I hid at the top of the stairs. I'm sorry. I know you told me to go back to the room but I... Well, what about what she said about Petra? Are you really going to marry her?"

"I'm not marrying Petra."

Marling nodded, more than a little relieved at this news. "But your mom said she'd make you do it."

"She can try, but I'll be king the day after tomorrow."

And then Marling's mind switched back to something else he'd said when his mother confronted him. "Did you mean it when you said you want to, uh, propose to me?" Marling asked, forcing herself to look into his eyes.

A gasp sounded from the other end of the room and Marling remembered that A: Kyran existed and B: he was sitting on the bed with wide eyes and a huge half smirk on his face. All he needed at this point was popcorn, and his gawking would be complete.

Marling turned her face back to Viktor's just in time to catch sight of the melancholy glint in his eyes.

"I'd like to," Viktor said, in a quiet voice.

Kyran gasped again. "Oh my *God,* are you going to do it right here?"

This time Marling and Viktor both looked at Kyran, and though Marling gave her best scowl, Kyran just continued grinning right back.

"Marling, I know she say something about…" Viktor held up one of his slender, beautiful hands, hands that Marling had quite enjoyed during her acquaintance with him. "She say something about the fires. But I never hurt anyone on purpose."

"Did you really set fire to your school?"

"Just one room. It was a accident."

Just like always, despite how serious everything was, his use of 'a' instead of 'an' made her smile, even if sadly. "You burned your dad, too?"

The sadness in Viktor's eyes shifted to something like shame. "I was angry. But I learn to control it since I was younger."

"Oh please, you two. Just kiss and get it over with," Kyran said.

Viktor shot Kyran a look. "You're so annoying," he said, his voice suddenly deeper and growly in a way that made Marling shiver. She was scared of him but also turned on, which was confusing. Especially with Kyran sitting in the room with them.

"I know I am, faerie boy. Now kiss her or something, so I didn't just waste my time watching the worst romantic dramedy of the year."

Marling glared at Kyran, but then, before she knew what was happening, Viktor took hold of her and kissed her so hard that she had to hug him around the waist to keep from falling. When Viktor broke the kiss, Marling attempted to coax her lips into forming words but they felt a little numb. "Well," Marling said, breathlessly. "Now that you two had your pissing contest, maybe uhhh… well, maybe we should all get some rest."

And Kyran and I can finish figuring out how to destroy your mom.

"Marling's right, you should go. You can't have your bride until the wedding, you know," Kyran said, standing up and sauntering toward them. "Really. Go!"

Viktor dropped one more kiss to Marling's forehead and then opened the door. "Try not to leave the room tonight. I'll come find you in the morning." He hesitated in the doorway but then he waved and walked away. Marling had to fight every instinct in her body that screamed at her to follow him.

Kyran closed the door. "He's so skinny. Does that weird you out a little? I mean like, *so skinny.*"

"It hurts," Marling whispered.

"Eww. See, that's what I'm talking about. Way too skinny. I wouldn't want to hold a guy with bones sticking out at weird angles. A little meat's good on everyone."

"No, I mean… the unlove spell. It hurts, physically. So much."

Like a missed connection, like frayed ends, like seared tears, like burned nerves. It hurt like loneliness, but worse.

chapter twenty-two

F ive years ago, New Year's Eve)

"You're not like Henry, are you? From the Time Traveler's Wife?" Marling whispered, her eyes idly bouncing from the streetlights, to the store signs, to the night sky, and back again, as she walked with Viktor.

"I don't know what that is."

"That book. He travels through time, appears in different parts of their relationship. Sometimes he's with her when she's a kid. Sometimes he's with her when she's... well, he just keeps disappearing and reappearing and she's always waiting for him." She dared to turn her head then, angle it up so she could look at him.

They'd been pressed close together ever since they'd solved the Great Eggroll Crisis, finished their Chinese food dinner, and stumbled back out onto the street together.

Marling felt overly full and sleepy and deeply afraid of something she couldn't understand. Maybe it was because it was New Year's Eve, or maybe it was Viktor. He'd been awfully quiet since they exchanged their fortunes and left the restaurant. In their four days together, that was anything but unusual. He felt like an enigma to her, sometimes inexplicably quiet and distant, even when he stood next to her, as if his mind was tethered to a ghost of some other world.

But now his silence seemed heavier than it should, so she held a bit tighter to him.

"You're not going to disappear, are you?" she asked, attempting to laugh and cover it over as nothing but a lighthearted inquiry. But the laughter caught in her throat and turned into a ragged cough.

"Disappear? No."

"Promise?"

They stepped around a group of loud-mouthed teenagers and just when Marling thought maybe Viktor hadn't heard her question, he looked down at her. "Disappearing is a trick I save only for those I don't like." Viktor stopped, too quickly. Marling tried to continue on and was abruptly halted by Viktor's hold on her.

"What's wrong?" Marling demanded. His face had changed. His lips were curved down and his eyes reflected pain as plainly as if someone had just struck him. "Viktor, what's wrong?"

He whispered something that she couldn't understand and his cheek twitched, his gaze somewhere far away from Marling or Manhattan or bad Chinese food or questions about sad books.

Marling concentrated all of her being on one of the spells that Lady Grieve had taught her, an empathy spell. It was only supposed to be used in moderation, because some witches had used it so often that they became crippled later with attachment to the pain of others.

What were the words again? Marling searched her memory and then silently whispered the words to herself, reaching up to brush her fingertips along Viktor's jaw, his neck. She begged the energy of his skin, the caverns of his soul, the traceprints of his blood to speak to her, to share their secrets in the language that only magic or love can comprehend.

Something was gone. Something had been subtracted from him, in a flash like a camera snapping a final photograph.

Marling's eyes filled with tears and she saw the tears mirrored in his eyes too.

"You did something to me," he said, his voice accusatory and heavy with emotion. Viktor pulled away from her, walked away with his head down. He only made it a few paces, though, before he stopped and turned around again. The tears had disappeared from his eyes, but the pain had not. "I'm sorry. I'm sorry, I shouldn't have done that." He let out a great sigh. "What did you do to me? You did something."

Marling felt as if she'd been caught stealing, and though Viktor's sadness and her own fear haloed her, she found anger the easiest emotion to latch onto. "What do you mean?" she demanded, narrowing her eyes at him.

"You did something with magic. You looked at me."

"I'm looking at you now!" Marling said.

"No, you looked at me differently. Inside."

"You're crazy," she said, but without conviction. She waited as a group of young women in sparkly dresses pushed between her and Viktor, and then she relented. "Okay, okay. I used a little magic. But only a little."

"Don't ever do that again, Marling, not to me. Understand?"

Now, Marling could understand that most people wouldn't want someone poking around in their mind or their memories. But just as many people felt curious, even if only a little, about what it felt like to have magic clash with their boring existence. So why was Viktor so insistent?

"Okay," she said, and then nodded. "Fine! Okay, whatever. I won't."

She waited for him to relent, but neither of them moved, and eventually Marling realized she was cold and that she wasn't really angry anymore.

"I'm sorry I did that without asking," she said, but only because she meant it. She'd never been one to apologize easily, not even to handsome Russians. "Lady Grieve said that when someone's hurting, sometimes you can help them if you understand what's wrong."

"You could have asked."

"What's wrong, then?"

"What did you see?" Viktor asked her, quietly.

Marling shrugged. "Nothing. Just... absence. Something was gone, I don't know. What was it?"

Now it was Viktor's turn to look apologetic. "I don't know either, Marling."

"But it hurt you?"

He hesitated, and then nodded. "Very much."

Then, finally, Marling closed the distance between them again and hugged him. "Let me help you," she whispered. "Please let me help you..."

"If I can, I will."

They walked away together, this time holding hands, and Marling did her best to talk about anything and everything to distract from whatever nameless ghost had stolen him away from her a few moments before. "Remember when you said you were a Russian spy?" she asked, poking him in the ribs. "I had an idea about that. Maybe you could dress up in a trench coat and go into that place I applied to and tell them they have to hire me." She waited for his laughter, but only got an unconvincing smile in return. "Or, you know, you could tie me to the bedpost and question me." She got another distracted, half-hearted smile.

That wasn't a good sign, especially when bedposts were part of the proposition.

"I was handcuffed to a bedpost once, but it wasn't anything sexy. My stupid cousin thought it would be funny to do while I was taking a nap. I was 7, so I thought that I'd been arrested while I was asleep, and that the cops were going to haul me off to jail. I cried so hard that my mom yelled at my aunt about it."

Viktor laughed, quietly. The world balanced again, even if only a little.

"We should get coffee," Marling said, squeezing Viktor's fingers tighter.

"Isn't it a little late for that?"

"It's New Year's Eve! We'll be up forever and ever!" Marling said. "Because I want my kiss. You'll be my New Year's kiss, right?"

He answered by letting go of her hand, slipping his arms around her, and hoisting her up just enough that she could wrap her legs around his waist. Marling had never done that with anyone before. She was relieved to note that Viktor leaned against a wrought iron gate, otherwise she would have been worried she might topple him over. But wow. He was stronger than she'd guessed he was.

And then he captured her lips in a kiss that could have set the city on fire.

Marling clung to him and lost herself in the kiss. His mouth was just the right amount of firm, confident but not commanding. Gentle but not disinterested. He drew breath from her and gave it back, traced the tip of his tongue over her bottom teeth. He tasted warm and inviting, eager to give himself over to her if she wanted.

Just as Marling felt dizzy with his adoration and attention, Viktor's temperature plummeted so palpably that she pulled away from him. It seemed to be good timing, as he tipped toward her, gasping. "What's wrong this time?" she demanded, wondering if maybe he was sick or something. His behavior in the last hour had been unusual, even if her Viktor-gauge was still forming.

Viktor spun and cast a glance at the gate as if it had personally antagonized him.

"Did you hurt yourself on the gate?" Marling asked and then blushed. "Oh, was it me? Did I hurt you...?"

"No, no, no. No. I'm... uh, allergic to iron."

Marling blinked at him. "Oh. Well, that's kinda lame. But my friend in high school was allergic to strawberries, nuts, and cauliflower. I think that's worse. Well, maybe not the cauliflower part. No one really needs cauliflower in their life." She bit her lip. "Are you... okay?"

He nodded, so Marling slipped her arm around him and they crossed the street together, talked about cats and then, somehow, Marling found herself arguing with Viktor about whether peanut butter or almond butter was better.

They were just about to cross a street when Viktor's cell phone rang. Even before his face fell, Marling knew something had happened. Something had changed, and nothing in all the world could stop it.

chapter twenty-three

A knock at Marling's door drew no response, so Viktor slipped inside quietly. He found Marling and Kyran asleep next to each other. Odd.

Viktor knelt beside Marling's side of the bed and tucked some of her tangled dark hair behind her ear before lowering his head and whispering her name. Marling flailed, staring at him in mute surprise.

"Marling," Viktor whispered.

Marling sat up, patting nervously at her hair and sinking into herself as if she was embarrassed for him to see her. Her hair hung around her head like a messy, lopsided halo, and Viktor found himself smiling and reaching up to help her straighten her hair. Marling wasn't a soft, gentle sleeper. Upon waking, she always looked like she'd just been on a safari that involved crocodile rolling. Aggressive crocodile rolling.

"Uh, hey there," Marling said and then cleared her throat a few times. "Did my voice just sound weirdly deep? Sorry."

"Do you want to take a bath or shower?"

Marling's eyes widened. "Does my hair look that bad?"

"I just think, you might want to take a shower."

"Oh God. Do I smell?" Marling asked, raising an arm to sniff at her armpit.

"Marling. Do you want a shower?" Viktor demanded, and got a nod in response. "Alright, come on. You can use bathroom in my room." Viktor glanced at his wristwatch, wondering just how much time they would have together alone before the ceremony preparations stole him away.

Kyran chose that moment to wake up with a loud yawn and obnoxious stretch. "Good morning everyone. What time is it?"

"What's he doing in here, anyway?" Viktor pointed at Kyran.

"Oh, he's afraid of the dark."

"I am not afraid of the dark! That room you gave me is haunted, *thank you*. And I'm not talking about friendly ghosts. There's some serious Japanese horror movie action just waiting to take place in there." Kyran straightened his clothes and climbed off the bed. After staring at himself in the mirror across the room briefly, he turned around. "Ugh, did you see the bags under my eyes? These are like, 'the levee's about to break' sandbags. Marling, did you bring eye cream? I left all my Kiehls at home."

"You kidnapped--" Marling said and then abruptly stopped, remembering Viktor didn't know about the kidnapping situation. "You kidnapped my makeup bag, remember? So no, I don't have any eye cream."

Viktor stood up and offered his hand to Marling. She accepted it and climbed off the bed, locked her fingers tight against his as they crossed the room together. "I was invited to make appearance on a talk show, back in New York City," he said, glancing back at her.

Marling's eyes widened. "When? Because I'm totally up for going back to New York City. We can leave now, if you want. I don't even need a shower first."

"Next week. I think that after the ceremony, I'll fly back." He sucked in a deep breath, and said the one thing he'd wanted to say all morning. "We could go together, if you want."

"Must be nice to just get in a fancy plane and fly to another country. And it must be nice to have someone drive you to your interview, so you can go on TV and talk about how great your book is while a zillion fangirls drool over your skinny ass in tight pants. I mean, you just have to let your hair hang in your eyes a little, right? Play the complicated, moody artist card and you're all set to be the next big star. Is it great? It seems great," Kyran said.

Viktor turned his head slowly, having forgotten entirely that Kyran was even there. "You think my life is great?"

Kyran shrugged. "It doesn't look too bad, aside from the crazy mom."

"Everyone has many light and many shadow in them. I don't doubt you've suffer. But I can't prove the pain that makes up my soul, or the ecstasy that... that a book or a word might bring to me. You can not see my inside and perhaps for you I am only a... a spoiled prince."

Silence hung in the air for a long time. Finally Kyran said, "With shiny hair." Somewhat begrudgingly he added, "How? *How is it so shiny?*"

"We are all only one thing to everyone else. But inside we are many things," Viktor said. "That's all I can tell you."

"Right, right. Admittedly that was kinda poetic. But stop being such a Russian tragedy, Vik. It's cheesy."

Viktor shuddered at the nickname Kyran had thrown about so easily, when Haven had been the one to bestow it on Viktor in the first place, and no one used it anymore.

"And really, how do you get it that shiny? Is it almond oil or something? Magic? Magic almond oil? Coconut oil? Do you get blowouts, Vik? I mean, is that what princes do, when they aren't making television appearances to promote their new book?"

Temper flared gently in the back of Viktor's mind, traced his spine, and bounced across his fingertips, but he silently whispered to the fire to stay put. "If I am so offensive to your... your pretentious..." Viktor struggled with the English words he was looking for. "You're welcome to leave. I'm sure there are a lot of things in nature that you'd find less offensive."

"Nature? Viktor, these are Rag & Bone pants. Do I look like the kind of guy who likes nature?"

Marling slipped her hand into Viktor's hand. "Let's go," she said, giving Viktor the smile of someone who is anticipating a shootout, and would like a better place to hide.

"No really, you can go," Kyran said. "I'll just wait here and try not to find myself slain at the hands of your lunatic mother. Besides, I need to catch up on my Nabokov. I have a feeling that'll help you and me get along much, much better."

Viktor exited the room before he said something he would regret later.

"I ask Petra to find clothes for you," Viktor said to Marling as they arrived back to his bedroom a few minutes later. He led her into the bathroom and pointed at the tiny stack of clothes.

Marling's face twisted. "Petra? Great." She muttered something that sounded like 'horse lady' and then plastered a big smile on her face. "So, uh, where's the shower? This bathroom is about as big as my apartment building back home." She waved a hand in the air. "And considering that I don't see a shower or bathtub, I'm starting to believe this is only a small part of the monstrosity that you call a bathroom."

"Oh, yes, follow me."

"Do you have a bathroom attendant? Or three servants to surround you and lovingly remove your clothes and lower you into a bathtub filled with rose petals and magical potions?" Marling asked, as Viktor led her into the bathtub-cove.

"You sound like your friend Kyran."

"No, no. See, he's just commenting about everything because he's jealous. I'm commenting because I'm genuinely afraid I could get lost and end up wandering a maze of gold-plated bathroom tiles for the rest of my life. Or offend three beautiful servants who just want to lather me in fancy lotions and wash my hair." Marling fell silent, staring at the bathtub. "Is this considered a pond, or is it a lake?"

Viktor couldn't stop himself from laughing. "It's not that big."

"No, I mean, I'm sure the president has a bigger bathtub, but this is pretty impressive. I think I'll choose the bathtub over the shower, if that's okay. Though, I'm sure the shower is probably spectacular too." Marling approached the tub slowly, studied it. " I'm a little confused, I'm not going to lie. There's four faucets…"

"Here, let me help you." Viktor drew a warm bath for Marling, turning the third faucet just enough to allow a slow, steady stream of soaking solution into the water. "This, it is very relaxing."

"It smells heavenly."

Viktor straightened. "Do you want me to leave?"

"No! No, stay." Marling peeled off her clothes in record time and sank into the warm bath water. It felt as heavenly as it smelled, soaking almost immediately into her tense muscles. "Come sit with me."

"Is the water alright?" Viktor asked, kneeling beside the bathtub.

"I can say with complete honesty that this is the nicest bath I've ever had. And probably the nicest I'll have for the rest of my life. Unlike you and fancy pants Petra, I'm not used to the royal treatment."

"You must understand about Petra, Marling. She is not like you, she is not like me, but she's not my mother either. She's not evil. She save my life, several time. And she love me, in her own way."

Marling pulled a face. "I'm not jealous. Well, not very jealous. I just think she's a snob."

"She is, but she has always been there for me when I needed it most."

For a long time, neither of them spoke. Marling seemed to be almost as consumed by heaviness as Viktor was, but finally she said, "Remember how I put the unlove spell on myself?"

"You shouldn't have, not for anyone."

Marling shrugged, dropping her gaze to the water. "It's starting to hurt."

Viktor reached one hand out, traced his fingers over the side of Marling's soft, round face. "I don't have a spell, but I hurt too," he whispered.

"You do?"

"I think of Eggroll Crisis all the time. And when you yell at your boss, and when we get lost in Central Park and I think of... of... of afternoon, the day we go see your fortune teller. Remember in your apartment, before we leave...?"

"Uh yeah. Believe me, I remember very well."

"Tonight I have... practice ceremony, for the coronation. If you wait a few more days, I'll take the throne. I will always belong to them; I can never belong to myself." Viktor sighed. "But I promise, I will find a way to belong to you, too, if you want me to."

"Of course I do! I do, I do." Marling hesitated. "That's why I came here. That's totally why. Uh." Marling shifted in the bath, leaned up and caught Viktor's face between her hands. She kissed him with such conviction that he almost forgot all of his worry and fear. Almost.

Viktor untangled himself from Marling after a very long time. "You should finish your bath. I'll take your old clothes and I'll make sure they're cleaned." *And inspected thoroughly for measurements, so the tailor can have the blue dress ready for you by tomorrow.*

These weren't ideal circumstances for a proposal, but it didn't matter at this point. Viktor couldn't let Marling go again, not unless she was the one who said goodbye first.

chapter twenty-four

Twenty-Four Years Ago

Viktor tugged at his scarf and awkwardly shuffled through the snow behind his brother. Haven marched ahead with the flourish of one of the performers that had recently visited the palace for the elder prince's 10th birthday. Haven had declared, upon the performers bowing and saying their goodbyes, that he could be a member of the circus if he wanted. He'd claimed he could jump through a ring of fire, too. Viktor believed it.

Haven's feet fell so lightly against the ground that he walked on top of the snow, leaving only the slightest indention where he stepped. Viktor's steps felt heavy and clumsy in comparison, his boots crunching through the snow and causing him frustration. He wished he could walk as fast as his brother, but it was impossible. He easily lost sight of Haven time and time again, and felt very lost and alone, only to have his brother reappear with a laugh and an admonition to *hurry up Viktor*!

Petra had joined them earlier but then she'd wandered away to look at some tracks that she thought might belong to a firehorse.

"This place will be an ice palace," Haven said, motioning to a pile of sticks and some gathered snow. "Petra and I are going to make a big kitchen and two bedrooms. She can sleep in one and you and I can sleep in one." He walked toward the sticks and picked one up, waving it around like the performers had waved sticks of fire.

"But we have rooms," Viktor said. Warm rooms. Rooms with toys. And food. The idea of sleeping in the cold seemed a bit foolish.

"Don't be stupid, they're not going to be real rooms. Just rooms for our ice palace. You know, we can sleep in them when we don't want to sleep in the other rooms." Haven squinted in the sunlight and poked his stick in the snow. "It's gonna be huge. Almost as big as our house."

Viktor turned and looked at their house and then looked at the pile of sticks. Hmmm.

"But Petra and I have a lot of work to do," Haven said, and sniffed. "And I don't feel like working on it right now. Come on, Vik." Haven threw his stick down and walked away, making sure to dance about a bit as he did. Viktor trudged after him.

Eventually they reached the edge of the lake, and Haven stepped out onto the ice without hesitation.

"You know what's down there?" he asked, holding his hands out at his sides like he was balancing. But Viktor knew he wasn't really balancing, because Haven always had perfect balance. He was like a cat that way, just like Mom always said.

Viktor leaned forward a little, staring down at the ice. "No," he said.

"Fish," Haven said. "Fish, eating each other and laying eggs and having fish parties and going to fish school and fish dancing."

Viktor had never known that fish went to parties.

"And you know what else? *Monsters!*" Haven said and cackled. "Now come on, we need to get to my hiding place in the woods."

"Is it safe?"

"Is what safe? Are you scared of monsters, Vik?"

Viktor shook his head. "The ice…"

"Don't be stupid, I'm walking on it, aren't I? Come on, or I'll leave you here!" Haven skipped across the lake, singing something the performers had sung. He turned around as he reached the other side. "If I leave you out here, you're probably going to get eaten by the glen-dragon! Snap snap, yummy little prince, all in one delicious bite! SNAP SNAP!"

Tales of the glen-dragon had been generously passed between the boys ever since Haven had read about them in one of his books. He was convinced that a glen-dragon lived somewhere in the woods behind their home, and passed his time munching arbitrarily on animals and humans alike.

Better to be safe than sorry.

Viktor walked across the lake as quickly as he dared, praying he wouldn't fall through. His nerves made the fire flare up in him, though, and he felt a wave of heat wash from his feet to his face. "Don't leave, Haven!" he called. "Please don't leave me!"

He'd almost crossed the lake when he heard something loud and terrifying, and Viktor felt himself slipping downward. Cold water hit his face and enveloped him and he barely managed not to open his mouth and scream. Viktor kicked furiously, flailed his arms and tried to return to the surface, but he was all turned around and his boots weighed him down.

Viktor's head bounced against ice and he struggled, slapped at it, pounded it with his fists. More from stress and fear than anything else, the fire in his fingers rushed forward and he felt the ice give way. He broke surface and gasped. "Haven! Haven!" he cried, slapping at the cold water. He caught sight of his brother, who seemed too stunned to do anything but stand with his mouth hanging open. "Mom! Mom! Haven!" Viktor sank beneath the surface of the water again and fought his way back up, then sank again, each time managing to catch a breath of desperate air. His magic warmed him enough that he could still move, but his teeth chattered and he could only think of one thing: *so cold.*

"Viktor!"

Petra grabbed one of Viktor's hands, and somehow she helped tug him out of the water and up, up, up, onto the ice. "Stop wiggling! Be careful or you'll fall through again!" Petra shouted.

Viktor did as he was told and finally, after what felt like an eternity, he and Petra managed to make it off the ice and safely to where Haven waited. Haven threw his arms around Viktor and hugged him so tight that it hurt. "You're cold, you need to go inside now," Haven said. "Come on, hurry up."

Viktor had lost one of his boots in the incident, so he limped and hobbled along behind his brother and Petra, shivering all over. He silently begged the fire in his hands to keep him warm, but doing so was exhausting. By the time they reached the palace, Viktor lost his balance, and Haven had to catch him. Petra ran and told the grown-ups what had happened, and Gloriana descended upon them with a fury.

"You stupid little boys! Do you realize you both could have been killed?" she shouted. "Haven, do you know what would happen if I lost you? You're the elder prince! You're my heir!"

"But I didn't fall through the ice, it was him," Haven said, pointing at Viktor.

"You could have been killed!"

Eventually Gloriana lifted Viktor into her arms like she'd done when he was really really little. She carried him inside and tended to him, but all the while she scolded him for endangering Haven.

"I'm so cold, Mama," he said, something he hadn't called her since he'd turned five and Haven said only babies called their mothers *mama*. "So so so so so cold."

"You have to be careful with yourself, my sad little beauty," Gloriana said, taking his cold face in her hands. "You're not like your brother." And then, finally, she hugged him and he cried until his chest felt heavy, and his nose and eyes hurt.

Eventually Gloriana let him go and she slipped out of the room, telling him to stay in bed and sleep if he could. Viktor cried for a little longer, mostly out of exhaustion, and was too distraught to even notice when Haven snuck into his room.

"You crying, Vik?" Haven whispered.

Viktor shook his head so hard that it hurt, but tears rolled down his cheeks anyway. Haven stared at him for a long time, as if unsure of what to do, but then finally he climbed up on Viktor's bed and hugged him. "That was amazing when you melted the ice," Haven said. "I wish I could do that!"

"No you don't."

"Yes I do. I can't do anything except climb trees and hide. You have real magic. I bet you're stronger than Mom!"

Viktor wiped his nose on his sleeve. "No. Mom is the strongest in the world."

"Oh please! She can't make fire come out of her fingers. I bet she's jealous of you." Haven nudged his brother, but more gently than usual. "We all wish we could do what you do."

Viktor sniffled, and then both boys jumped when they heard their mother yelling Haven's name.

"I gotta go. But hey, I'll come visit you later through the secret door!" Haven said, leaping off the bed and running to the door. He paused just before leaving. "I won't tell anyone you were crying," he promised, and then ran away. Viktor knew he would keep his promise.

chapter twenty-five

"We have to do it soon," Kyran hissed, the second Marling stepped into her room. "Tonight, maybe."

"Listen, Viktor will become King tomorrow and I'll get him to free the witches, alright? I know he'll do it for me."

Kyran shook his head. "Oh really? And how exactly do you know?"

"Because I know Viktor," Marling said, feeling heavy and guilty and even more pained than she had earlier. "Just give him a chance."

"Oh please. Are you going to give him a chance to write a 600 page novel where a witch leaps in front of a train at the end? He's not gonna help us, Marling. He's fae. He might translate well on camera, and he might want to marry you, but that doesn't mean he cares about Lady Grieve's life."

Marling hesitated. "He... he told me where they are." She waited out Kyran's expected parade of shocked words, facial expressions, and hand gestures, before letting out a heavy sigh. "You need to keep it down, Kyran. Someone could hear us talking."

"You tell me every single word of what he told you, Marling Ellis, or I swear I'll use a truth spell on you. And don't think I won't! I've done it many times. I could do it in my sleep!" He leaned closer. "Where are the witches? Where's Lady Grieve?"

"I don't have the full details but I know they are, uh, frozen." She swallowed heavily, forcing herself to make eye contact with Kyran. "Behind the house."

Kyran's eyes widened, and he flailed his arms around a few more times. "You didn't think to tell me this before *now*?"

"His mother can't find out that he told us, or who knows what would happen. Listen, if we can just give him until tomorrow, he'll be King. Then he can do anything he wants! Will you please, please, please trust me, and just let me handle this?"

"You're such a bad witch, though."

"Kyran, you brought me along for a reason, right? Just trust me. I have a knack with people, I always have. It's why my boss hired me at Moonhorse in the first place." She sighed. "Viktor will free them, I know he will. He's never going to be anything like his mother."

"And you're going to marry him and have ten babies and blah blah, right?"

"I don't want ten babies."

"Marling, I know this guy fluffs your toast just right but you need to remember a couple of key things." Kyran held up his hand and pointed at one finger. "A: he's a pointy eared freak." He pointed at another finger. "B: He's Russian." Another finger. "C: His mother threatened to kill both of us. I know mother-in-law issues are common, but this situation seems over the top. Do I need to go on?"

"But I love him."

"That's the unlove spell."

"No! I mean, I really do love him," Marling said, while praying to herself that it was true. She could feel the difference, right? She could distinguish real love from some stupid spell she'd put on herself. "I really do, Kyran."

Kyran finally sighed and rolled his eyes. "Alright, geez, okay. Don't start crying. I'm a sympathetic crier, and I'd rather not have swollen eyes right now. We'll give him a chance. *One chance.*

Just one. And I still think you should find yourself someone a little less elf-y, but whatever. It's not my life."

"He wants us to meet him in a few minutes."

"Will his mom be with him?" Kyran demanded, crossing his arms over his chest.

"I don't know! I don't think so! Come on, just follow me." Marling shuddered as she stepped out of the room, though, because it felt as if eyes hid in every corner, above her and below her, watching her always. The air even felt heavier, as if clouded by an invisible rage. She watched as servants darted here and there, speaking among themselves and carrying chairs, boxes, trays. She followed one of the men carrying a big box, and ended up at the top of the staircase, unsure if she should follow him any further. Wasn't Viktor supposed to come find them?

Marling turned around with a heavy sigh, meaning to speak to Kyran, but she found Viktor standing directly behind her. She gasped and clapped a hand over her chest, startled. It was as if he had materialized from nothing, and his blue eyes were bright with something like excitement or fear. "We have rehearsal for tomorrow," he said. "Do you want to join me?"

"Aww, darling, so nice of you to think of your rehearsal," a voice said, and Marling immediately knew it to be Gloriana's voice, maybe because of the shudder that ran from her head to her feet. "I wondered if you'd make it at all, since you disappeared so abruptly."

Marling slowly turned around, expecting to see a floating bedsheet, but instead she saw nothing but servants darting around in the distance.

Creepy.

"And tomorrow… are you planning to be here?" the voice continued, behind Viktor now. Marling gently pushed Viktor out of the way, trying to see the body that matched the voice, but all she saw was Kyran's open-mouthed, shocked expression. "Or do you have some commitment elsewhere, firedancer? Maybe a radio interview? A television appearance? I know how fond you are of those."

Marling tipped her head up, because now it seemed as if the voice was above her. She saw only the fancy paintings on the roof above, though. She cast a nervous glance in Viktor's direction and realized that the color had fled his face.

"I'll be here," Viktor said, and then pressed his mouth into a thin line. "Why are you hiding yourself?"

"Hiding? Whatever do you mean?" a voice asked, from directly in front of Marling, and then a shape appeared so quickly that Marling wasn't sure if it had actually always been there, and she'd just missed it. The shape took on a womanly form, petite and impossibly beautiful, with full lips and almond shaped eyes that seemed full of mischief, and age, and something impossibly cruel. "My little firedancer, you didn't tell me she's fat."

Marling had been called 'fat' only a few times in her life, and all but one of those times had been in jest among friends, the kind of insult that only stings a little when you think about it later. But to hear the word fall from Gloriana's pouty lips, to hear it uttered in that whispery, important voice... Marling blushed bright red and dropped her gaze self-consciously downward.

"She's beautiful," Viktor said, his voice dangerously tight.

Gloriana smiled. "I suppose you've always had strange taste." She flickered from view and reappeared beside Viktor, which made Marling feel even more uncomfortable. She'd never encountered a ghost before, and certainly not one as... substantial as Gloriana.

Viktor bent just enough at the waist to offer some sort of mocking bow to his mother. "I'll see you at the rehearsal."

"Your clothes are waiting on your bed, Viktor. I can't wait to see you in them. Prince of the Skyler bloodline... prince of the fae!" Gloriana's face lit up in such a manner that Marling felt physical warmth against her skin. "Though you forget who you are sometimes, you'll always be drawn back to us. And soon you'll love being King as much as you ever loved some silly human career like writing." Gloriana glanced at Marling. "Or some human girl."

Marling stepped forward before she could stop herself. "Just because you're a queen of *something* doesn't mean you're the queen of *everything*. And it doesn't mean you can go around acting so pretentious and snobby, and saying rude things to people you don't know. Especially people who genuinely care about your son."

The silence that fell around Marling felt almost suffocating, but she forced herself to hold steady and stare evenly at Gloriana.

"Well, you're certainly not as submissive as Viktor is," Gloriana said at last. "I hope it's not catching." She flickered from view. "I'll see you at the rehearsal, my little firedancer."

And then nothing.

Viktor surged toward Marling, capturing one of her hands and squeezing it a little too hard. "You have to be careful, do you hear me? Please be careful with your words. Until tomorrow you're still in danger," he whispered.

"But she's so mean to you. And she called me fat."

"I know," Viktor said. "But please. Promise you'll be more careful."

Marling had never been particularly good at holding her tongue when she should. Actually, she was terrible at holding her tongue, ever. But Viktor was right about the danger, and Marling and Kyran needed more time, if they were going to rescue the witches. She finally forced herself to nod. "I'll try. But only because I'm way better than a person who floats around calling people fat and then evaporating."

Viktor called for a passing servant, waving her over. He spoke to her in Russian, motioning at Marling and Kyran. The woman cast a disapproving glance their way, but nodded to Viktor. "She'll take you to the throne room," Viktor said. "Stay there until I find you, alright? Please, Marling. This time, please do as I say."

Viktor rushed away from them and Marling found herself walking beside Kyran toward the throne room, her mind whirring and buzzing with confusion about everything she'd just witnessed. Half-bodies were ghosts, but also kind of not ghosts? And they were incredibly insulting, if Viktor's mother was any indication.

"That was awesome," Kyran hissed to her. "You standing up to her, I mean. You have guts!" He patted her on the back. "I knew I chose you for a reason."

Marling couldn't help feeling the tiniest bit proud of this, even if it was only a half compliment. Her inability to keep anything in her brain from spilling out of her mouth continued to be a point of both admiration and contention among her peers, and while it usually just meant she'd lose a friend or two, this time it might mean she lost her head.

Or, ended up frozen in a field behind the house.

As if things couldn't get any worse, Petra stood just inside the throne room like some kind of tiny, smug sentinel. She strolled toward Marling and Kyran, and crossed her arms over her chest. Her dress today boasted a graphic pattern befitting of Alexander McQueen. Marling had to admit the dress looked stunning on Petra's womanly but petite figure. But she would never say it out loud, of course. Ever.

"Is that... McQueen?" Kyran asked, letting out a wheeze.

Petra's smile widened. "Hmmm, is it? I've forgotten." She spun around slowly, with all of the grace and swagger of a runway model. "Yes? I think it is."

"It's so beautiful." Kyran sounded as if he might cry. "Can I touch it?"

Though Petra rolled her eyes, she danced a bit closer to Kyran. "Go on, then."

Kyran pinched a bit of the colorful fabric of the sleeve and then let out a long, deep sigh. "One time I spent an hour standing outside of the McQueen store in Manhattan. I couldn't go inside. It was just too much. I think I would have burst into flames in the doorway. I'm not worthy."

Marling tried not to laugh, because that would be rude. But it was a struggle.

"Speaking of clothes, you look quite nice in the outfit I picked out for you." Petra pointed a finger toward the gray blouse and black skirt that Viktor had given Marling to wear. "I had a feeling that the right clothes could fix at least a few of nature's mistakes. If only we could do something about your hair, though."

"I like my hair the way it is."

"You need to own a mirror then." Petra shrugged. "I bet he liked that shirt on you. Gray's his favorite color."

"Viktor's?"

"Gray, silver, he loves them."

Marling searched her mind for any conversations they might have had about favorite colors, but came back only with a vague recollection of her telling Viktor how much she loved red cars. And he'd said that he loved black cars, and then they'd gotten into a short but intense argument over coffee beans. She had no idea how they'd jumped from cars to coffee beans.

"He's never liked anyone like he does you," Petra said, balancing one delicate hand on her hip. "Viktor drifts in and out most of the time. But he's terribly fixated on you."

Warmth flooded Marling's face.

"Be careful with him. He's never been like anyone else." With that, Petra turned and walked away, taking their servant guide with her.

"McQueen," Kyran whispered with the reverence of a man on his way from church.

Marling cleared her throat. "My hair isn't really *that* bad, is it?"

Kyran's gray eyes were still unfocused as he turned his head and glanced at her. Then he winced and shook his head really

215

hard, letting out a quiet gasp. "Your hair *is* that bad, Marling, we've had this discussion. Split ends? Remember?"

Thankfully, Viktor arrived only moments later, surrounded by a group of women in black capes, flustered servants, and a few old white-haired guys. Viktor remained in the center of the crowd, a bright spot among a lot of chatter, arguing, and instruction. When he spotted Marling across the room, he broke away from the crowd and made a beeline for her.

Marling, for her part, couldn't help staring wide-eyed and open mouthed at Viktor in his navy blue uniform. It looked like something directly out of the past, all shiny buttons and silver epaulets, strong shoulders and clean lines. Viktor seemed taller, more intimidating in his uniform, like a handsome soldier prince of fate.

"Is this your coronation costume?" Marling asked when he stood in front of her. Viktor nodded. "It's really impressive." Marling moved forward to touch the rich fabric. "You're going to be the most handsome king of Russia ever."

"Not king of Russia, Marling. Just of the... just of my people. And the Skyler bloodline."

Whatever. In Marling's mind it was pretty much the same thing. She turned to look at Kyran, motioning at Viktor. "Isn't it wonderful?"

"It's not McQueen."

One of the old guys yelled for Viktor. "Find a chair and get comfortable," Viktor said to Marling. "This could take a long time."

He wasn't kidding. Just the set-up took longer than Marling's cousin's entire wedding. And Marling's cousin was a diva. Once everyone was in place, the old guys perched on chairs and the black-robed ladies gathered along either side of a lush sapphire-colored carpet that had been laid out. Across the room, an orchestra practiced playing something that sounded extremely depressing.

"I bet this is comparable to the Oscars," Kyran whispered. "Everyone's quiet and bored, and it's going on for way too long. And the old guys in the room own half the planet. If Rupert Murdoch isn't sitting over there, I'll hand you a million dollars."

"I don't think he's sitting over there." Marling held a hand out. "Give me my million dollars."

Kyran ignored her joke. "Well, it can't really be the Oscars. Not enough free booze. And only one McQueen."

Gloriana appeared at the other end of the room, beside the throne, glowing like a stream of floating candles.

"Oh, good," Kyran whispered. "Billy Crystal's hosting again."

Marling laughed out loud before she could stop herself, and several people stopped to turn and look at her. Ooops.

The orchestra broke into a full-fledged, intensely emotional symphonic piece that wouldn't have sounded out of place in a miserable period costume flick. Petra walked into the room with her head held high and she took her place beside Viktor, hooking arms with him.

"Why are they so cozy?" Kyran whispered.

"They grew up together." Marling looked at Kyran. "Why do you care so much about her all of the sudden, though? Are you on her team now, because of her dress?"

"Just because she owns a McQueen dress doesn't make her any less of a pointy eared freak." He shrugged. "Besides, you're prettier."

Sometimes Marling really liked Kyran. Now was one of those times.

Viktor and Petra walked to the throne and Petra bowed to Viktor, stepped aside. Viktor sat on the throne with his back rigid and his chin raised, as if he was facing a firing squad.

Kyran leaned closer to Marling. "Is that the crown? It's a bit more tasteful than I expected."

The crown in question sparkled even from a distance, thanks to giant jagged crystal shards, and something that looked suspiciously like a giant blue diamond.

"It does kind of look like they found that necklace from *Titanic,* so I suppose that's impressive at least." Kyran held something out to Marling. "Vodka?"

"Where did you *get* that?"

"I had a few nips left in my bag, and they're not providing free champagne at this gig. Go sparingly on it, though, it's the last of what I have."

Before she could take Kyran up on his generous offer, Marling's attention was dragged back to the ceremony as a little old lady placed the crown on Viktor's head, and everyone stood up and clapped. Together, they recited something that didn't sound like Russian... or any language that Marling had ever heard. It sounded creepy, and old, and strangely sad. Marling sank deeper into her chair, feeling uncomfortable to witness it.

"Okay, is that the end? Please tell me it's the end," Kyran muttered.

Marling couldn't tear her eyes from the grim look on Viktor's face, the slight sheen of tears in his eyes. "The end? Maybe the end of a lot of things," she whispered, and though Kyran laughed quietly at her response, she couldn't bring herself to smile. It hadn't been a joke.

chapter twenty-six

Sounds cut back in, slowly, as if Viktor was waking from a dream. At first they were only a murmur but then words became distinguishable to his ears.

"That was beautiful, beautiful," one woman said, reaching out and brushing her fingers against Viktor's arm. "My King, my Lord. But tomorrow you should walk faster, when you approach the throne."

"No, walk slower," someone else said. "Much slower, with your head held high. And speak louder."

"Yes, louder. Project, Prince Viktor. Send your voice throughout the room." That voice belonged to an elderly fae that Viktor hadn't seen since he was young. He remembered the old man in great detail, mostly because of his frightening red eyes and ultra-pale skin. He looked like a walking corpse, and usually smelled like one, too.

"Aww, my little firedancer. They're right, you must send your voice out further. Not just to the back of the room, but around the world. You'll be King, Viktor," Gloriana said, her whisper echoing through Viktor's mind as the crown was removed from his head. "Remember, you're doing this for Haven."

"I'm doing this because Haven is gone," Viktor corrected, quietly, and stood up. He gently pushed his way through the crowd that sought to devour him, and located Marling and

Kyran where he'd left them. "Marling, you always say, you might marry a prince one day. What do you think? Still interested?"

Marling tipped her head back, staring up at him while biting into her lower lip. "Well, of course I can't judge you for how long and--"

"That was more boring than watching golf on TV," Kyran said, quirking one well groomed eyebrow. "But I liked the part where the old lady almost dropped the crown. That kind of thing creates interest. I was on the edge of my seat for maybe, like, eight seconds."

Viktor barely caught himself from laughing, though a smile did stretch across his face despite his efforts to stop it. "Are you hungry?"

Of course Marling said yes, and she sprang from her chair as if she'd been waiting for this offer for hours. She grabbed his hand immediately, without hesitation or fear of anyone watching. Viktor squeezed her fingers, heartened by her bravery.

The kitchens were stocked nearly to overflowing with harried servants, bumping into each other and balancing heavy trays of food, shouting orders at each other. Several of them froze when they spotted Viktor. They made a show of bowing to him, but he waved it off.

"Please don't worry about us. I can make something."

After several half-hearted, nervous offers to help him, the staff returned to their frantic work, and Viktor was able to help himself to enough ingredients to put together sandwiches for himself and his two guests.

"Well, I can add this to my list of dreams come true," Kyran muttered as Viktor pushed a plate toward him. "I've been served by royalty. And hey, maybe 1% of the world's population will recognize that fact."

"Even that's too big a number," Viktor said, sitting down between Kyran and Marling. "Many years ago, there were more of us. But the world changed and it's hard to be... it's hard to be different, in this world, without danger. And many witches kill fae."

"Let's get this right, buddy. You guys kill us too."

Viktor turned his head and fixed Kyran with the... what had Marling called it? The evil-eyed stare? It was something that had always come as second nature to Viktor, a silent ability that he had inherited from his family. If you made eye contact with someone for long enough, they almost always backed down.

Kyran, for his part, blushed, but he didn't look away. "You've heard of the Silent War, haven't you? It's not some cute sitcom rivalry." Kyran paused. "It's more like *Gone with the Wind*. Without the romantic subplot."

"*Gone with the Wind...?*" Marling repeated. "How are you connecting this to *Gone with the Wind?*"

"Shut up." Kyran looked at Viktor again. "Anyway, point is: maybe you guys wouldn't be so scarce if you'd stop making other people scarce."

"I don't make people scarce." Viktor held Kyran's gaze a little longer. "Usually."

Marling cleared her throat and leaned around Viktor so she could see Kyran. "Viktor said that his people come from Iceland," she said, with the exact tone of a parent who is trying to change the subject before her children murder each other with dull dinner knives.

"Right, and I bet they were Santa's elves back in the day too," Kyran said, looking away from Viktor. He picked up his sandwich and nibbled at it in a finicky manner, but at least silence fell between the three of them until everyone was done eating.

One of the servants snatched up their plates the instant they were finished with them, and nervously asked Viktor several times if he wanted something else to eat, anything else, anything at all. Dessert maybe? Coffee?

"They seem to enjoy serving you," Kyran muttered. "And here I am, working long hours without pay, and I don't even have *one* personal assistant."

Viktor stood up from his chair, scoffing. "I'm King tomorrow, they're afraid, that's all." To demonstrate, he pointed at one of the girls who was busily scooping butter into a bowl. She dropped what she was doing immediately and asked what he needed. "Nothing, don't let me interrupt you." He cast a sidelong glance at Kyran.

"So? Your mom's terrified everyone into behaving. That's really nothing to brag about." Kyran shrugged. "Out of curiosity, though... can I get your mom to do that to the kid I'm tutoring for extra money?"

"Viktor? I need to you talk to you," Petra said, sweeping into the room with a great deal less elegance and smugness than usual. Her face was tinged pink, and her eyes shined with something unfamiliar.

"Let me talk to Petra. I'll meet you back at your room in a few minutes," Viktor whispered, and Marling hugged him like she'd never see him again. "Only a few minutes, really."

Kyran tugged on Marling's arm and she let go of Viktor, but reluctantly. She turned around to wave at him just once before she disappeared from sight, dragged away by Kyran.

Petra leaned in closer to Viktor, as soon as Kyran and Marling were gone. "Something's going on. I don't know what it is yet but it has to do with your mother." She pinched Viktor's arm hard enough to hurt. "Are you listening to me? This is serious. I can feel it, just like always... dark, dark magic."

"Is it because of Marling?" Viktor whispered, his mind immediately leaping to all of the worst possibilities of such a thing.

"Well, what do you think, when you've brought a witch right into your mother's home? You need to be careful," Petra said, and for once, she looked afraid.

A voice from the doorway startled them. "Prince Viktor! Prince Viktor!"

Viktor's stomach dropped, already sure the news would be bad. "What's... what's wrong?"

"She wants to see you," the girl whispered, wide-eyed with the terror that only Gloriana could put into someone. Viktor had never seen the girl before, and he couldn't help wondering just how young she was. Fifteen? Sixteen at the most? She might never grow up, if she found herself caught in the crossfire of Gloriana's rage. "She said, tell you she's in the field. She said you'd know what that means." She shivered. "She wants you right now."

"I'll find her. Thank you."

Petra followed at Viktor's heels, her energy almost crackling with nerves and fear. "Be careful," she said, as they rushed outside. "Be careful, Viktor, please, be careful!"

When Viktor found his mother, she stood in the middle of the field, with her witch captives frozen around her, and a book lying open at her feet.

"Do you know what this is, Viktor?" Gloriana asked. Her voice was the gentle rasp it had been when he was young, when she stopped by his room to say goodnight to him. But Viktor knew her well enough to recognize the strains of rage in her words. "Do you see this page? Look." The book's pages rustled, and turned as if by invisible hands. "I know English isn't your strength, firedancer, but see if you recognize any of those words."

Viktor hesitated.

"LOOK AT IT!" Gloriana's voice rang in his ears until he felt dizzy. "Pick it up, Viktor, and read the book your friends carried in their bag."

Viktor crouched down, his eyes passing quickly over the words. Half-body. Ah, of course... an old term for the form that Gloriana currently existed in. Someone had written notes by hand about spells that could destroy half-bodies.

"They mean to destroy me," Gloriana hissed. "They came here to destroy me!"

"Marling came here for me. If anything, they're nervous, that's all. You've frightened them."

"Nervous? They've devised a plan to destroy me because they're nervous? Do you suppose they've also studied ways to murder you, just in case? Do you think that girl has practiced how she might slip a blade into your heart?" Gloriana laughed humorlessly. "I wish she *had* stabbed you. If you had suffered, if you had bled until you could barely hold onto life, perhaps you would finally realize that you can't trust witches. That girl came here to free her friends, and she brought her failure of a teacher with her. I know their kind. I've been almost destroyed by their kind before, don't you remember?"

Viktor thought of Marling's professed reasons for appearing in Russia, and everything that had happened between them since they arrived. "No. She wouldn't lie to me."

"I've let you become too naïve, Viktor. You were always so frail and sad, but I should have forced the truth on you while there was still time. Your brother knew the truth of what they are. He knew that they want only to sell us to the highest bidder, and burn whatever's left."

The wind picked up and Viktor shuddered against it, even as heat rushed to his fingertips.

"This is your last chance. Kill them, Viktor. I'll help you do it," Gloriana said, holding her hands out toward him. "Call for her."

"Leave her alone."

"Bring her out here and we'll kill her. And, if you're too weak, I'll do it myself!" Gloriana said, sneering at him.

For the first time in almost a decade, Viktor let go of the mental control he kept on the fire in his hands. Flame fell from his fingertips and melted the snow at his feet, set stray branches to popping and hissing. "I said, leave her alone."

Gloriana's face twisted into a sad smile. "You think I'm afraid of your flames? Don't forget who tended to the burns you caused when you were young. Your tricks might impress a circus, but they strike no fear in my heart." She squeezed one of her tiny hands into a fist and then splayed open her fingers. The flames at Viktor's feet disappeared, as if they'd never existed at all.

"I won't let you hurt Marling," Viktor said, silently commanding the fire between his hands to grow and grow, until it glowed above his skin in a huge circle of light and dangerous heat. "You claim you're not afraid of me, but I burned you once. You locked me in the shed overnight, because you were so angry." Sweat rolled down Viktor's neck from the heat of the flame. "You wouldn't have done that if I didn't hurt you. You wouldn't have done it if you weren't afraid of me."

Gloriana shook her head, looking away from Viktor. "You know, many times I've wondered… what might have happened if Petra hadn't pulled you out of the lake? Would Haven have learned his lesson about wandering away? Might I have him here still?"

It took every fiber of control in Viktor's being to keep from striking. But not yet, not yet. He stepped closer to her. He needed to be able to touch her, to force her to stay substantial, if he was going to hurt her.

"We all know one thing," she said, with a sorrowful, horrible sigh. "It shouldn't be you here now, Viktor. It should have been him…"

Viktor drew the fire back into himself and seized hold of his mother. He heard her scream with pain, but she slipped away from him, and flickered out of view.

"It should have been him!" she said again, louder, and then Viktor realized that he couldn't move, couldn't speak, couldn't do anything at all but stare sightlessly where his mother had stood only seconds before…

chapter twenty-seven

Marling winced and lurched forward.

"That was dramatic," Kyran said, looking up from his phone. "What's wrong? Did you just remember you left the stove on at home or something?"

"Something happened to Viktor," Marling whispered and winced again.

Kyran's eyes widened. "Is the unlove spell telling you something? What happened, what happened?" He stepped in front of her, grasping her forearms gently. "Marling, stick with me, what's going on?"

"I don't know! Just... something bad." In all of her years, Marling had never experienced anything like this, except one time just before her birthday, when she had a powerful premonition that she shouldn't go to a party that some of her school friends were going to. Later she found out that almost everyone who had attended the party ended up with a severe case of lice. But this was different from that. It felt stronger, and far more painful.

A knock at the door startled both of them.

"That's probably Viktor," Kyran said, his tone falsely reassuring. "It's okay, Marling. I bet he's here to apologize. You know how those pointy-eared freaks are... Bossy, and annoying, but at least alright when it comes to manners." He walked to the door and swung it open, but it was Petra, not Viktor, that pushed inside.

"Gloriana's lost it," Petra said, her voice lacking any trace of snark for once. "She found your witch book, and she figured out why you came here. She confronted Viktor about it and he tried to burn her and she's... she's done something to him. I think she's frozen him."

Marling and Kyran exchanged a glance. "Where's your book?" Marling asked with a gasp, grabbing Kyran's arm.

"It's in my bag!" Kyran opened his bag, tearing through it. "It's in here somewhere, it has to be! I put it in this section..."

Petra shook her head. "No. Gloriana's got the book."

"What did she do to Viktor? Can it be undone?" Marling demanded, snatching up her trench coat and pulling it on.

"I don't know, but she might still be out there."

Marling took a deep breath. Her hands shook and her legs felt like they'd turned to jelly, but she marched past Petra and out of the room anyway. "Show me where he is, Petra!" she said. "Show me now."

Kyran chased after her, catching up as she reached the staircase. "We don't have the book, Marling! We can't just go out there; she'll turn both of us into popsicles. Or worse, she'll stuff us! Marling, Marling, at least let me call Primrose. Stop, *stop!*"

"You brought me here for a reason, right?" Marling asked, without slowing down. Petra followed along at her side, head held high and her mouth pressed into a tight line. "Well, I think it might just be because I'm the only person you know who's never afraid of anything I should be afraid of."

"Yeah, but... but Marling! We're not prepared! I know that we need to force her into a solid shape and... and I think we'll need to throw something painful at her... but I haven't memorized the last part..."

Marling stopped long enough to catch Kyran by the shoulders. "Then think up the rest. You're one of the best witches I've ever known. You trained under *Jeremiah August*. If you have to turn her into a gorilla, do it. Just... help me right now, Kryan. Please."

Kyran's cheek twitched and he took what felt like a million years to think it over. Finally, he nodded. "Alright. But I'm not used to winging it."

"That's okay. I wing everything."

Together, they followed Petra out into the cold. Marling barely registered the harsh temperature as she tripped and trudged her way through the snow, closer and closer to what she knew might be her end. She'd lied to Viktor about her motives for coming here, and she'd put him in danger. If nothing else, she at least needed to try to fix all of this.

Petra motioned for them to follow when they reached a gateway, and Marling pushed her shaking hands into the pockets of her jacket. How was she going to fight a powerful ghost, if she was this afraid?

Because she had to. Because Viktor was in danger. Because she cared about him. Maybe even loved him. Just as quickly as the nerves had taken control of her, they dissipated.

Calm. Lady Grieve had always told her to be calm. Primrose had always told her to face danger with deep breaths and both eyes open. Her mother had always told her to stop talking so much when she was nervous.

Calm.

A field dotted with frosted statues awaited them beyond the gate. Marling's eyes flicked over the statues, taking in the frantic, pained, and fearful expressions. These statues were not made from marble, though. They were made from people. Even at a distance, Marling recognized Lady Grieve... and then, somewhere in the middle of the group, she saw Viktor.

Marling trudged toward him, guilt tugging at her as she caught sight of the betrayed expression on his face.

"How sweet," a voice said, in Marling's right ear. "And I thought you'd run away as soon as you heard of the trouble you'd caused. You're either crazier or more violent than I first anticipated." Gloriana half-appeared in front of Marling, peering up at her through heavy eyelashes. Her legs and feet were missing, as if she was half buried in the snowy ground, and her face and one of her arms were dark blue as if she'd been bruised or burned. "But then, your mission was to free your friends, wasn't it? You broke my son's spirit for the sake of your teacher, your colleagues. Tell me, do you feel anything, seeing him this way?"

"I love him!"

"So I've heard. Look what your love has done to him. No matter. When I'm finished with you, I'll release Viktor. I'll have to break his mind, of course, but I don't need much of him to finish what I've started." Gloriana's eyes flicked behind Marling, to where Petra stood. "Petra Marsh, thank Mab for you. You'll help me, won't you? You've been a daughter to me. Just carry on the Skyler bloodline, Petra. Swear you will!"

The twisted meaning behind Gloriana's words hit Marling full in the stomach. She turned slowly, glaring at Petra. Had she led them out here to set them up? Did she really plan to stand by as Viktor was reduced to nothing but a senseless puppet to provide heirs for Gloriana's precious bloodline?

"Swear it, Petra," Gloriana said again.

Petra's eyes flicked between Viktor, Gloriana, and Marling. Finally she nodded to Marling. "Her true name. You need her true name, to destroy her."

Though Marling was surprised at this, she forced herself into action. "Do it, Kyran! Take hold of her!"

Gloriana screamed, snow exploding up from the ground around her. "Petra, what are you doing?"

Kyran stepped up, shouting the magic words in a perfect rhythm, each of them uttered with the accent that Lady Grieve always scolded Marling for not being able to replicate. He surged forward and grabbed for Gloriana's arm, but his fingers slipped through her like she was made of air.

"Kyran, no!" Marling shouted, shaking her head. No, you had to do something. You had to do something! What was it? Why hadn't she paid more attention when she learned about ghosts and half-bodies and naming spells?

Marling squeezed her eyes closed, searching through memories of her many jobs, her many bosses, her classes with Lady Grieve, her late night sessions on Tumblr, her first four days with Viktor. Where was it? Where was it...? The information was locked away in her brain *somewhere*, she just needed to access it.

Wait. Viktor's voice, his words. *Believe in yourself.*

Marling kept her eyes closed as she reached out and took hold of Gloriana's cold arm. It was solid under her touch, and quivering.

Immediately Marling's head filled with an angry voice, with prompts and commands to let go, fall down, give up, wither, die. She struggled to push away Gloriana's voice, to reclaim her own thoughts.

"Marling!" Petra shouted. "Marling listen to me. Listen to the name!" The name Petra shouted was foreign and strange, nothing Marling had ever heard before. She would have to say it right, or the spell wouldn't work. She would die, Kyran would die, Viktor and Petra might die too.

Believe in yourself.

Marling spoke the name aloud, and Kyran's voice buzzed in her ears, reciting words that Marling was unfamiliar with. She felt Gloriana twist and squirm in her hold, screaming commands. Gloriana cursed her again and again, fighting with all her might. But then, all at once, Marling felt Gloriana's arm dissolve in her grip.

"I won't let you, I won't let you!" Gloriana screamed as Marling opened her eyes. The fae queen's voice carried higher and higher, taking on a wordless scream that sent Kyran crashing to the ground. "You can't hurt me, you pathetic little girl. You've never known any real *pain*."

Marling held tight to Gloriana. "You're wrong!" she said, recalling Viktor's face when she told him she hoped she'd never see him again. She summoned every shred of pain that their fight had caused her, focused on the memory of his defeated expression. She thought of her own warm tears rolling down her cheeks as she begged his forgiveness, begged him to stay, swore she would never forget him.

"That? Is that your *pain?* That is nothing," Gloriana said, but her voice was strained. She screamed again, stirring snow up. A burning sensation shot up Marling's arm, and Gloriana hissed. "You can't do it, little witch."

Marling thought of Viktor walking away, likely to never return. What had Marling yelled at Viktor? She'd called him something stupid, during their fight. She'd called him some harmless French word, but she'd been so angry that it might as well have been a real curse... "*Ananas!*" Marling shouted now, as loud as she possibly could.

Gloriana dissolved into nothingness with a howl, burning Marling's hand as she did so.

And then there was only cold wind against Marling's face, snow fluttering in the air in front of her. She shivered and stumbled forward, to the side, falling against one of the frozen witches. To her surprise, the man caught her.

"You must rest!" the man said, in a soft French accent.

"Is she alright?" another voice asked, and Marling felt a hand on her shoulder, a hand on her back. When she tipped her head up finally, she saw that all of the figures had been freed, and most of them were crowded around her.

"Where's Kyran? Where's Viktor?" she asked, her throat hurting from all of the yelling she'd just done.

"Marling." The crowd parted, on cue, and Viktor fell on his knees in the snow in front of Marling. He pulled her into a tight hug and kissed her all over her face.

"I'm sorry, I know she's your mom but…" Marling said and closed her eyes, returning his hug. "I had to, Viktor. I'm so sorry."

Viktor pressed a kiss to the side of her head. "No, you had to."

"I'm so sorry I lied to you about why we came here. But I wasn't lying about any of the rest of it! I promise I wasn't. I never lied to you about… about wanting to see if it would work out and… and I really do want to be with you. I'm so sorry, Viktor, I--"

"It's okay, I know," he said, his voice hoarse.

"Where's… where's Kyran?" Marling carefully regained her feet; she and Viktor worked their way to Kyran. He was sitting up, at least, even if he was groaning and grumbling about his head hurting.

"Are you okay?" Marling asked, offering him a hand. "Can you stand?"

"Can I stand? I need a drink. Oh my head, oh my head." Kyran stood, slowly, and grabbed Marling's hand for leverage. "Oh my *head*. Does your head hurt? Why doesn't your head hurt? Oh my gosh, we did it, Marling."

Before he could say anything else, Viktor hugged Kyran and pressed an enthusiastic kiss to each of his cheeks. Despite everything, Marling had to laugh at Kyran's wide-eyed, horrified expression.

"Thank you, Kyran," Viktor said, pulling back from him.

"Don't… ever, ever, ever do that to me again." Kyran straightened his shirt and his face flamed red. "I… you… you're too skinny."

Marling sidled up beside Viktor, slipping her arm around his back. "Not too skinny for me, though." She thought she was going to get one of those storybook kisses that makes the heroine nearly burst into flames (ha ha ha) but Lady Grieve poked at her. Of course she did. That woman had the world's worst timing about pretty much everything. "Excuse me,"

Marling said, and stepped away so she could talk to her teacher somewhat privately.

"Marling Ellis. I'm… well, to be honest, I'm flabbergasted. But maybe I was too hard on you in the past," the old witch said, shaking her head. Gauging by the tiny peek of a flower print shirt sticking out from under her jacket, she'd been on her way somewhere warm, before she was captured. "I want you to make you my second."

"Well, this whole rescue attempt was Kyran's doing," Marling said. "And if it weren't for him, I couldn't have done any of this. He's… he's so dedicated."

Lady Grieve eyed Kyran from a distance. "Yeah? I'm glad he came for me when I called him, of course. But he mixed up that spell…"

"He kidnapped me and flew me to Russia so that we could rescue you. Really, I think he's your man. He'd be the best second you could ever ask for." Marling shrugged. "I'm not sure that I want to be a witch, anyway. It was fun, but I'm terrible at it. The only reason I managed any of this…" She looked around, motioning with a shaky hand. "Well, it's because I accidentally put an unlove spell on myself so that I'd only ever love Viktor."

Lady Grieve's face fell into a scowl. "A what? What did you say, Marling Ellis?"

"I know. It was so stupid! But I guess it all turned out alright, right? Because of all of this?"

"You put an unlove spell on yourself."

Marling sighed. "It was an accident. I'm not very good at magic, *okay?*"

"No, I mean, if you think that you put an unlove spell on yourself, you're a worse witch than you know. There's no unlove spell on you, because there's no such thing as an unlove spell. Why do you think it's the 'easiest spell in the world'?"

Marling stared at her for a long time, waiting for the older woman to laugh. Or at least smile. Or maybe shout, *just kidding!* "I… No, you're wrong. I felt… I… all of these years I've…"

"The unlove spell is a lot of nonsense, Marling. It's for charlatans and idiots. Mostly idiots."

Oh. "So… all of this time, if I had feelings for Viktor, those were mine?"

"Well, I should hope so! Honestly, Marling, did you ever listen to anything I taught you?" She groaned. "You're right. You'd make a terrible second." Lady Grieve let out an exaggerated sigh, reminiscent of sighs Marling had heard from Kyran many times. "Now, get your prince friend over here. I came to Russia with important news, but that idiot Gloriana wouldn't listen to me. Next thing I know, I'm stuck here. I've long ago missed my cruise by now, dammit."

Marling shook her head. "I'm so confused."

"I found out that the elder Skyler prince is alive. Great, right? Well, I show up with the good news and everyone wants to turn it into some big, ugly scene. If she would have let me *speak*, she probably would have been real happy, but fae are notoriously difficult to deal with." Lady Grieve straightened her hair. "I need to call my travel agent."

"Wait, are you saying that Viktor's brother is alive?" Marling demanded.

Lady Grieve grimaced. "Alive? I'm sure he's been passed from hand to hand by slavers, thanks to that bastard Gorey Billings, but I've been told he's alive."

That was all she needed to hear. Marling ran back to Kyran, Viktor, and Petra, almost tripping over her feet. "Kyran, go talk to Lady Grieve. Right now! I'm pretty sure I've just convinced her to take you back as her second," Marling said. She waited until Kyran had walked away to turn her attention to Petra. "Thank you," she said, and found it didn't burn as much as she'd expected it to. Which was a miracle, in and of itself.

Finally, Marling took Viktor's hands in her own and looked into his eyes. "Viktor… Lady Grieve said your brother is alive."

chapter twenty-eight

Viktor found himself trailing between the window and the door, back and forth, each time telling himself that soon he would spot a car in the distance, and his brother would return home.

It was three days after Gloriana's fall, and Viktor had ordered the coronation to wait until the elder Skyler heir could return. In the three days since, Kyran had milked his small amount of injuries for everything they were worth, spending most of his time in the pool with a never-ending stream of alcoholic drinks on hand. Lady Grieve had returned to America on the first plane she could catch, and Marling had been tended to most tenderly for the wounds she'd taken.

The freed witches had scattered, though not before thanking Viktor for his generosity in allowing their freedom. Some of them had been very vocal in suggesting that the Silent War was long over, and should be forgotten.

Viktor, for his part, still felt incredibly sore from his captivity. Gloriana had, apparently, done something to him that she hadn't done to the others, and it left him in pain, even days later. Not surprising, really.

Viktor wandered to the window for the millionth time, and this time he saw a car approaching. He ran for the door and threw it open wide. He'd sent most of the well-meaning members of the household staff away, instructed them to wait for his orders, and then he'd hired three fae doctors to set up a medical bay for the elder prince.

Viktor half-expected to see a little boy meander his way to the door, gangly and dark eyed and holding a stick in one hand. Or maybe he would see some strange reflection of himself, just with brown eyes and lighter colored hair.

But the figure that appeared in the doorway, helped on either side by servants of the Skyler household, was an odd mixture of both of Viktor's visions. He was impossibly petite, standing easily a head shorter than Viktor, and his eyes were as brown and cat-like as they had been when he was a child. His skin had lost its glow, though, and he looked frail as balsa wood.

And even at a distance, Viktor could see scars tracing their way across his face and throat.

For a long few seconds, the brothers only stared at each other, and then the tiny figure smiled and said in English, "Well, I guess little brother isn't so little anymore...?"

Viktor swept forward and caught Haven in a hug that lifted him clear off his feet.

"Ow, ow, ow! Careful with me, Vik. You're a lot stronger these days, you know," Haven said, coughing as he laughed. Viktor gently set his brother back on his feet, but didn't let him go yet. Haven laughed again, tipping his head back. "I always knew the fire would pay off. Look how tall you are! And my brains stunted my growth, wouldn't you know it."

"What happened to you? Where were you all this time...?"

The smile drifted from Haven's face, and he coughed again. "I'd like to sit down, Vik. Or if you have a bed or something, that would be super fancy."

"Yes, yes. I've prepared everything for you. Do you need doctor now? Or just some peace?"

"Is peace really an option? I like the sound of that. Peace it is!"

Viktor supported Haven's slight frame away from the door and through the palace, waving away anyone who ran toward them with offers of help. He took his time, making sure to stop every now and again so Haven could rest. Though he had no idea of the details, he could easily imagine the horrors his brother had experienced in their years apart.

By the time they reached the door of Haven's childhood room, the elder prince was audibly winded. He coughed and wheezed and Viktor all but carried Haven the rest of the way into his room. "Wait a minute… is that my stuffed horse?" Haven demanded, settling on his bed. "And this! Is this the monkey that I shoved in the…?"

"You shoved it in the oven, yes."

Haven turned his eyes to the floor, where his book still lay open, just how he'd left it. "I was reading that."

"Yes."

"Did you leave *everything* the same?"

Viktor glanced around the room and shrugged. "Your bookshelf collapsed a few years ago, but we fixed it. And one time Queen Mab, my cat, she sneak in here and play with the monkey."

"You have a cat? I'd like to meet her." Haven cleared his throat and lowered his head, but Viktor spotted the shine of tears in his eyes before he could hide them. "Funny, I thought you'd throw all my things in the snow like you were always threatening to do, whenever I picked on you."

"No. We missed you."

Haven shoved a stuffed animal out of the way and shifted on the bed until he could prop himself up against the headboard. Somehow, he didn't look a lot different than he had the last time that Viktor saw him there. Just sadder. Slower. "What have you been up to, Vik? Aside from growing too much and sending rescue teams after me."

A million answers crowded into Viktor's mind, fighting for attention. The books he'd written, the school he'd attended, the friends he'd made, the wonderful night he'd had too much to drink and had met a girl named Marling. His first trip to Paris, the evening he'd spent alone, walking the streets of London while nursing a freshly broken heart. The time he'd burned his father's hand, the first time Viktor had ever controlled his fire when it sought to escape him.

"Still just as talkative as ever, huh?" Haven snickered. "Really, though. Tell me you've crashed some expensive cars, and you have six kids, all of them in different countries."

Viktor walked to the bookshelf, which he had helped to repair, and he withdrew two books from it. He carried them back to Haven and held them out in offering. "I added these, because I thought you'd like them."

Haven's gaze dropped to the books. "What's this? Viktor Arson? Is that you?" He flipped though the top book until he reached the back. "Ah! It is you! Look at you, all photogenic. You wrote these?"

"My first two, they're written in Russian, and translated into English for the U.K. and for United States. The last one, I write it in English."

"I knew you'd learn eventually. See!" Haven flipped through the pages, his little white hands marked all over with scars. What had happened to Haven in his time away? "Is this a glen-dragon?"

Viktor tore his eyes from the scars on Haven's hands and nodded, a smile stealing his face. "Yes, I- I wanted everyone else to know about the glen-dragon. I tell the illustrator, he has to draw him just right, just how you always say it is. Do you like it?"

Haven nodded, turning the page. "It's not bad." He turned another page. "And you even included our little imaginary friends, Bee and Cee." Haven cleared his throat once, and then again. "They look just how I imagined them. And this… I'd forgotten about this monster girl. We made her up to scare Petra."

Viktor laughed at the memory. "She was so scared. But I was scared too. I just keep it a secret."

"Oh, people like these books, do they?" Haven said, turning the book over and looking at the reviews. "This one says it seems like you speak from experience. Of course you do! You're an expert on everything in this book, Vik." Haven turned his face up to his brother. "May I borrow these? I'd love to read them while I recover. Looks as if you've added lots of juicy new details. I've been away so long, too, I need refreshing on all our stories and monsters and ghosts."

"They're for you. The books."

"Really?" Haven asked softly. "Well, I like them. Thank you."

Child Haven never would have spoken so politely, unless he was mocking someone. Something had changed in their years apart, and it ran a lot deeper than the scars on his hands. No, this was something that echoed the endless pools of sadness in Haven's dark eyes.

Viktor sat on the edge of Haven's bed. "Soon, I want you to meet Marling."

"Is Marling your girl? Someone told me you're in love. What's she like?"

"She's- she's not like us." Viktor considered. "She says too much, always. Not like me. She's not like me at all."

"Like you? I think everyone should strive to be more like you, Vik." Haven set the books aside and drew his knees up to his chest. "I'd like to meet her. Bring her to see me. I'll do my best not to frighten her away!" Haven snickered and then it turned into a cough.

"Maybe this evening?" Viktor suggested. "In a few days, I take her back to America."

"Oh? Then what? Do I smell a wedding, little brother?"

"Maybe. I haven't really asked her yet."

Haven waved his hand. "International flights give you plenty of time. And think of the immediacy of the situation!

'Look, we're in a flying deathtrap. Isn't it romantic? Marry me!' It's perfect timing, if there is such a thing. And of course she won't say no. Not to the King of the fae."

Viktor let out a heavy sigh. So Haven must have heard that their mother died, and whether he knew only of her official death five years ago, or the events of this week, it surely contributed to his sadness. He'd been so close to their mother, through everything. It would be awful to tell him the truth. "I'm still only prince," Viktor said.

"Mother...?"

"When you disappear, she lose her mind. She's never the same." Viktor closed his eyes. "I'm sorry, Haven. She wasn't how you remember her."

Though Haven nodded and his face betrayed no sign of any emotion, his eyes flickered pain. "I heard. But why haven't you taken the throne? It's been five years!"

"It's not mine."

"It's as much yours as mine, and it always has been," Haven said. "You were loads more responsible than me. And you knew a lot of stuff. Like the names of countries! That kind of thing comes in handier in the real world than I ever could have guessed."

Viktor considered this. "I'm not good at making important decisions."

"For someone who's bad at decisions, you've sure figured out a lot of important things. I might never have made it home if it wasn't for you listening to that witch woman. Or so I've been told. Someone might have been trying to talk you up to me, ha ha!"

All at once, Viktor felt a wave of unfamiliar pride. He stood up and gathered blankets together from the other side of the room, settling them at Haven's feet. "You're tired, I'm sure. Maybe you should sleep?"

"Oh, I'll sleep and sleep and sleep! All I do is sleep!" Haven cackled. "I'm just a sickly, sleepy kitty these days."

"You won't be for long. Soon no one can keep up with you, again," Viktor said.

"Think? Well, no tree climbing or apple throwing for me. Not yet! Maybe after your doctors are finished with their tricks."

That felt like a cue to leave. Viktor nodded, standing and heading for the doorway. "Yes, I'm sure of it. And in a few days, we finally have our rightful King."

"Well, if they made the coronation uniform for you, they're going to need to chop it in half. I'll be swimming in it!" Haven said, with a tired cackle.

"I'm sure that's easy fix."

Haven cackled again, but it turned to a cough. "It had better be! I'd look incredibly foolish in your old trousers."

"Petra said she wants to come see you as soon as you're ready for her. But for now, you should rest. Just call if you need me, okay?"

Haven laughed sadly. "I've been calling all these years, don't you know? You're the first one I call for any time I'm in trouble, Vik."

Once, so many years ago, Haven had told Viktor that it was bad luck to do anything in doorways. And he'd believed that, in some childish way, for long enough to miss out on thanking his brother before his disappearance. To shy away from saying something he should have. "I'm sorry I couldn't answer. I'll be here now."

"You were there all along. I always thought, 'Well, if Viktor was around, this is what he'd do.' All of your stupid good advice… And I always told myself that I needed to get back home, eventually. Can't let little brother be right about how dangerous my adventuring is!"

Viktor felt tears burn and blur his vision. He nodded and tried to say something, but his voice was a syrupy, unintelligible mess. Thankfully, Haven saved him from needing to speak.

"You have books to write!" Haven said. "Go on, go on! It's your turn to go on crazy adventures, and it's my turn to laze around indoors all of the time, learning important things."

"I'm glad you're home," Viktor said, doorway or not. "I love you, Haven."

"I love you too, little brother."

Out in the hallway, Viktor spotted Petra fast approaching. He met her halfway, and though she hesitated, she finally threw her arms around his waist and pressed her face against his chest. Viktor returned her hug, resting his chin on the top of her head.

"Is he alright?" she whispered.

"He's tired. Very tired."

"Should I wait til later to see him?" Petra asked, her voice sounding terribly less confident than usual. "Is he sleeping?"

The three of them had gone on so many adventures as children, and now, standing with only a few shadow lengths between them again seemed surreal. Viktor felt the warmth of tears against his shirt, and as much as he searched his memory for another time that he'd seen Petra cry, he couldn't think of one. "You should go see him," he whispered, and kissed the top of her head. "Just don't ask him about what happen. He'll tell us when he's ready."

Petra pulled away from Viktor, blinking away her tears and making a bit of a show of pulling herself back together. Even then, though, she looked up and caught Viktor's sad gaze, and her forced smile slipped again. "I'm glad you're alright, Viktor," she said.

"That's because of you and Marling."

"More her than me. She really does love you." She angled away from him, patted at her hair. "I... I'll go see Haven now."

As Viktor walked away, he felt as if twenty year of heaviness lifted from his shoulders.

chapter twenty-nine

Marling squirmed in her airplane seat, scrolling through her 68 unanswered Tumblr messages. Sometime during her time away, a few of her followers had discovered the photos of Marling and Viktor at Benjamin's party, and the messages had come rolling in.

Omgggggg are you dating Viktor Arson?

Girlfriend, please tell me you're dating Viktor Arson!

You are my favorite tumblr ever. Also, are you dating Viktor Arson?

MARLING!!!! Is it true that Vitkor Arson has a Huge tattoo on his back of angel wings???! Someone has he has a couple tattoos like one on his hip. Tell me tell meeee!

You have to see this picture of Brandon Flowers from the Killers. Why haven't you been on the tag? We miss you!

Marling can you please helpo me my boyftiend and I just broke up. It was a big fight please help I told him he's need to stop being so mean to me because he's always telling me what to do and he said I'm controlling so we broke up. Help!

"So, your fans miss you?" Viktor whispered in Marling's ear, and she almost jumped clear out of her seat. "Well, you know," she said, angling the laptop screen away from him. It might not be best if he saw the question about the hip tattoo, even if he *was* the owner of the laptop she was currently using. Viktor had offered to lend it to her for the long flight back to

America. "Tell that woman that I only show my hip tattoo to the highest bidder."

Marling twisted to look at him better. "Are you telling me there's money exchanges involved in your personal life?"

"Maybe," Viktor said, lowering his voice and raising an eyebrow. "How much you have on you, Marling?"

"Hey, I happen to know you do not have a hip tattoo."

"Well, maybe not last time you check."

Marling's gaze traveled toward his belt before she could stop it. "Really…"

"A little mystery, it's the best way to conduct yourself in the world of social media."

"Well, not in the world of me! I'll need to have all the details as soon as possible!" Marling said, a bit too loud. Several people turned and glanced at her, though they pretended to only be coughing or stretching. Honestly, people on planes were so nosy. She hadn't even been that loud! "Okay but... Do you really have a hip tattoo? And if so, can we go the airplane bathroom immediately so I can see with my own eyes?"

Viktor shrugged and returned to scrolling through tweets on his phone, a slight smirk tugging at his lips.

Hello Marling, I have a question for you. I am 24 and have not found a boyfriend. I would like to have a boyfriend, How can I get a boyfriend? I am pretty skinny and I'm beautiful, people say. What should I do?

MARLING OMG OMG OMG OMG TELL ME ABOUT VIKTOR!!!!!!

Then there were a series of messages from an anonymous person:

How do you know Viktor Arson?
How do you know Viktor Arson?
How do you know Viktor Arson?

"Wow. I think your fangirls have migrated to my blog, Viktor. This one is *very* insistent for me to tell her how we know each other. Should I mention the hip tattoo?"

"Enough with the hip tattoo, *please*. Really, I beg of you. I don't need that image in my head," Kyran said, from the seat behind Marling. "Can't you two talk about kittens or baby pandas or like, diphtheria or something? Please. Anything that's less repulsive than imagining a tattoo on Viktor's bony hip."

A loud dinging noise sounded, and then the pleasant voice of their pilot requested that everyone shut off all electronic devices because they would be landing soon. Marling closed the laptop and turned off her phone, putting everything away in her bag. Kyran leaned forward to tap her on the shoulder.

"So we need to talk about this plane. The food is not good. The drinks were not that great, either. Admittedly we're not on the cargo level of *Titanic* but we're not exactly traveling Rose's mother's style, either," Kyran said, and then looked at Viktor. "You couldn't spring to get us on something a little nicer, rich boy?"

Viktor shrugged. "I travel the same as anyone else."

"That's very charitable of you, but I'm sort of a war hero now."

This was the seventh time Kyran had said this, during their ten hour flight back to New York City. Marling had kept a tally, and she was beginning to think that Kyran had set a stopwatch so that he could remind them every hour.

"Are you sorry you missed Dame Marrow last night?" Viktor whispered to Marling, as soon as Kyran settled back into his seat.

"What? No, not really. I mean, considering everything that's happened in the last few days, I think she would have been a *little* bit anticlimactic." Marling shrugged, staring at her hands. "You know, she was right about one thing though. She said I was in love. It wasn't the unlove spell… that was all me and you."

Viktor captured one of Marling's hands and kissed her knuckles. Ugh. Somehow what was even hotter than the leather pants he loved to wear.

When they landed finally, Kyran was on his feet before Marling could even unfasten her seatbelt. He had let his beard get quite full during their time in Russia, and had spent an extra-long time fluffing his hair before they got on the plane. If Marling didn't know any better, she'd think he was trying to impress someone.

"Here's your jacket," Viktor said, standing up as best he could. He had to duck his head because he was too tall for the overhead storage. Marling had no such issue, considering she was still around the height of a tall twelve year old.

Marling let out a happy sigh as she slipped her arms into the fur jacket that she could now call her own. Viktor had let her choose a jacket, a hat, and a necklace from Gloriana's costume room. She'd been disappointed to discover that the Blue Dream Dress was missing from the room, but then, it wasn't surprising was it? If Gloriana had somehow found out how much Marling loved it, she'd probably burned it or something.

Aww, poor dress.

It was fine, though. Marling was happy with the fur jacket, fur hat, and ruby necklace. Real rubies can really work a number on anyone's disappointment.

A few minutes later, Marling, Viktor, and Kyran shuffled along the aisle and exited the plane together. At first they stayed close, maybe a little clingy after the dangerous adventures they'd taken part in together, but then Kyran broke away from them and looked left and right, left and right.

"What's he doing?" Viktor mumbled, watching Kyran.

"OHMAGAWD YOU GUYS!" someone squealed, and Marling knew it was Emma even before she saw her. Emma bounced from foot to foot, clad in a bright yellow dress and high heeled black boots. Her black hair looked unusually full and lush, which made Marling suspicious that it was a wig. "You're home! You made it!"

"Hey!" Marling said, smiling at her friend. "Yep, we're safe. It was..."

Emma ran right by Marling and hugged Kyran. Weird. Emma had seemed to be pretty Team Viktor since before Marling even knew who "Viktor Arson" was, so why was she missing out on her big chance to meet him finally?

"What happened?" Emma demanded of Kyran, breathless and wide eyed. "Lady Grieve said you had to fight the fae queen! Did the book help? Oh darling, I'm so glad you're alright!" Emma brushed her hand over Kyran's cheek, causing his face to turn pleasantly pink. "I like this beardy look on you. You're beardier than last time I saw you."

"Oh, you know. Destroying a half-body will do that to you," Kyran said. "All that adrenaline and testosterone from doing cool stuff."

"And you did it without proper tools! Brave, brave man!"

"Yeah," Kyran said, in a casual tone. He shot Emma a smug little smirk. "I guess you could say, I winged it."

"Kyran Gray, you've got me all flustered!" Emma said, in her most embarrassing bad English accent. She giggled. "You won't believe what I saw on the telly this morning! It was this program about medallions from the 18th century, and I thought of you right away. Remember when you demonstrated that one spell for the class and used a medallion?" Emma hooked arms with him. "Well, you simply have to hear what they said, you'll love it..." They walked away together toward the luggage pick-up area.

Viktor cleared his throat. "I thought he was gay...?"

"I don't know."

"Are they a couple...?"

"I don't know." Marling shook her head. "Nothing about him makes any sense at all, so I shouldn't even be surprised."

Marling and Viktor picked up their luggage, and worked their way slowly through the busy airport. At one point, a short guy with bright blue hair ran into Marling without apologizing, yelled "*Lola!* Wait for me!" and then tore after a skinny girl with a pink mohawk. It felt brilliantly homey, after the stark and conservative colors and manners Marling had experienced in Surki.

"Oh Viktor, I'm so happy to be back in New York City," Marling said, and she meant it with every fiber of her being. There was just something incredibly satisfying about returning home after an unexpected adventure to Russia, especially when the aforementioned adventure includes almost dying at the insubstantial hands of a ghost fae queen. Or half-body. Whatever.

Marling's phone chirped with a text from Emma, saying that she and Kyran were going to grab dinner and catch up on everything that had happened. "Well, we're on our own," Marling said, as much to herself as to Viktor. "We can just catch a cab back, I suppose."

Now, Marling could count on one hand how many times she'd brought a guy back to her apartment, because that number was exactly twice. The first time had been when her coworker, Stanley, had offered to fix Marling's computer. He'd turned out to be allergic to the neighbor's cat, and had all but run out of the apartment only fifteen minutes later, with red eyes and a stuffy nose. The second guy was a friend of a friend who paid Marling two hundred bucks to sleep on the couch for the night so he could audition for a play.

He didn't get the part and later Marling heard that he'd ended up in prison for something involving cocaine, a missing painting, and a camel statue. But she didn't like remembering that incident. And hey, two hundred dollars is two hundred dollars.

When Marling marched into the apartment with Viktor in tow, both of her roommates paused in eating their spinach and quinoa or whatever, and stared.

"This is Viktor," Marling said, trying to sound casual. "He's kinda famous."

"Oh, Viktor Arson?" Tim said. He hadn't spoken to Marling in so long that she'd actually started to think he preferred sign language or telepathy with his wife. "Viktor Arson. Did I see you on TV?"

Viktor stepped forward, holding his hand out. "Nice to meet you." He shook Tim's hand and everything got really quiet in the room for a long time. A really, really, unbearably long time. And then finally Tim cast a meek look at his wife and they returned to eating their weird healthy food and Marling dropped off her stuff in her room.

"This place is… it's a bit smaller than your old place," Viktor said, poking around a little in Marling's room.

"Well, the apartment is a lot bigger, but I'm not alone." Marling perched on the edge of her bed. "I do miss the old place sometimes. Even with the crazy neighbor. You know, it was him that kept the rent so low, I think."

"Did he stay quiet after I leave?"

"Oh, very quiet. I didn't hear a peep from him until the day the cops showed up to arrest him for shooting a hole in the roof."

Viktor laughed, but he seemed more disturbed than anything. "Well… maybe it's time you have a bigger place."

"On my current budget? I think I'll be living on the street. Which *is* bigger, if you want to be technical about it."

With another quiet laugh, Viktor slung the strap of his bag across his chest and offered his hand to Marling. "It's getting late, and I think we belong somewhere else on New Year's, don't you?"

Marling hesitated, staring up at him. Her mind replayed their last New Year's Eve together, and she couldn't help fearing that she would dance through the steps again, one after another, and they'd break up before the clock struck midnight. But that was superstitious, wasn't it?

Finally, Marling climbed to her feet and picked up her purse. "Alright, let's go."

When they reached Times Square, it was filled to overflowing with tourists, locals, drunks, crooks, crazies, and romantics. Marling couldn't help smiling as she walked with Viktor through the crowds, bumping into all manner of people along the way. It was so claustrophobic that she actually wondered if she'd have a panic attack later, when it sank in just how crowded everything was.

"It's 10:30," Viktor shouted to Marling, over the noise. "I have something for you."

Oh. Oh, was he going to propose to her? Was he going to give her some massive ring that had once been worn by Russian royalty? "Before midnight?" Marling asked, unable to stop herself.

"You planning to break up with me?"

"No."

"Good." Viktor opened his messenger bag and removed a white box. It looked like one of those fancy dress boxes from expensive department stores. "Here."

"Is this a late Christmas present? Because I completely forgot Christmas. Well, I forgot it, but then I remembered. And it was an inconvenient time because of your brother coming home and all of that. I talked to Petra about it and I mean, she's still not my favorite person, but she's not *quite* as bad as I thought. She suggested I get you something when we came back to America, because then I wouldn't have to like, fly it back."

"Marling. Just open the box."

Marling opened the box with shaking, cold fingers. She felt lightheaded with anticipation and nerves and considered suggesting she just finish opening it later. But no. She could do it now! Faintness and nerves be damned, she'd fought a ghost and won, so she could do anything, really. Marling tossed away the top of the box and ripped the tissue paper out from inside it.

There, folded neatly and looking absolutely gorgeous, was the Blue Dream Dress.

Wait.

The blue dream dress.

"But it disappeared!" Marling said with a gasp. She struggled not to drop the box.

"I told the tailor to have it made to your measure," Viktor said, grinning. "When you leave your clothes with me, I give the measurements to him. Do you like it?"

"So... it'll fit me?"

Viktor laughed, sounding a little nervous. "Well, I hope so."

Marling half considered stripping and putting the dress on right there, but ultimately decided she didn't want to go to jail for public indecency tonight. Instead, she threw her arms around Viktor's waist and hugged him and jumped up and down a couple times for good measure, all the while clinging to the dress so it wouldn't fall to the ground. A dress like this was too good for getting trampled by drunk revelers.

"Marling?" Viktor said.

She stopped jumping. "Sorry! Too much jumping? I'm excited!"

Viktor took one of Marling's hands and knelt in front of her. Almost immediately, a drunk guy tripped over Viktor's ankle and fell on his face, so Viktor had to help him up and apologize and send him on his way. After making sure the man wouldn't fall again, Viktor returned to Marling and knelt again. "You say, you want to have this dress because it's in your dream, and you say you want to marry a prince. So I got you the dress. Marling Ellis, will you marry me?"

Marling squealed a yes and kissed Viktor so intensely that she finally had to kneel too, to keep from falling over. And though she couldn't be sure, she felt as if she kissed him clear until midnight. Or maybe that didn't happen, but it didn't matter. Nothing mattered except for Viktor and the Dream Dress.

"Marry a prince, have this dress. Was there anything else you always wanted?" Viktor asked her, when they broke their kiss.

"Hmmm." Marling pretended to mull over his question. "A professional chef. I think I can budge on the time travel thing, though."

"Oh? Good. I don't have time machine."

Marling laughed and kissed him again. This particular kiss might have brought them back to that public indecency thing, but Marling's phone chimed with a text from her boss, interrupting them.

Oh, yeah. She was still employed, wasn't she? Ooops.

afterward

For the first time, Marling walked into her boss Kim's office with some element of confidence. As she sat across the desk from Kim, she couldn't help smiling. A lot had changed during her time in Russia. And wearing a ruby necklace is a great confidence booster.

"Well, this is surprising. You were absent for two weeks, you never answered my emails, my phone calls, or my texts. Patrick Jones-Wiley said you were incredibly rude to him at Benjamin's party. I'm disappointed, because I liked you, Marling." Kim looked up from her work, eyeing Marling with clear disdain. "I'm surprised you bothered to show up at all, after ghosting on us."

Ghosting. Ha. "Well. Here I am!" Marling said, waving her hands to indicate herself.

"Marling. You're fired."

Marling's confidence faltered a bit, but she forced her smile not to budge. "Viktor Arson agreed to publish his next book with us. You know Viktor Arson, right? The crazy famous guy who writes books about fae? The one who was just interviewed on Cazzy's Breakfast Show two days ago? Did you see that? The female host got all swoony when he took a bite out of an apple, and she almost fell off her chair. It was pretty funny."

"Viktor Arson wants to publish with us?" Kim demanded, narrowing her eyes. "Are you joking, or did you really get him to agree to that?"

"Yep!"

Kim let out a sigh of relief. "Thank God! You're not fired. Let me get you on the schedule for next week." Kim leaned forward in her chair, tapping her brightly colored fingernails on her computer's keyboard. "Would you like your desk back? Because I gave your desk to the Glory Boys, for their overflow paperwork." The Glory Boys were two annoying Moonhorse employees who looked freakishly similar to each other, but weren't related. One of them always smelled like moldy cheese, and the other liked to brag to people about his huge reptile collection. Both of them were complete workaholics, though, so Kim loved them.

"No, no, I quit," Marling said. "But Viktor's still publishing his next book with Moonhorse."

Kim's fingers froze over the keyboard and she glanced up. "What?"

"I don't think I was ever really cut out for this part of the publishing world. Desks and 8AM clock-ins are just… not my thing," Marling said, with a casual shrug. She reached up and patted her ruby necklace, just in case Kim hadn't noticed it yet.

"So, you don't want your job back?"

"I'm sure the Glory Boys will make good use of my desk. You can always call me if you want me to pop into a party or two for you, though. I like parties."

"What are you gonna do?"

Marling wanted to say, *well my boyfriend just became my fiancé and he's actually a prince and we're going to travel the world for a while for his media appearances and spend long weekends never leaving our hotel, and occasionally we'll go visit his mermaid friend in Russia.* But instead she just shrugged again. "I'll figure something out."

For a long time, Kim just squinted at her. Finally, the other woman pushed away from her desk, crossed her arms over her chest, and nodded. "Alright, Marling. Well, I'm sorry to lose you."

"Thanks! I mean, uh, I'll miss you. You're a cool boss."

Kim gave a tight-lipped smile and another nod. "Thank you for your service at Moonhorse Publishing. I hope you find happiness elsewhere."

Marling stood and headed for the door, making sure to keep her chin high enough that the ruby necklace was on full display. "You too, Kim. I hope you find happiness."

"Hey, Marling?"

Marling turned around, because this was one of those moments when hard-earned wisdom and unsaid words of love were usually expressed. Maybe Kim had secretly always respected Marling, and she'd tear up and say something along the lines of, 'you've always been like a sister to me. I love you,' or maybe she would whisper something melancholy and profound in French.

Kim sighed. "For the love of God, get a haircut, Marling."

about the author

Kendra L. Saunders is a time-and-space traveling fashionista author who writes books about magical, dark-haired men, interviews famous people, and suggests way too many bands to you via whatever social media platform she can get her hands on. She writes with good humor because humor is the best weapon for a girl who can't learn karate (or ballroom dancing). She's the author of the Alien Pop Star series, magic realism novel Inanimate Objects, the dark comedy Death and Mr. Right, and the poetry collection Geminis and Past Lives.

www.ingramcontent.com/pod-product-compliance
Lightning Source LLC
Chambersburg PA
CBHW050740230626
47052CB00004BA/764